BLUE BUDDHA

Helen Christine Anderson

ISBN: 0692824669
ISBN 13: 9780692824665
Library of Congress Control Number: 2016921218
Helen Christine Anderson, Fletcher, NC

CHAPTER ONE

You probably didn't pay much attention to the story. It was all over the news for a day or two, but nowadays it seems nobody cares much about murder. I guess they have other things to worry about. Just take my word for it that once upon a time, a triple homicide was a big deal. And believe me, it makes an even bigger impression when your own kid is one of the victims.

At the time, I didn't know who to blame. I was too angry to think. Now that a year has passed, I can see I missed some things back then. It's only now that I'm able to sort it all out.

The first I knew about it was when that lawyer, Emma Faulkner, called me on a Thursday afternoon in August. I had never heard of this lady, much less met her. Out of the blue, she calls me at my office and lays it right on me. My daughter is dead. Shot. Found murdered with two other people up in Buckhead, assailant unknown. It never occurred to me to ask why this lady was calling, instead of the police. Like I said, I missed a few things that day. It was a shock.

Cynthia would have been twenty-one in November. I hadn't seen her for nearly two years, not since she stormed out of the house after our big blowup. She wasn't a bad girl, just confused. After her mother died, she was never the same. Twelve is a rough age for a girl to lose her mother. You know what the song says: "Sometimes it's hard to be a woman." Nobody was around to teach her how to be one, so she had to make it up as she went along. She might have gone too far. But I'm getting ahead of myself.

I met Emma Faulkner at the downtown morgue a couple of hours after she called. It was Cynthia, all right, no doubt about that, although I could only be sure of it because of the blue butterfly tattoo on her right shoulder—the one we argued about before she left me. But half of her head was blown off. That beautiful blond hair was all matted with blood, and you couldn't see her eyes at all. She had blue eyes, big and round, just like her mother's. Once I was sure it was Cynthia, nothing else seemed to matter. I didn't ask many questions that day, maybe because I'd been afraid for a while that something like this might happen.

Emma Faulkner didn't seem to know much about it, either. She said she was representing the estate of one of the other victims, a guy named Jack. I had never heard of him. The bodies had been found in his house, and apparently they had been there for a few days. Atlanta is hot in August. The gardener called the police when he smelled something bad. I didn't need to hear any more details that day.

I did think Emma was pretty young to be representing an estate, which turned out to be substantial—but I'll get into that shortly. It figures that she had to be at least thirty, but she didn't look much older than my Cynthia. She had a wild mane of brown hair and dark eyes—almost black. One of the cops once commented that she was "hot," and now that I think about it, I guess she was. Personally, I didn't find her particularly attractive, maybe because of the circumstances, but apparently a lot of men did.

The funeral was two days later. I don't remember much about it. My brother Charles was the only family member who came. We've never been a close family. My sister Terry didn't approve of Cynthia, so I guess she thought she'd get in one more jab at my girl by not showing up. That's the sort of thing you always expect from Terry.

After the funeral, Charlie and I stopped by a bar near my house for a couple of beers. Charlie lives in Chattanooga, about two hours away. He was staying overnight, so we figured it wouldn't hurt to get a little drunk close to home.

"Aw, Joe, don't blame yourself," he told me. I'm ashamed to admit I must have been crying.

"It's not that. I don't know who's to blame."

"Maybe nobody. Maybe it was something that just happened."

I thought about that. Does murder ever "just happen?"

"Maybe," I said. "I don't want to talk about it now. Let's have another drink."

We did. Then we had a few more. By the time we left the bar, it was late. Neither of us was in any shape to drive, and we needed some air, so we left my car in the parking lot and walked home, maybe a mile. On the way, Charlie asked me the question he must have been holding back when he was sober.

"Do you think she was hooking?"

"I don't know. She didn't have any money. She had to be getting by somehow."

"What did the cops say?"

"Nothing much. Just that there were four takeout meals from a Mexican restaurant on the table, and only three bodies. The fourth enchilada must be the killer."

"I guess that makes sense," he said.

We walked along quietly awhile. Then Charlie started asking me about why Cynthia had left home. We had never talked about it before.

"She never actually said," I told him. "We'd been arguing a lot for a few months—mostly about her staying out all night, coming home drunk, hanging out with people I hadn't met. You know, the usual adolescent rebellion, except she seemed a little too old for that. I always expected her to come back and go to college. You know, make something of herself. But of course she didn't."

"Sounds like she got in with a bad crowd," said Charlie.

"Yeah, the cops acted strange. Something about drugs," I said.

"Cindy was on drugs?"

"They asked me that. I told them I didn't know. I don't."

"If she was hooking, she might've been."

I didn't want to think about that possibility. I wanted to think about the day she started kindergarten. She wore a pink dress that day. She was a beautiful little girl. My little girl.

"I never understood her," I said. "Cynthia was always in a world of her own—imagined herself as a fairy princess, and I guess I must have treated her like one. It was cute then. But after her mother died, she pulled away from me. Spent all her time reading paperback romance novels and mysteries. It seemed like life was always too drab for her. But that last year or so, she really went off the deep end. I keep thinking I should have paid more attention. Maybe I could have saved her."

"Don't think about it, Joe. You'll feel better tomorrow. You can think about it then," said Charlie.

I lay awake most of that night. Alcohol does that to me sometimes. I couldn't stop thinking about Cynthia and the murders, wondering about the other two victims. Then I would think about my wife, Barbara, and the way she died—slow and painful from the cancer. They cut off both of her breasts, but she died anyway. Cynthia cried a lot, of course, but I never did. Not that I wasn't feeling anything, but instead of crying, I mostly drank. I lost a lot of sleep back then, too.

CHAPTER TWO

Charlie left the next morning, and I was supposed to go to work, but I was too worn out from the funeral and everything—and also hungover. As a county tax assessor, I made my own schedule, so nobody had to give me time off. I just took it. All day I stared at the TV, waiting for every news update, figuring they'd be arresting somebody by now. But it had been three days since the bodies were found, and the news had stopped covering the story. They had already moved on. I wasn't ready to do that yet.

In fact, I may as well admit that I was getting angry. I didn't know exactly who I was angry at, but my hands were shaking, and not just from alcohol. Then I got up and paced around the house, saying, "Fuck, fuck, fuck," under my breath. Which surprised me, by the way, because I rarely swear. In all my fifty-five years, I'll bet I haven't said that word more than three or four times. I always thought it was undignified. Hearing it coming out of my mouth was a weird experience, to tell the truth. It was like somebody else was inside my head, stirring me up.

After the six o'clock news, I made myself a sandwich and drank a couple of beers to calm down. It was raining outside. I looked out the window and didn't see my car parked on the pad; then I remembered that we'd left it at the bar. "Fuck," I said again and grabbed my raincoat.

It was about half a mile to the Fuzzy Navel Lounge on Tara Boulevard. Actually, I'd never been there before I stopped there with Charlie, and I had a little trouble finding it again. By the time I did, I was soaked through and feeling thirsty, so I went inside. Seated at the bar were two young men, obviously gay and huddled head to head. I sat down in the same booth where Charlie and I had sat the night before, and I ordered a beer.

"Did you want to order dinner, sir?" asked the waiter, who, now that I thought about it, was probably also gay.

"No thanks. I just ate," I said, looking at the pictures of Marilyn Monroe on the wall behind the bar. By now it was clear that this was a gay bar, and Charlie and I had completely missed that obvious fact. Or at least I had. I wasn't sure about Charlie.

"Mind if I join you?" asked a voice behind me.

I looked around. The voice came from a nice-looking young man, maybe mid-to-late twenties. I didn't want to be rude.

"Sure. I'm just having one drink. I'm waiting for the rain to let up."

"Okay," he said, sitting down across from me. "You just looked a little out of place, and I thought maybe you could use some company."

He was drinking something amber on the rocks—smiling, but not in a flirtatious way. I decided I liked him.

"I just lost my daughter," I said, surprising myself.

"Lost? Sorry, I don't understand," he said. I remember thinking he had kind eyes.

"She was murdered."

"Wow! Murdered? What happened?"

"That's just it. I don't exactly know," I said.

"Do they know who did it?"

"No. At least I don't think so. Nobody is telling me anything. The police won't call me back."

"Well, where did it happen?"

I thought about it. "Up in Buckhead, somewhere off Peachtree, I guess. I've seen pictures of the house. It was on the news."

"Yeah? Okay, I think I did see that on the news. That's rough. Sorry, man."

"Thanks," I said. Part of me wanted him to leave, but that angry guy inside me wanted him to stay. I don't have many friends, and it seemed easier to talk to a stranger than to anyone I knew. For some reason I took out my wallet and slipped a snapshot of Cynthia out of the back flap. It was the one I took at her eighteenth birthday party. She was laughing then.

"Beautiful, man. She's a beautiful girl."

"Was," I said. "Somebody blew her head off."

"Yeah, sorry about that. She *was* a beautiful girl."

I put the picture away. It only made me angrier to see her laughing like that. I wondered if she was laughing when they shot her in the head.

The guy took a sip of his drink and slumped back in the booth.

"My name's Daryl," he said, extending his hand.

"Joe," I said.

"Pleased to meet you, Joe." We shook hands.

He took a couple sips of his drink. "So what are you going to do about it?"

"What do you mean? What *can* I do?" I perked up. That was a question I hadn't really asked myself.

"Well, for starters…If I were you, I'd go up there," he said.

"Up where?"

"The scene of the crime. Up in Buckhead. I'd want to see the place for myself."

"What? Why would I want to do that?"

"Just to see the place—see where she died. You know."

I took a couple more gulps of beer. That idea hadn't occurred to me, but it made my heart jump.

"I couldn't do that," I said.

"Why not?"

"It's just not...me," I said. "I don't think that's allowed."

He laughed, throwing his head back. He was a good-looking guy. Blond, athletic. The kind of guy I would have wanted my Cynthia to bring home.

"*Of course* it's not allowed. Fuck! That's exactly why you should do it!"

I thought about that. For some reason it made sense. What did I really have to lose?

"Fuck, you're right!" I said. All the beers and lack of sleep were affecting me, and all of a sudden I was feeling bold. This guy Daryl was making me bold.

"Hey, man, if you're nervous about it, I'll ride up there with you. Whaddaya say?"

I tipped my glass up and drained it.

"What the fuck! Let's go!"

CHAPTER THREE

Buckhead is a straight shot up I-75, about half an hour from my place in Jonesboro. Daryl said he knew that part of Atlanta like the back of his hand because of all the clubs, so I let him drive. Don't ask me why I trusted him that much. Maybe I just needed to. Anyway, I didn't see any reason not to at the time, and like I said, I guess I was a little drunk.

We talked some more as we drove. He said he was a deputy with the Fulton County Sheriff's Office, and he worked at the jail. Said I reminded him of his dad, said we both reminded him of William H. Macy, and then started calling me Pops. Even though I wasn't sure just who this guy Macy was, or whether it was a compliment, it made me feel good to look like Daryl's dad. I told him about Cynthia and her mom, and he listened. One thing you can say about Daryl, he was a very good listener.

Before we left the bar, Daryl had looked up the news story about the murders on his iPhone and found the address on Tuxedo Road. Right here there's something you need to know about Buckhead— it's where a lot of the super-rich people in Atlanta live. Not the sort of neighborhood where you'd expect to hear gunshots, or where I'd have expected Cynthia to hang out, for that matter. All the houses are big, more like mansions, I'd say; and once you get away from the clubs around Peachtree Road, it's very quiet. Makes you feel like an intruder when you don't live there. I guess that's the idea.

By the time we found the place, it was getting dark. We pulled up at the curb in front of number Three Thirteen. I noticed a little red sports car parked across the street, but nobody was around, and there weren't any street lights. The rain had stopped, but it was still overcast, covering the moon.

It was easy to tell we had the right address, as there was a line of yellow crime-scene tape across both the driveway and the street frontage. Beyond the tape, a manicured lawn as long as a football field rolled uphill to the house. Almost all the other houses on the street were set back the same way. *These folks must want to keep their distance from the rest of us,* I thought. And maybe a gunshot wouldn't be so obvious here, after all.

As for the house, from the road it looked impressive, but somehow fake. I know that must sound presumptuous coming from me, but to my eye, everything about it seemed overdone—like an illustration in one of Cynthia's fantasy books. Right in the middle of the front lawn, there was a circular marble fountain with a couple of cupids holding up a big green bowl of some kind. I figured water was supposed to spill out of there into the large pool below, but it was dry. The front of the place looked like one of those plantations along the Mississippi, with half a dozen marble columns all across the veranda. Since the Civil War, we haven't had any real plantation houses in Atlanta. I guess that's why the place struck me as fake.

Daryl turned off the engine and started to open the door.

"What are you doing? We can't go up there," I said.

He laughed. "Come on, Pops. I thought we already settled that."

"Yes, but I don't think we're supposed to go past that tape. We could get arrested."

He just shook his head. Then he got out, and I watched him walk back and duck right under the crime-scene tape and start up the long driveway. I felt like a damn fool sitting there. After all, it was *my* daughter who was dead. So I got out and followed him.

The house seemed dark, or at least there were no lights on in front. The driveway was an uphill climb, and I felt a little winded by the time we got to the top. Or maybe that was just because my heart had started beating faster. Daryl didn't seem nervous at all, but I just figured that's young people for you. He started around to the back.

"Wait a minute," I whispered. "Shouldn't we at least ring the bell?"

"Nah, there's nobody home," he said. He continued past the row of garages and behind the house, so for a moment I lost sight of him.

"Daryl!" I whispered as loud as I could. "Stop! Wait for me!"

I caught up with him, my heart beating really fast now, mainly because the farther you went behind the house, the more you could smell that awful odor. The smell of death, I guess you'd call it. Daryl was standing on a flagstone patio behind some big windows, looking in. By the time I got there, I thought I was going to puke from that smell, but he didn't seem bothered.

"I don't think I can go any farther," I said. "That stink is going to make me pass out."

"You'll get used to it after a few minutes," he said. I looked at him with a question mark, and he shrugged. "I smelled a lot of that in Afghanistan."

"Oh," I said. Hearing that he was a veteran made me feel a little guilty for complaining. I never was in the military. My generation grew up between wars. He seemed confident, like he knew what he was doing, so I decided to shut up and follow him.

We crept along the back of the house, looking into the windows wherever we could see past the foundation shrubbery. It was a big house, maybe three or four times the size of mine. Along the way there were several doors open to the patio, and Daryl tried all of them. They were all locked. At the corner of the house, he stopped and motioned me back.

"That's funny," he said.

"What?"

"It's too quiet and too dark. See those lights up there? Those are motion detector lights. Why aren't they coming on? A place like this would have vibration detectors, too. Why didn't the burglar alarm go off when I rattled those doors?" He was more or less mumbling to himself, but I could hear him.

"Maybe the cops shut them off."

"No, they wouldn't do that. They would leave everything on to keep out burglars and…people."

"Like us, you mean."

"Yeah," he said and grinned. "People who might want in there for other reasons."

I had no idea what he was getting at, but it didn't matter. I was scared, and for some reason, I had a creepy feeling, like we were being watched.

He started back along the house and stopped at the first set of glass doors.

"I'm going to try something," he said. "Get ready to run if I signal you."

He grabbed ahold of the door knob and bumped the glass hard with his elbow. Nothing happened. He grinned. "That's what I thought. The system is turned off. See that little device up there? Vibration detector. If they had the system on it would have started flashing. Why would they turn it off? Strange." He seemed to be talking to himself again.

I didn't know what to say. Daryl seemed to know about things I didn't have a clue about.

"Come on," he said. Then he shocked me. He reached into his waistband and pulled out a small, squared-off pistol. I shook my head and backed away. This was getting too dangerous.

"Relax, Pops. It's just for self-defense. We've gone this far; let's do what we came for."

I was holding my breath, both because of that disgusting stink and because I was scared my breath would make noise.

"Give me a credit card," he said.

I saw what he had in mind, and I hesitated. "Come on, you have a credit card, don't you?" he whispered impatiently. He knew I did, because I'd used it at the bar.

I took the VISA card out of my wallet and handed it to him. Within five seconds the lock popped open, and he turned the knob. The deadbolt was not locked. Daryl slipped inside, and I followed, holding onto his shirt.

We had entered a large dining room, with tapestries on the walls and a long table that looked like it could seat maybe twenty people. But even in the dark you could see the room was a mess. All the drawers had been pulled out of the buffet, and there were broken dishes and linens all over the floor. There was even a big hole in the sheetrock of one wall. I'd never seen anything like it. Daryl still had his gun drawn and kept stopping every couple of feet to listen. I don't know what he expected to hear, but when we went through the archway at the end of the room and turned the corner, we could see that there was a faint yellow light coming from a room at the end of the long hallway. Then we heard a noise, like maybe a couple of footsteps.

"Somebody's in there," he mouthed to me, gesturing with the gun.

At that point I froze. "Let's go," I whispered. "We shouldn't be here."

But just then the light went off. Someone came out of the room and walked across the hall. There they stopped, and you could hear the sound of a keypad setting an alarm, followed by a rhythmic beep. My eyes were just getting used to the dark, enough so that I could see the silhouette of the person standing there. It was a woman. Before she turned and walked out the front door at the other end of the hall, I recognized who it was. It was Emma Faulkner.

Daryl pushed me back into the dining room. "Let's go!" he said. "We've got about ten seconds to get out before that alarm goes off."

I groped my way back ahead of him through the room and toward the glass doors. We slipped out onto the patio and got the door closed. Just then the patio lights came on all across the back of the house—the motion detector Daryl had mentioned. Emma must have switched it on when she set the alarm. Why had it been turned off? We crept behind a shrub and waited there for a couple of minutes, I guess to see if anyone else was around. When nothing happened we started back down the driveway. My car was still parked there on the street, but the red sports car across the street was gone.

CHAPTER FOUR

"I know that woman," I said, once we were back on the road and my heart rate had settled down.

"Yeah?" He didn't sound very curious under the circumstances.

"Her name is Emma Faulkner. She's a lawyer."

"Right," he nodded, keeping his eyes on the road.

"You know her?" I asked, surprised.

He didn't answer at first. Finally he looked over at me. "I don't exactly know her. You might say I know *of* her."

I was confused and must have shown it.

"Look, Pops, I know a lot of people in this town. In my line of work, you deal with a lot of people."

I didn't really see how a deputy sheriff could have gotten around all that much, especially at his age. But my own social circle was pretty limited, so it was hard to relate.

"Where did you meet her?" he asked after a pause.

"She's the lawyer who called me the day they found the bodies. I wonder what she's doing in that house with all the lights off like that."

"Good question. She has balls." He grinned but seemed to be talking to himself again.

"Well, she did say she represents the estate of one of the victims—the owner of the house. Maybe she had some business to take care of."

I could see his expression in the darkness as he turned onto I-75. He had a sarcastic smile on his face. "Yeah, maybe some business she didn't want anybody to watch."

Puzzled, I shut up again. We drove along quite a ways before either of us spoke.

"She must have seen my car, you know," I finally said. "I wonder if she recognized it from the other day."

"Most likely, if she's as observant as I think she is. The Clayton County tags would be a dead giveaway. You don't see many of those in this part of town, especially on a ten-year-old Chevy." He chuckled.

I was a little offended by that remark, but it made me think. If she did recognize my car and then saw the patio lights go on, she probably realized I was back there. And she must have suspected that I'd seen her. I wasn't sure what that might mean. I sank back in the passenger seat, mulling it over.

"So tell me what you've heard about this Emma Faulkner," I said.

"Just that she's a nut cracker and maybe a little shady. But then, if you ask me they're all pretty shady. It goes with the territory."

"What's her specialty?"

"Good question. The only kind I've heard about is criminal—big-time drugs, mostly. That's about the only kind of criminal client who could afford to pay for that little Maserati she was driving."

Now I was confused. If she was a drug lawyer, it didn't make sense that she'd be doing probate work, representing the estate. Even I knew better than that.

All of a sudden I started feeling paranoid. Too much to take in, and too many coincidences. I couldn't make sense of it. How did Emma contact me? And just how did Daryl happen to know her? And who the heck *was* Daryl, anyway? I decided to clam up.

We drove the rest of the way back in silence. I could tell that Daryl was chewing things over, just like I was. I wanted to ask him more questions, but after the business with the gun and everything, I just didn't trust him much anymore. I was glad when we pulled into the Fuzzy Navel parking lot.

He got out and came around to meet me. "So it looks like a dry run, Pops. Sorry about that."

"That's okay. It's probably best," I said.

"At least you got to see the place. Next time we'll get in there and look around."

I didn't want to hear about a "next time." After what had just happened, I was starting to think Daryl was a little off his rocker.

"Sure. Sounds good," I said, going around to the driver's seat.

"Just give me a call if you need anything, Joe. I'm sure glad we met tonight." He reached into his pocket and handed me a business card.

"Yeah, me too," I said, starting the engine.

I left him standing there, watching me pull away. I'm not sure why, but I decided to circle the block and cruise the parking lot again. When I came back around, I saw him again, going back inside the bar with another man who was wearing a gray three-piece suit. I sat parked at the curb for a few seconds, just long enough to notice that there were two cars in the parking lot with Fulton County tags—a silver pickup and a brownish Mercedes. I don't know why, but I wrote down their license plate numbers. Then I hightailed it home.

CHAPTER FIVE

The job of Clayton County Tax Assessor isn't very glamorous and won't ever make you rich. But what most people might not realize is that a tax assessor has access to a lot of information. Actually, any halfway clever person with a computer can get access, but it's a lot easier when it's all laid out for you. For example, from my computer at work, I can find out who owns what—and usually what it's worth. Not that I'm the type to abuse my position, since I did take my oath of public service seriously, but there are times when information comes in handy. This was one of those times.

I had trouble sleeping again that night, after I left Daryl. I know it sounds nuts, but when I got home, I was still shaky and confused and felt like I needed a drink. So I poured myself a tall glass of vodka, hoping it would knock me out so I could get some rest after the previous night's insomnia. No such luck. I should have known better. I did fall asleep, but after a couple of hours, I woke up and looked at the clock—not quite 2:00 a.m. Knowing from experience there was no way I was going to get back to dreamland that night,

I got up and made myself some coffee and tried to sort through what happened the evening before.

None of it made sense. I was almost ready to believe I'd dreamed the whole thing until I looked at the framed graduation picture of my innocent Cynthia on the mantle and remembered how she looked lying there on the slab in the morgue, with her eyes missing. It was real, all right—the whole crazy thing.

I took the picture down from the mantle, and, odd as it seems, I carried on a conversation with my daughter for about an hour. We reminisced about some of the good times before her mother died and about little things like her middle-school soccer team and our trip to Disney World. I kept apologizing, telling her how I wished I'd done more to protect her. She kept smiling back at me, insisting that she wasn't dead.

When I couldn't take it any longer, I headed out to the car. No idea where I was going, really, but I needed to drive. With that photo propped up on the dashboard, still whispering to me, making me feel guiltier and crazier by the minute, I cruised around the deserted streets of Jonesboro for quite a while. Eventually I ended up at the county building, sitting in front of the computer in my office. It seems that even when I'm an emotional wreck, my basic instinct is always to go to work. And that's where my access to information comes in.

I sat there in the dark for a while and then switched on the computer. The first thing I did was a title search for the address up in Buckhead: Three Thirteen Tuxedo Road. The name that came up didn't make any sense. Based on what Emma Faulkner had told me, I was expecting it to be a Jack Something-or-other, but instead the property was titled in the name of somebody named Dawn Marie Sterling. Who the heck was that? I double checked, and sure enough, the title had been transferred from its previous owner just a year earlier in a bona fide sale for $3,327,000.00, according to the tax stamp. That sounded about right for Buckhead, given the spread I had seen at that address.

Feeling more frustrated than ever, I ran the license tag numbers for the two vehicles I'd seen at the Fuzzy Navel. The first was a silver Toyota pickup belonging to a Daryl Spinks. The tan Mercedes belonged to somebody named Jonathan Lebeaux, who had a Buckhead address. I could tell that by the zip code—30305. *Quite a coincidence,* I thought. Finally, just out of curiosity, I ran a reverse check for vehicles registered to Emma Faulkner. Sure enough, she was the owner of a late-model Maserati, red in color. Although it was interesting, none of this information was particularly helpful.

I sat at my computer for quite a while, studying the familiar black-and-white screens with their lines and boxes, numbers and signatures. Strange to say, they gave me a lot of comfort, even though I couldn't make heads or tails of the information at that point. I'm sort of a black-and-white guy, I guess. When you start throwing a lot of color at me I get nervous.

While I was sitting there thinking, I realized that I could access quite a few other databases from my computer, including Fulton County government. Quickly I logged onto the personnel records page and verified that Daryl Spinks was employed as a deputy sheriff. One mystery cleared up. Maybe I could trust the guy, after all. At least I knew he was telling the truth about *something.*

My next search was especially brilliant, if I do say so myself. I logged onto the Fulton County Probate Court internal records and located a list of all the current estates being litigated. There was only one filed in the preceding two weeks for someone named Jack or Sloan. In fact, it had been filed earlier that same day. It was the estate of Ervin Jackson Sloan, filed by Emma Faulkner, attorney at law. Bingo! Whatever else may be true about that woman, at least she was really a lawyer, and she really represented somebody named Jack. Besides that, the court filing didn't tell me much except that there was no will, the decedent was forty years old, and the person filing the petition was somebody named Diana Diamond, who claimed to be his common-law wife.

But just when I was beginning to think my paranoia the previous evening was out of line, I did one more search that changed my mind. I looked up the news story that Daryl had found on his iPhone in the car and skimmed through it. It listed the names of the murder victims: Ervin Jackson Sloan, Dawn Marie Sterling, and Soraya S. Romero. No mention of my baby daughter, Cynthia Ann Brock! And just as strange was the fact that after reading through the story three times, I realized there was no mention of the address where the murders happened. Daryl must have known the address all along, even before we met. Why had he pretended he didn't?

I got up and paced around the office for quite a while. My mind was racing. What the heck was going on? If there was one thing I knew for sure, it was that Cynthia was dead. Why wasn't she listed in the news story? Could it be a mistake? I had to find out. And then I had to know what was going on with this Daryl Spinks.

The more I thought about it, the madder I got. It does seem paranoid now, even to me, and maybe it was the shock or the alcohol and lack of sleep, but it felt like somebody was playing a cruel joke on this lonely old guy, and I saw no humor in it. Besides, it seemed like they were trying to deprive me of my few remaining memories of Cynthia and my time to grieve. It was as if she never even lived. By the time the sun came up, I had made up my mind to find out who killed her, and I was ready to do about anything it took to avenge my little girl.

CHAPTER SIX

W hen I heard security arriving to open up, I slipped out the back door of the building. It was almost eight o'clock, and I wasn't ready to face anyone at the office yet. When your kid gets murdered, you don't feel much like listening to sympathy from people you barely know. There's nothing anybody can really say, so the best thing is just to say nothing, but most people don't realize that.

Besides, I was sick of sentimentality. Right then what I wanted were facts. I needed to find out everything the police knew. So I turned Cynthia's picture face down on the dashboard, turned onto I-75, and headed for the Atlanta PD without really knowing what I would do once I got there. The desk sergeant sort of blew me off until I told him I had information about a murder. Then he told me to sit down and wait for the lead homicide detective. That turned out to be Lieutenant Frank Dupree, a black guy about my age with a lot less hair than me, but in quite a bit better shape. He showed me into his office. I told him my daughter had been murdered the week before.

"Sorry for your loss, Mr. Brock," he said. He was shuffling papers while he said it, so it didn't seem very sincere. I shrugged and said thanks.

"Now what's this about information? You have some info for us?"

"It's about the triple murder that was on the news. Up in Buckhead."

That seemed to perk him up. "I just thought I might be helpful, Lieutenant. I did some research and noticed some things that seem wrong."

"Oh?" He was leaning forward by this time, and not shuffling the papers any more.

"Right. Well, for starters, the names of the victims. My daughter Cynthia was one of them. I identified her body a few days ago, and there's no doubt it was her. But the news reports list somebody else's name—Soraya or Dawn or something. It doesn't make sense."

He turned to his computer and tapped a few keys to pull up a file. It took him a few minutes to look through it.

"Looks like we identified the bodies by the usual means—photo IDs and next of kin. You say your daughter was one of them?"

"She was shot. Her face was more or less blown off, but I know it's her because of her tattoo. A little blue butterfly right here…" I showed him where.

"Okay, yeah, now I see the problem," he said, reading something on his screen. "It says here that the woman we ID'd as Dawn Marie Sterling was born Cynthia Ann Brock. That's your daughter, right?"

"Yes, sir."

"Well, it seems she changed her legal name at some point, and her driver's license, too. We didn't figure that out until one of the attorneys involved in the case told us about the name change. It's been corrected on the report, but evidently the news didn't get it right. It wouldn't be the first time."

"By any chance would that attorney be Emma Faulkner?" I asked, seeing a few things starting to add up.

"Ye-e-ah, that's right. She apparently represents somebody or other in the case, not sure just who. Anyway, we know Emma pretty well around here. And if memory serves, she also represented Jack Sloan once or twice before he died." The detective had a funny look on his face.

I nodded. "I met her. She's the one who took me to see Cynthia's body, but she didn't say a word about this name change business."

"Man, like I said, I'm sorry for your loss, but it looks like a case of snafu in the original ID. I wouldn't make any more of it than that."

He was trying to end the conversation, but I wasn't ready to leave.

"So do you have any idea who did it yet? Any clues?"

He sighed and shook his head. "Afraid not. But since you're here, I do have a couple of questions for you."

"Sure...anything," I said.

"Was your daughter involved in drugs to your knowledge?" He sat back, studying me.

"The other officer asked me that. I really don't have any idea. She never used drugs when she lived at home, that much I know for sure."

He sort of smiled. "Well, no offense, Mr. Brock, but most parents don't know when their kids are using drugs. But that's not really what I meant. The male victim of this crime is someone we've suspected for quite a while to be heavily involved in marijuana and heroin traffic. We've been out to his place with search warrants a couple of times, but we couldn't make a case, other than a couple of busts for possession."

This was interesting information but hard to accept. Cynthia involved with a drug dealer?

"You mean this guy named Jack?"

"That's right. I probably shouldn't be telling you this, since the investigation is just getting cranked up. I think you should probably expect to hear further from the investigating detective before long."

"But do you have any idea who might have killed them?" I wanted the bottom line.

"Not yet. We're working on that. For now, we're assuming it was a mob hit."

I understood what the detective was saying, but it just didn't seem to fit. "I don't understand. Why would anyone kill Cynthia? She was barely twenty years old, for God's sake!"

"She was living with Jack Sloan. Not a very safe place to be living, if half of what I hear is true. And apparently she'd been with him for quite some time."

I didn't know what to say.

"Listen, Mr. Brock. We'll be sure to let you know if there's an arrest made. You might even get involved in a trial if there is one. Give me a call if I can help in any way. But for now, I'd advise you to go home and rest. You look like you could use it." He handed me a business card from a plastic holder on his desk.

"I haven't been able to sleep. Strange things have been happening. Do you know somebody named Daryl Spinks? Tall, blond guy?"

The detective shook his head. "Can't say I recognize that name. Should I?"

"I don't know. He's a Fulton County deputy sheriff. I met him last night, and I'm beginning to wonder if it was accidental."

"Can't help you there. I've never met him. But I wouldn't worry about it too much. When you're exhausted from grief, things can get blown up in your mind. Things you wouldn't think twice about under normal circumstances."

I started to say something about our visit to the murder scene but then realized I better not. "Maybe you're right. I'm probably imagining things," I said. But I was pretty sure I wasn't.

CHAPTER SEVEN

My stomach was growling for food, so I stopped at a Denny's just off the freeway and ordered an omelet with a side of pancakes. It was the first real food I'd had for days, and it made me relax a little. As I sat there, I watched my waitress serving some other customers. The badge on her uniform said Nicole. She looked a lot like Cynthia—blond, blue-eyed, wholesome. Couldn't be more than eighteen or so. I imagined what her life must be like. Possibly a student, maybe in college, with her whole life ahead of her. Hopefully a long life.

As I sat there, eating my Denny's breakfast and speculating about Nicole, something hit me like a ton of bricks. That big house up in Buckhead worth over $3 million was titled in the name of Dawn Marie Sterling, a.k.a. Cynthia Ann Brock. Wow! Cynthia must have come into some real money to be able to buy that house. And as I recalled, there was no mortgage on it. Cash purchase, free and clear. And I was her only heir.

I jumped up from the table, threw down a couple of bucks for the tip, and headed for the cashier. Then I doubled back to the table, reached into my wallet again, and pulled out a twenty-dollar bill. I walked over to Nicole and handed it to her. She looked surprised and whispered, "Thanks." I just smiled and said something like "No, thank *you!*" Then I was out of there.

I made a U-turn off of I-75 and headed north again. Now that it was daylight and I'd had some nourishment and a stiff dose of adrenaline, I was feeling pretty good. I wanted to see that house again. *My* house? Could that really be true? It excited me no end, but to tell the truth, the memory of the previous night made me feel more scared than elated. The more things fell into place, the more unreal they seemed.

I turned off the freeway and drove around until I located Tuxedo Road. The place looked a lot different in the daytime— still sort of phony, but not nearly as creepy. There were a couple of cop cars parked on the curb, and the crime-scene tape was still in place. I was feeling confident by now, so I ducked under it and climbed up the driveway. Halfway to the house, a uniformed officer stopped me. He had a hare lip.

"Sir, this is an active crime scene. You can't come up here."

"Sorry, officer. I don't want to intrude, but I'm the father of one of the victims, and I just found out that this is probably my house."

He looked at me like I was crazy. "I don't think that's right, Mister…"

"Brock."

"Mr. Brock. This house belongs to a man named Jack Sloan, who is now deceased. We're investigating his murder."

"I understand that," I said. "But I think you're misinformed. I'm a tax assessor, and I've researched the ownership of this property. It belonged to my daughter, Cyn…I mean Dawn Marie Sterling."

"The gal who was killed was your daughter? The blond gal?"

"That's right," I said, feeling more entitled.

"Hold on a minute, Mr. Brock. I need to go consult with my detective."

He turned and walked back up the hill toward the house. After a few minutes, he came back.

"Come this way, Mr. Brock. Sorry for the third degree."

When we got to the top of the hill I could smell the odor of death again, and it made me gag, even in broad daylight. The officer looked at me and saw my problem. He handed me a mask.

"Here, put this on. It won't block the smell completely, but it helps," he said. "It's smeared with Vicks VapoRub to cover up the odor."

About that time a short, square-built man in plain clothes came out the front door and walked down to where we were standing. He had steel-gray hair, cut military style. He extended his hand, and we shook.

"Mr. Brock? I'm Lieutenant Virgil Drake, lead detective on this case."

"Pleased to meet you," I said, adjusting the mask on my nose. The other officer was right, it didn't really help.

"I understand you were related to one of the victims here? Ms. Sterling?"

"Well, yes, except I knew her as Cynthia—my daughter, Cynthia Brock. I found out this morning that she changed her name. I hadn't seen her for a couple of years, and I guess a lot has happened during that time."

He nodded. "Looks that way. Sorry about her death. She was mighty young to die under circumstances like this. I lost my son in Iraq, so I have some idea how you must feel."

"Thanks," I said, suddenly feeling like I might cry. But I didn't.

"Now what's this about the house? You say you're the owner?"

"Well, that might be a stretch, at least as of now. I looked up the title and saw that it was in my daughter's name—her new name. So since she had no other heirs, I thought…"

"I see," he said, stroking his chin. "Well, it might not be that simple, but I get why you would see it that way."

I didn't understand what he meant. "I just wanted to go inside and look around. I won't touch anything. Just wanted to see the place, you know?"

He hesitated and stroked his chin some more. "Mr. Brock, it's understandable why you'd want to do that, but you might want to think it over. It's pretty rough in there. Not like what you might have seen on TV."

I swallowed and set my teeth. "Sir, I realize it probably hasn't been…cleaned up. But I do want to look at the place, if it's all right."

He shrugged. "Okay then. We're about to release the crime scene, so suit yourself. It's not exactly regulation, but I'll make an exception. All I ask is that you keep your hands in your pockets; don't touch anything or pick anything up. We'll walk straight through the place and then right back out. Understand?"

"Yes, sir," I said.

We walked up to the front door, which was a grand two-story entry at the back of the deep front verandah. The doors opened into a large central hallway with wide plank floors—the same one I'd seen Emma Faulkner exit from the previous night. Of course, I didn't mention that to the detective.

There were several large rooms on the first floor, and except for the kitchen and dining room, I really couldn't tell one from another. All were furnished in obviously expensive but pretentious furniture—sort of French style, maybe Louis the something-or-other, with a lot of curves and gold trim. We walked together through a front parlor and a back parlor, and then across the hall into a room that looked like a library. From what I remembered, this could have been the room where Daryl and I saw the yellow light, but I couldn't be sure. The dining room was like I remembered it: littered with garbage, with a huge crystal chandelier hanging over the table.

In the daylight I could see that it wasn't just the dining room that was completely trashed. I don't mean just messy; I mean turned upside down. Everywhere you looked there were papers, magazines, books, CD cases, videotapes, liquor bottles, bric-a-brac—you name it—thrown around like a tornado had hit the place. There was a lot of white dust all over everything—fingerprint dust, I assumed. I kept my hands to myself, like the detective said, but even without picking it up, I could see that a lot of the trash was hard core porn. I'm no prude, but this stuff looked really filthy. Pictures of sex with all kinds of bondage gear, naked kids in sexual poses, even people doing it with animals.

Detective Drake turned around after we stepped into the first room. He could tell I was shocked. "Don't say I didn't warn you," he said.

"Who made the mess?" I asked, baffled.

"Can't say. We did do a thorough search of the place, of course, but this is pretty much how we found it. Seems somebody was looking for something, and they apparently meant business."

We finished the tour of the downstairs and then walked around the bedrooms and study upstairs. In the master bedroom there were photographs all over the floor, mostly of naked people performing sex acts. One whole wall and the ceiling were mirrored. In the corner, hanging from some hooks, I saw what looked like a couple of ropes with handcuffs tied to the ends. Over the bed was a large photograph with a shattered frame, showing a good-looking, dark-haired guy and a cheap-looking blonde with enormous breasts and a lot of make-up, both of them nude, standing back to back and smiling sideways into the camera. The man had a huge erection. Even the detective seemed embarrassed, and we didn't hang around in there very long. But besides that smell, there was nothing about the place that seemed like a murder scene. Then we went down to the basement.

CHAPTER EIGHT

By this time I had started getting used to the smell of death, just like Daryl had predicted the night before. But when Detective Drake opened that basement door, the stench almost knocked me over. I might have turned around and left right then, but I saw that the detective seemed amused at my reaction, so I decided to keep going.

As we descended the basement stairs, we came into a big room, the size of a small theater. In fact, I guess that's exactly what it was—a private theater. At the far end of the room, there was a screen that almost covered the wall, and at the near end there was another wall, painted off-white with an opening for a projector, not completely visible from where I stood. Off to my right was a long white sofa, and in the middle of the room were rows of cushy swivel chairs, maybe fifteen or twenty in all, on a slanted platform. Directly in front of us was a carpeted area just big enough for a large, black grand piano. On the opposite side of the room, across from where we stood, was a long bar with a smashed mirror behind it and several barstools covered in white leather.

As I reached the bottom of the stairs, I saw straight ahead of us the source of the stench. On the floor under the piano was a three-foot circle of blackened blood and clots of tissue, crawling with little white maggots. I guess I might have expected to see something like that at a murder scene, but the sight of those maggots really got to me. Disgusted and about to puke, I turned around to go back up the stairs. From that angle I could see the sofa head-on. On the wall behind it were two large splotches of dark blood and chunks of tissue, close together. The sofa was soaked with blood, too. You could tell that the people whose blood was on that wall had been sitting there together. Maybe they were watching a movie, or maybe listening to the piano—who knows? Whatever they were doing, the blood under the piano was obviously from somebody else, as it was at least six feet away from the others.

The detective crossed his arms. "There you have it, I'm afraid," he said.

I did my best to look composed. "Which one is my Cynthia?" I asked.

"The one on the left side of the couch was identified as Dawn Marie Sterling," he said. "I guess that would be your daughter."

I looked at the explosion of black blood and the chunky streams of gore running down onto the sofa and tried to picture my girl sitting there. Some things your mind just won't let you do.

"Who was the third victim?" I asked.

"A gal named Soraya Romero. We don't have a very clear picture of her yet—maybe a hooker, just a case of being in the wrong place at the wrong time. She was about thirty years old, apparently from somewhere out west. She had a Texas driver's license, but it's fake. The photos don't match up with state records. She doesn't look Hispanic, but she could still be an illegal. We're trying to track it down."

"How do you figure one person could have killed all three of them?"

"Well, it's just a theory," he said, backing up toward the piano to illustrate. "But if the killer was somebody they trusted, he could have stood behind the male victim—like this—and nailed him through the back of the head so he fell back this way. The murder weapon was a little Glock 27, which happens to fit the empty holster that was inside this guy Jack's waistband. That gun is missing."

"So you think they were killed with Jack's own weapon?"

"Sure looks like a possibility. After the killer nailed Jack, he would have popped both women with a headshot. It would have taken less than three seconds for somebody who knew how to shoot, so the girls wouldn't have time to react. The killer would have had an even easier shot if Jack was kneeling or sitting in front of the girls. That's the best I can figure."

"Okay," I said. "I've seen enough."

We walked back upstairs. In the front hall, I stopped to catch my breath.

"Sorry you had to see that," said Detective Drake.

"No, it's all right," I said. "I asked for it. Now I know where Cynthia died. I don't know why, but that helps."

He shrugged. "You might want to take a look out back. There's a nice garden out there."

He pointed outside, which of course I already pretty much knew about, and I walked through the kitchen out to the patio. It looked different in the daylight. There was also a large swimming pool beyond the patio, and a little guest house with a well-kept formal garden, which I'd completely missed the night before. It looked like the property stretched way back into the woods, and I couldn't see any other houses behind it. From my experience working for the county, I calculated a property of this size was probably at least an acre. In Buckhead that was a big spread.

The detective had followed me outside.

"Who's going to clean up the mess in there?" I asked, gesturing toward the house.

"Beats me. People think the cops do it, but that's not our job. I guess whoever owns the house is going to have to clean it up. From what you tell me, that just might be you."

"I still don't understand why the place is so torn up. Somebody looking for something—but what?"

The detective smiled. "Well, to tell you the truth, with a guy like Jack Sloan involved, it could have been anything—maybe drugs or money. He could have had a pretty good stash of either or both, and chances are he didn't keep it piled up on the coffee table. These drug dealers get pretty paranoid sometimes, and they can be very creative about their stash."

"Do you think they found whatever they were looking for?" I asked.

"Hard to tell. We sure didn't find anything worth all this trouble, and we're pros at it. My hunch is it wasn't the killer who did all this. They would have wanted to get out of here quick, right after the murders. But they might have come back later. Or maybe somebody else did. Like I said, the power had been turned off, so none of the alarm equipment would have worked. The place would have been wide open to anyone who wanted to come in and look around."

My stomach did a flip. "So if they didn't find what they were looking for, they might be back?"

Detective Drake shook his head. "Yeah, that's always possible, but we've got the alarm system set now, so it would be harder. We've changed the code, so anybody trying to get in would be out of luck, even if they knew the old one. Hey, I wouldn't worry about it too much. You weren't planning on moving in anytime soon, were you?"

I hadn't even thought about that. "No, I guess not. Not anytime soon, especially with the smell and all. I know the mess can be cleaned up, but do you think that smell will ever come out?"

"Oh yeah, you'd be surprised. There are cleaning crews that do it all the time. They've got a bunch of chemicals that will eventually fade it down to nothing. If you want, we can try to hook you up with one of those companies."

"No thanks," I said, not wanting to think about it right then. "I do have one more question, though. When do you figure all this happened?"

"Last Monday night sometime. They'd all eaten Tex-Mex within an hour or two of the murders, but we can't be absolutely sure of the time because the bodies sat in the heat for at least three days. In fact, it looks like the killer—or somebody—deliberately turned off the power when they left. I guess they wanted those bodies to rot. Or else, like I said, they wanted to be able to get back in."

"It sounds like the killer had some sort of grudge, other than just drugs or money."

"Yeah, it does seem so, although these drug gangs can be brutal. Like I said, it looks like the killer was somebody they trusted, and they'd been hanging out together. The male victim was seen ordering four dinners at the Dos Amigos restaurant a few blocks over in Peachtree Hills, just shortly before the estimated time of death, between nine and midnight Monday."

I had heard about as much as I could take. The detective gave me his card, and I thanked him and walked back down the driveway to my car.

It was nearly three o'clock, and I was tired, but I wasn't ready to go home just yet. Maybe it's just me, but once I get interested in something, I can't seem to let it go. In this case, it wasn't just the possibility that I might be about to inherit a fortune. It wasn't even the consuming need I've already mentioned to find out who killed my daughter. It was mainly that nothing seemed to add up, and all the loose ends and question marks were turning into an obsession. I knew it was foolish for an aging accountant like me to involve myself in what should have been strictly a police investigation. Not only foolish, but possibly dangerous. But by then I didn't care. I was all in.

I turned into a strip mall and parked in front of a Radio Shack. For years I'd been resisting the purchase of a smartphone, thinking it was just so much gadgetry and feeling like it was bad for your mental health to be hooked up to the Internet every minute of every day. But now I was starting to see the advantages of being connected. The clerk in the store set me up with a late-model phone with a two-year contract and helped me get online. The first thing I did was look up the address for the law offices of Emma Faulkner.

CHAPTER EIGHT

Lawson, Faulkner, and Craig, PC, was located in the Atlanta suburb of Vinings, near the Chattahoochee River, in a sleek, glass professional building. I knew I could have called ahead, but suspected that Emma wouldn't talk to me on the phone. After everything that had happened recently, I wasn't about to trust anyone, especially this woman who misled me about my daughter and failed to tell me about the name change. What else had she failed to tell me? Not only that, but I was curious about this person named Diana Diamond, who was represented by Emma and who supposedly was somehow involved with Jack Sloan's estate. Instead of calling, I followed my new GPS to Emma Faulkner's office.

I circled the parking deck before driving in and saw the little red Maserati parked on the first level in a "reserved" spot. Obviously the lady was in. For a few minutes, I sat behind the wheel, debating whether to phone from there or just go on ahead. I decided on the latter and took the elevator up to the top floor. The office was posh and quiet. There didn't seem to be anyone around except the Asian-looking receptionist, who seemed surprised to see me.

"May I help you, sir?"

"I'm Joe Brock. I'd like to see Ms. Faulkner if she's available, please," I said politely.

"Ms. Faulkner is in court today, sir. Can I direct you to one of her associates?"

"No, I need to see her in person. If you don't mind, I'll wait."

"It could be hours. Sometimes she doesn't even check in after court." This receptionist was good at her job. Very smooth. I knew she was giving me a line of crap, of course.

"That's all right. I've got time; I'll wait," I said, sitting down in one of the expensive leather chairs.

"As you wish, sir. May I get you some coffee?"

"No thanks."

But after almost an hour of waiting, fiddling with my new phone, I wished I hadn't turned down the coffee. I was tired and out of sorts, especially since I knew Emma was back there somewhere. It was nearly five before I decided I'd had enough. The receptionist was putting on her jacket, getting ready to leave. I walked up to the window.

"Listen, Ms. Whatever Your Name Is, I know Emma Faulkner is in there because I saw her car in the parking lot. Please tell her that Joe Brock is here, the father of Dawn Marie Sterling."

She frowned and disappeared into the inner sanctum. After about a minute a door opened into the reception room, and out stepped Emma herself. She was dressed in a red suit with a sheer blouse—so sheer you could just about see through it. She wasn't wearing a bra. I stood up.

"Hello, Mr. Brock. I didn't expect to see you again quite so soon," she said.

I followed her down a corridor to the corner office, which was a spacious, dramatic glass box overlooking the Chattahoochee. She pointed to a wingback chair across from her desk, and I sat down.

"Now tell me what's going on. What brings you all the way up here to see me?"

All of a sudden I felt tongue-tied. "I don't know exactly. I've been looking into my daughter's death, and there are a few things that don't seem right. I thought maybe you could give me some answers."

"I'll try—if I can," she said, smiling. She had a lot of large, very white teeth.

"It's about this guy Jack Sloan—the one you said you represented…"

"No, Mr. Brock, you misunderstood me. I don't represent Mr. Sloan now. He's deceased, of course. I represent his wife, who is heir to his estate." She smiled again.

"That's what I was wondering about. His wife. Her name is Diana Diamond?"

She seemed surprised that I knew the name. "Right. Miss Diamond is petitioning for his estate in the Probate Court, and I'm representing her. We have to sort out inheritance of his property— his house, vehicles, other assets…"

"But I understand that the house he was living in…over in Buckhead? I understand it's in the name of Dawn Marie Sterling. And that person happens to be my daughter…or was."

Emma steepled her hands and studied me across the desk. I could tell she was impressed that I'd figured out about the name change and knew about the title and the probate case. Her dark eyes narrowed.

"Mr. Brock, in the legal system, things are not always as they appear. Sometimes the name on a title doesn't mean what you might think."

I thought about that. "Well, I'm no lawyer, but in my job, the name on the title means quite a bit. It means ownership."

She smiled again. "That's why we have courts, Mr. Brock—to sort out appearances from reality."

"That's exactly what I've been trying to figure out. The appearances don't seem to add up to any kind of reality," I said.

She rolled her chair back from the desk and crossed her legs, showing a lot of thigh below her skirt.

"So I gather you've been doing some investigating, have you?"

"Well, not really investigating. Just checking things out. Like I said, I keep finding out things that don't make sense."

"Such as?"

"Well, for starters, why did my daughter change her name? And why didn't you tell me about that?"

She paused for only a second. "Oh, so that's it. Mr. Brock, I can certainly understand why that would bother you. Believe me, I had no reason for keeping anything from you, other than sparing your feelings. I thought it was hard enough for you to have to see the body without dealing with the other…circumstances."

I turned over what she had said in my mind. It wasn't entirely implausible. But then I thought again about seeing her set the alarm on Tuxedo Road, and knew I shouldn't trust her.

"Okay then," I said. "You seem to know quite a bit about these circumstances. Tell me about them."

She pulled back up to the desk and rested her elbows on it. "What would you like to know?"

"What about Cynthia's relationship with this guy Jack? What was that deal?" The truth was that after seeing all the pornography on Tuxedo Road, I wasn't sure I wanted to know any more, but I had to start somewhere.

"Okay then. Let's talk about that," she said. "Jack Sloan was a jazz pianist—a very good one. He owned some businesses, including a nightclub downtown. He made a good living that way. He was also a very attractive man. Your daughter was working as a waitress at the club. They hit it off, and after a while they moved in together. It was a love story—simple as that."

"Miss Faulkner…"

"Call me Emma. Everybody does."

"Okay, Emma. Forgive me, but I can tell it's not all that simple. Why was that house in my daughter's name—her *phony* name? She couldn't have earned enough as a waitress to pay cash for it."

"Ah! That's a reasonable question. Actually, I'm not sure— you'd have to ask his CPA—but it was probably purchased in her name for tax reasons. You know something about taxes, I gather. Well, the club business is largely a cash business, and sometimes people like to conceal their cash from the tax collectors. Not exactly honest, I'll grant you that, but it happens."

"So he gave Cynthia a gift of a three-million-dollar house just so he wouldn't have to pay taxes?"

"Not a gift. No, it definitely was not a gift. It did belong to him, of course, since it was his money that paid for it. It's part of his estate. I haven't filed the inventory in the probate court yet, but the house will definitely be listed. And it, along with everything else in the estate, rightfully belongs to Jack's wife, Diana Diamond."

This was more than I could follow. I chewed on it for a moment or two.

"Okay then. So who *is* Diana Diamond, and where was she all this time her husband was living with my daughter?"

At that point, Emma rolled her chair back again and stood up.

"Look, Mr. Brock, we shouldn't be having this conversation. I've tried to be helpful because I understand your grief at losing your daughter, but we've come to a fork in that road. It's not my job to advise you about the facts of this case. I have ethics to consider."

I looked back at her, and we sort of locked eyes for a minute. It was finally clear to me that Emma was no friend. She was an adversary. I needed to get a lawyer.

CHAPTER NINE

When I pulled into my driveway that night, I knew right away that something was wrong. I never use the garage because over the years it's gotten filled with junk—Cynthia's stuff, which I couldn't bear to look at after she left home, plus a lot of old furniture, tools, boxes of books and papers, and assorted knickknacks. You know—everything you should have thrown away but thought you might want someday. Anyway, the reason I knew something was wrong is that the side door to the garage was standing open. It had been locked from the inside for years.

I walked up the front sidewalk to the porch and tried the door. It was unlocked. Now I was sure there was a problem, as it's almost a religion for me to lock the door after myself when I leave. Funny as it may seem, I started wishing I had Daryl with me so he could draw his gun. It was probably stupid, but after the day I'd had, I didn't want to call the police. So I pushed the door open gently and stepped inside.

You've probably already figured out that I wasn't living an extravagant lifestyle. My job pays a decent five-figure salary, but with a mortgage and other bills to cover while trying to put a little aside in savings, I hadn't accumulated much stuff. Even so, when I walked through the front door and saw the condition of my house, I felt positively sick. Someone had torn the place up from top to bottom. All the upholstered furniture was slashed open, and the stuffing was everywhere. Tables were turned over, drawers pulled out, papers and junk tossed around, everything pulled out of the kitchen cabinets, and the refrigerator emptied onto the floor. They'd even taken the mattress off my bed and chopped it up; then they went after the box springs. Out in the garage it was even worse.

Call me crazy, but I didn't even hesitate. The phone hadn't rung twice before Daryl picked up. I told him what had happened.

"Wow, Pops, that's a pisser," he said. "It's a good thing you weren't home. They might have gone after you."

"What should I do?"

"Call the cops, I guess. Or maybe not. Let me think about this. Can you think of anybody who would have it in for you?"

"Yeah, but I can't tell you who they are. I think it might be the same people who trashed the house up in Buckhead. I took a tour of the place this afternoon. Same story. The whole place is a wreck. The cops said it was probably somebody looking for something—a stash."

"No kidding! You got in there?"

"Right. That's another story. It turns out that my daughter owned the place. It might be mine now."

"Wow! Listen, I'm just getting off work, and I'm coming over. Don't do anything until I get there," he said. He had hung up before I could give him directions. But I knew he had that iPhone, of course, and those smartphones seemed to know everything.

I waited outside, and within an hour Daryl's truck pulled up. He was in uniform.

"I've been thinking it over," he said. "It won't do any good to report this to the Jonesboro Police. They'll just treat it as a routine burglary, and from what you tell me, it sounds like a lot more than that. I have some contacts in the Atlanta PD I can call. They can connect it up with the murder case. You know—keep both hands working together."

I reached into my pocket and pulled out the business card that the homicide detective downtown had given me. "This guy said to call if I needed anything," I said.

Daryl looked a little annoyed. "I never heard of that guy. You can't trust everyone down at APD headquarters, you know. A lot of them are crooked. Let me just call my buddy, Hugo." He already had his phone in his hand.

I didn't know what to think, but as I had no experience with this sort of thing, I was glad Daryl was being proactive. My doubts about him the night before seemed unimportant compared to this new development.

We waited outside for Hugo to arrive, mainly because I was still nervous about going back in. He turned out to be a tall, slim guy with dark hair and a pencil mustache, dressed in plain clothes. He flashed his badge, too quick for the last name to register with me, and then started right in about how there was no doubt this was related to the "Tuxedo murders," as he called them. That didn't make me feel any better. He and Daryl told me to wait while they went in and checked the place out.

Honestly, by that time it had been two hours since I got home, and I was hungry and needed a drink and a bathroom. But I waited for them on the front porch for what seemed like a very long time before they came out and told me I could go inside with them. I followed the two guys back in, feeling disgusted, angry, scared, and confused, all at the same time.

"Don't touch anything, Joe," said Hugo, standing in a pile of torn-up *National Geographic* magazines on the living room floor. "You might disturb evidence. Daryl might disagree, but I think for starters, we need to get Jonesboro PD over here to dust for prints and take pictures. Don't worry, I'll make sure they get hooked up with the right people in Atlanta. Meanwhile, you need to be careful about talking to the Atlanta cops. Just a word to the wise."

"I don't get it," I said. "Why would they steer me wrong?"

"This Tuxedo deal isn't just any murder case, my friend. It has a lot of layers underneath and on top. People you'd never suspect of being involved, and unfortunately that might include a few people in uniform. You can't really trust anyone in a case like this, I'm afraid. And that's about all I can say about it right now."

"So you think I should call 911?"

"Yeah, that's probably okay. Just don't mention anything about Daryl and me being here. No point in confusing the issues. I'll get with my buddy on the Jonesboro PD later and make sure they follow up with the right people in Atlanta homicide division, though I don't have any doubt about the connection with Tuxedo."

I sank down in what was left of my Lazy Boy recliner, shaking my head. "It just doesn't make any sense. None of it does. Why would anyone want to do this? I didn't even know the people who got killed, except my daughter, of course."

"So maybe that's the connection," said Daryl. "Maybe your daughter knew something, or the killers thought she did. Maybe she had something they wanted that they couldn't find up at Tuxedo Road."

"Sure seems that way," agreed Hugo. "Did you have any contact with your daughter in the weeks before she died?"

"No. I hadn't heard from Cynthia for nearly two years. Of course, she did have a key to the house, and there were a couple of times when I suspected she might have come home while I was at work. Nothing in particular—just a feeling I had. I never stopped hoping she'd come back, you know."

"Yeah, that must have been tough," said Hugo. He didn't really seem very sympathetic, though. Just a hardened cop reading the script, I guess.

Just then I remembered my visit to Emma Faulkner's office. "Say, do either of you know a good lawyer I could call?"

They looked at each other. "What kind of lawyer?" asked Daryl.

"I'm not sure. Not criminal. Maybe probate? I need somebody to help me figure out what my daughter actually owned when she died. Her name was on the Tuxedo Road house, but there's some other woman claiming to be the owner. Pretty confusing."

"Yeah, Pops, I do know a good lawyer who could probably help you. He's in general practice—got me a settlement from a car wreck a couple of years ago, but I'm sure he knows about probate, too. His name is Lebeaux—Jonathan Lebeaux. Has an office downtown. I think I still have his card here somewhere." He thumbed through his wallet.

I took the card, realizing I already knew that name. But I decided not to mention it.

"Thanks, Daryl. I'll give him a call in the morning," I said. Then I dialed 911.

CHAPTER TEN

The city of Jonesboro only has twenty-five to thirty officers, and when you've lived there a long time like I had, you get to know them by name. As luck would have it, the cop who showed up the next morning was Fred Crick, a balding guy in his early forties with a bulging gut that stretched out the buttons on his shirt. Officer Crick was at least a nine- or ten-year veteran of the Force. When Cynthia was in high school, her friends used to call him Officer Prick because of his overzealous traffic stops along Tara Boulevard. Unfortunately, he had also ticketed me the previous month for driving with an expired license. Apparently he'd gotten promoted to burglary. I wasn't happy to see him, especially because I'd spent the night on my bedroom floor with all the lights on, listening for the return of the Tuxedo killers.

Crick took the report and looked around the place. He seemed to lose interest when I told him nothing was missing and there was no sign of forced entry. I tried to tell him what had happened to Cynthia up in Buckhead, and that I thought this burglary had something to do with it, but he didn't seem concerned.

"Looks like a bunch of punk kids to me. Vandalism."

"But why would they tear everything up like this? Don't you think they must have been looking for something?"

"Like what? A sack o' diamonds?" he asked, dripping sarcasm as he looked around my modest digs. "You're lettin' your imagination run away with you, Mr. Brock. I've been doin' police work for nigh onto twenty year now, and in my experience if there's nothin' stolen, it's gonna be plain vandalism. We get a lot of that around here these days. The whole county's gone over to the punks."

"What about the front door? I'd swear on a stack of bibles that I locked it. I always do."

"Apparently not this time," he said with a condescending smile that made me mad.

"Well, don't you think you should at least dust for prints?"

He laughed. "What in the world for? Y'all have been here for a couple decades, and in that much time, your average house will collect a hundred sets of full and partial prints. You'd never sort out what's suspicious and what's legit. Besides, your burglars probably wore latex gloves. That's what they do nowadays. Take my advice, Mr. Brock. Just call your insurance agent and collect a nice fat check, and use it to redecorate the place."

He handed me his card (I was acquiring quite a collection by this time) and told me in his official voice how sorry he was about Cynthia, and then he left. When he was gone, I made myself some coffee, turned the kitchen table right side up, and sat down to think. That front door bothered me most. I couldn't figure it out. Then it dawned on me. Of course! Cynthia had a key. Whoever got in there must have gotten it from her, one way or another.

While I showered and got dressed, I turned everything over in my mind. The more I thought about it, the more certain I felt that it was Cynthia's key that had opened my front door. The idea that her killer had been there in my house really shook me up.

Whatever else was true, it was for sure I needed a lawyer. The visit to Emma Faulkner's office had convinced me of that much. But could I trust this guy Lebeaux, who came with the endorsement of the questionably trustworthy Deputy Daryl Spinks? I remembered seeing Daryl going back into the Fuzzy Navel with that guy dressed in a three-piece suit, and the tan Mercedes registered to Jonathan Lebeaux. Now that I knew he was Daryl's lawyer, that didn't seem so strange. Still, something about the whole picture felt out of focus.

For a minute or two, I let my helpless feelings get the better of me, and I considered just giving up and letting Emma and Diana Diamond have the damn Tuxedo house. After all, I hadn't done anything to deserve it. Besides, I had this lingering, uneasy feeling like I'd be biting off something bigger than I could chew if I got any more involved. But then I thought about that bloody splotch on the wall that used to be Cynthia's brains, and the smirk on Emma Faulkner's face.

I decided I needed to have another conversation with my baby girl. So I went out to the car, got her graduation photo, and brought it back inside, intending to put it back up on the mantle. But I guess I was still pretty shaky, and I didn't quite open the hinged cardboard flap enough to stand the frame upright. It came tumbling forward and crashed onto the brick hearth, shattering the glass. I stood there a minute, ready to read this mishap as an omen, until I noticed something weird about the photo. It was bulging out of the frame, like there was something stuck behind it. I guess the glass must have been holding it in before it broke. I lifted the photo and pulled out a folded up piece of paper. It was a marriage certificate from the State of Nevada, attesting to the marriage, less than a month earlier, of Jack Sloan and Dawn Marie Sterling. It looked authentic, with an embossed seal at the bottom.

Cynthia was married! She must have really cared for this guy Sloan. If I needed my mind made up, that did it for me. I dialed the number on the card Daryl had handed me. Much to my surprise, Lebeaux answered the phone himself. I told him who I was and that Daryl had referred me. Then I tried to explain my legal problem but realized I wasn't really sure what it was. Once I mentioned Tuxedo, the marriage certificate, and "common-law wife," he seemed to get interested.

"I'll be damned," he said. "Well, I think we'd better get you over here ASAP. How soon can you get downtown?"

An hour later I was sitting in his office, which was in a little brick building downtown, off West Peachtree, and looked none too prosperous, at least compared with the fancy glass digs of Emma Faulkner. I remembered his Mercedes, though, and figured appearances could be deceptive and that he must be making good money somehow. He was a sharp dresser, too—sort of a handsome guy about my age, with a square jaw and reddish hair that looked like it came out of a bottle. Something about him looked familiar, and I wondered if maybe I'd seen him advertising on TV.

"So you're up against my good buddy Emma, are you?" He laughed, lighting a cigar. "She's a piece of work, I'll say that much."

I wasn't sure exactly what he meant by that. "To tell the truth, I'm not really sure *who* I'm up against," I said.

"Okay, let's talk about that," he said. "Looks to me like the first thing you need to do is file an objection to this Diana Diamond person acting as administrator of the estate. From what you tell me, this common-law wife business is a crock of shit. Your daughter is almost certain to have a better claim."

"Slow down, Mr. Lebeaux. This is all new to me. Exactly what is a common-law wife?"

He leaned back in his chair. "It's history, that's what. No such thing anymore in Georgia—or very many other states, for that matter. Used to be that if you shacked up with somebody, told people you were married, said some private marriage vows, then the law would recognize you as being married. Most people think you had to live together for seven years, or some such thing, to have a common-law marriage. But no. Not in Georgia. Theoretically, one night would do it, as long as you swore in court that both parties agreed to be married. It was a giant legal boondoggle for gold diggers, both male and female, claiming they were married and therefore entitled to something from the other person—or their estate, as the case may be. Thank God the Georgia Legislature did away with that one a couple decades ago."

I wasn't following. "So doesn't Emma Faulkner know that? Why would she put it in her court papers if it's not legal anymore?"

"Oh, but there's a catch—there always is, of course. If you can prove you had a common-law marriage *before* the law was repealed, the court still has to recognize it. I haven't seen paperwork yet, of course, but that must be what this Diana Diamond is going to allege."

"What about that house? Doesn't Cynthia's name on the title mean something?"

"Sure. Of course. But there are a couple of major snags that could wipe out her rights. First of all, people put property in other people's names all the time. When they do, it's usually presumed to be a gift. That's what you'll argue. But if Emma can prove it wasn't meant as a gift, but just as some sort of convenience, she can wipe out the legal title, and the court will award the property to whoever put up the money, in this case probably Jack Sloan. And this Diana person would be his heir."

I nodded. "Okay, I get that. Emma told me Sloan put it in Cynthia's name to avoid taxes."

Lebeaux laughed and shook his head. "And maybe he did. But let's not go *there*, Joe. You can bet Emma won't bring that argument up in court. If she did, the whole estate would end up with an IRS lien against it. No, let's just assume it was a gift to his fiancée, given out of love and affection."

I hadn't thought of it before, but the idea of the government getting involved made me even more nervous. Drug gangs and hit men were bad enough—but the IRS? That was scary.

"I don't know. Maybe I should just back off…" I said.

"I wouldn't worry about it, Joe. If the IRS could pin anything on Sloan, they would have done it long ago. No, your biggest obstacle right now is Emma. She's smart, but she's got some major hurdles here. Let's say the court does decide the house wasn't intended as a gift but actually belonged to Jack Sloan. Now you have to look to see who his heirs are. If he was married at the time of his death, with no children and no will, everything goes to the wife. But in this case you have to figure out *which* wife. Sloan couldn't legally be married to two women at once, and there's no such thing as a common-law divorce. This Diana gal is going to have to get on the stand and convince the judge of something that happened between two people at least twenty years ago, and that there was no divorce, so the guy couldn't have legally married your daughter. That's tough, especially since Sloan obviously didn't consider himself married to Diana when he flew off to Vegas to marry your daughter. It's a pretty big stretch even for Emma, if you ask me, but exactly the sort of thing I'd expect from her." He chuckled under his breath.

"Jesus," I said. "This is way too complicated. Give me the bottom line. What do I need to do?"

He took a couple of puffs on his cigar. I hate tobacco smoke, especially in small spaces like Lebeaux's office. "Okay. Like I said, you need to file in the Fulton County Probate Court. Object to Emma's petition and ask to be appointed temporary administrator of the whole estate. Whoever gets appointed will have control of the property, and that's ninety percent of the game. Once you're made temporary administrator, the chances are overwhelming you'll end up with it permanently."

"Let me get this straight. You're talking about the whole estate? Not just the house?"

"Sure. You can claim the whole enchilada. The judge will have competing petitions. Two women claiming to be married to the same man. Very interesting stuff. Fortunately, like I said, there are rules for deciding that. If Jack wasn't married to Diana at common law, then everything goes to you, as your daughter's only heir. If he was married to Diana, then the most you'll get out of it is the house—*if* it's ruled to be a gift. And it's up to Diana to prove it *wasn't* intended that way—hard to do when the donor is dead. Worst-case scenario, you'll walk away with nothing. But the odds are definitely in your favor."

I sat there a minute, thinking it over, remembering what the police had said about the drug dealings. "Would that mean I'd be responsible for whatever Sloan owned? Like maybe a stash of money or drugs?"

Lebeaux smiled. "Well, if there are any drugs involved, that's a whole different problem. But yes, you'd be in the driver's seat. You'd have to manage it—investigate, gather in the assets, report to the court, the whole deal. Under the circumstances, you might not be comfortable doing that. But of course, that's where I'd come in. I'd take care of everything for you. If you hire me, that is."

"Mr. Lebeaux, I'm not a rich man. All this sounds expensive."

"Oh, don't worry about that. I'm used to dealing on a contingency. I'd take a cut of whatever you get."

"Like…how big of a cut?"

He rolled his cigar between his thumb and forefinger. "Standard is forty percent in a contested probate case. Considering the numbers involved here, I'd be satisfied with that."

"Forty percent of three million? But I'd have to sell the house to pay you," I said.

"True. But you weren't planning on living there anyway, were you?"

I reflected on that. "No, I guess not."

"Do we have a deal then? If so, I'll print out a contract right now."

I shrugged. What the hell. "Okay, go ahead."

CHAPTER ELEVEN

I've tried to reconstruct the next few days, but honestly they're mostly a blur in my memory. I got the insurance company out to clean up my house, and they moved me into a motel near the freeway while the work was being done. I ended up with a pretty generous check, just like Officer Prick had predicted. And by the following Monday, I was back at work, nodding and thanking everyone for their sympathy, even though none of them had ever met Cynthia. I drank too much and slept hardly at all.

Meanwhile, Lebeaux got busy right away and filed a lot of paperwork with the probate court. He called to let me know that the hearing to decide on the temporary administrator of the Jack Sloan Estate was set for the following Thursday. This temporary hearing was really important, he said. If we won, it would give us a big advantage when it came to the final trial.

It all seemed to be moving too fast.

"What am I supposed to do at this hearing?" I asked on the phone. "I don't know anything about this guy Jack Sloan."

"Don't worry, I'll handle it," he said. "It's basically a matter of submitting paperwork on our side. All we need are certified documents—the marriage certificate and the deed, et cetera. On the other side, Emma will have to put up witnesses to prove this Diana character was married to Jack. I'm not worried about that. Judges never did like common-law marriages. Plus that, I'm pretty sure Emma isn't expecting to see that marriage certificate. I can't wait to see her face."

The next Thursday, I met Lebeaux in the courthouse coffee shop half an hour before the hearing. I was getting nervous, but he again reassured me. "Listen, Joe, this is a piece of cake. Trust me."

We walked upstairs to the courtroom, where Emma was already sitting at the table, wearing a blue suit with a long slit up the side. Next to her was a skinny woman who looked to be about my age, with frizzy, dyed black hair and blue-rimmed glasses.

"Isn't she a little old to be Jack's wife?" I asked, remembering that Sloan was supposed to be about forty.

"Looks that way. You never know what to expect where Emma's concerned," said Lebeaux.

Judge Osgood Mitchell entered from behind a wood-paneled door. He was a chubby guy, a little older than me, with a pink face and a stringy gray comb-over, pleasant-looking.

After some arguing between the lawyers about the "discovery" papers Lebeaux had sent to Emma, and other legal matters I couldn't follow, I was called to the stand and sworn in. I apparently had to go first because we were the petitioners.

"State your name, please sir," said Lebeaux.

"Joseph P. Brock," I said.

"How are you employed?"

"I'm a tax assessor for Clayton County. Been doing that for twenty-five years."

"And how are you related to Ms. Cynthia Brock?"

"She is…was…my daughter."

"Do you know whether she had any other heirs?"

"Objection!" shouted Emma. "Calls for a legal conclusion."

"Sustained," said Judge Mitchell.

"Well, let me ask you this: To your knowledge, did she have any other living relatives?"

"No, sir. Her mother died several years ago. Cancer."

"No brothers or sisters?"

"No. She was an only child."

"And what, if anything, do you know about her legal name being changed?"

"I found out she'd changed it to Dawn Marie Sterling. Not exactly sure when."

"Was your daughter employed, Mr. Brock?"

"I'm not sure. I heard she was a waitress…"

"Object to the hearsay," said Emma.

"Sustained," said the judge, yawning.

"Well, to your knowledge, did your daughter have any means of earning a living?"

"No. She was a high-school graduate. No job skills."

"Did she have any assets?"

"No money—at least not when she left home. She was pretty much broke. But by the time she died, she owned a three-million-dollar house in Buckhead."

"And would that be Three-Thirteen Tuxedo Road, Fulton County?"

"Yes, sir."

"Do you know where Cynthia was living at the time of her death?"

"Apparently she was living in that house—the one that was in her name. I think that was the address on her driver's license, too," I said.

"And to your knowledge, who was she living with?"

"Objection! Calls for speculation," said Emma.

"Overruled. You may answer the question, Mr. Brock, if you know."

"She was living with Mr. Jack Sloan. They were both murdered two weeks ago in that house on Tuxedo Road."

Lebeaux reached into his file and pulled out the marriage license. Emma saw him doing it and stood up. Lebeaux came toward me and handed me the paper.

"Mr. Brock, have you recently learned anything about your daughter's marital status at the time of her death?"

Emma came forward. "Your honor, I renew my previous objection at the bench to this evidence."

"Overruled, Ms. Faulkner. This is a certified document," said the judge.

"Mr. Brock, have you seen this document before?" asked Lebeaux.

"Yes. I found it behind a photograph at my house. I believe my daughter must have hidden it there."

"Your honor, I tender this document, marked Movant's Exhibit One, a certified copy of a Nevada marriage license between Jack Sloan and Dawn Marie Sterling."

"My objection stands, your honor. We have not been able to authenticate this document. Until they prove it's authentic, it's hearsay."

"The document is admitted," said Judge Mitchell.

"All right, Mr. Brock, that's all for now," said Lebeaux.

Emma stood up. "No cross-examination, Your Honor."

I got down from the witness stand, and Lebeaux offered a certified copy of the deed to the Tuxedo house and a certified copy of Cynthia's name change in evidence. The judge accepted them with no objections from Emma. Then Lebeaux rested his case.

Emma called Diana Diamond to the stand. She got up and walked past me, leaving a trail of flowery perfume. She was wearing a black pantsuit and was sort of plump through the middle, but her arms and legs were so skinny the fabric flapped when she walked. She was sworn in.

"State your name, please," said Emma.

"Diana Yvonne Diamond." She had a raspy voice, like somebody who'd smoked cigarettes for a very long time.

"And are you related to the deceased, Mr. Jack Sloan?"

"Yes, ma'am. I was his wife," said Diana, gazing down at her fingernails.

Lebeaux started to stand up but then stopped himself.

"And when were the two of you married?" asked Emma.

"That was back in 1995. We lived together back then," said Diana.

"Did you have a marriage ceremony in 1995?"

"No, not exactly. Not public, anyway. It was private, between Jack and me. We didn't need a piece of paper to prove we were married."

Lebeaux rolled his eyes and whispered to me, "Wish I had a dollar for every time I've heard that one…"

"Please tell the court about your relationship with Mr. Sloan," said Emma.

"Well, of course Jack was a lot younger than me," said Diana, smiling up at Judge Mitchell. "He was only nineteen years old when we first started living together. I was thirty-eight at the time, old enough to be his mother, you know. I imagine that was the attraction, since he had lost his parents at an early age. But it turned into a pretty steamy relationship, if you get my meaning…"

The judge was looking down, flipping through papers, and didn't seem impressed.

"Go on," said Emma. "You and Mr. Sloan had a sexual relationship, I take it?"

"Oh yes, very sexual. Jack was a very sexual person, and so am I."

"And when was the last time you and Mr. Sloan had sex?"

"Well, we weren't seeing each other very often toward the end, you know. I live in Midtown, and he'd bought that place up in Buckhead. But he spent the night with me just a couple of weeks before he died. I have witnesses to that."

"And did you have a continuous marital relationship for the entire time you were together, even after you came to Georgia?"

"We sure did. It was what you might call an 'open marriage,' though. Like I said, Jack was a very sexual person, and I didn't object to him having sex with other women. I also had sexual relations with other men. We had an understanding that way."

I thought about the porn I'd seen all over the Tuxedo house and the pictures of buxom women. If Jack was having sex with them, it was hard to imagine he had much interest in Diana.

"I see," said Emma. "Now tell the court, if you would, exactly when and how you and Mr. Sloan became husband and wife."

"Well, it was on his twentieth birthday. I had bought him a little gift and made him a birthday cake—chocolate fudge, as I recall. That was his favorite. Anyway, when we were celebrating and drinking champagne, he reached into his pocket and pulled out this ring…"

She displayed a gold band on the third finger of her left hand.

"Go on, Diana. Tell the court what he said."

"I'll never forget it," sighed Diana. "He said, 'I will always love you, my darling, and with this ring I'm making you my wife.'"

"Were you surprised?" asked Emma, smiling.

"Oh, no, not really. Jack was very sentimental, and he loved symbols. I had just finalized my divorce from my first husband a few weeks earlier. I know Jack was waiting for that to happen before he proposed."

"But he didn't just *propose*, did he?" asked Emma.

"Objection! Leading the witness," said Lebeaux.

"Sustained," said the judge.

"Well, tell Judge Mitchell what you said to him after he told you he was making you his wife."

"I said—and this is a direct quote—'We are already married, darling. I don't need a ring to prove it.' Then we kissed. And from then on we called each other husband and wife."

"And did anyone else know you were married?"

"Oh, of course, everyone knew it. My two children knew it. They're outside, waiting to testify. They knew Jack and I were married. We did lots of things as a family. They were only a little younger than Jack, of course, but that didn't matter. He loved them as his own kids."

"Did you and Mr. Sloan have any children together, of your own, that is?"

"No, we didn't. I had a hysterectomy when I was about forty, so we couldn't have any together. Jack was broken-hearted about that," said Diana, with a sad look on her face.

"And finally, Diana," said Emma, "were you and Jack Sloan ever divorced?"

"Oh no. No way. We were married for life, until *death did us part*," said Diana, wiping away a tear.

"All right. Now, do you know anything about the assets Mr. Sloan owned at the time of his death?"

"Oh yes. I know all about that. He owned a club in Midtown, of course—the Blue Buddha. There is also a hotel down by the airport. I think it's called the Fly Away. He had several cars...a BMW, a Jaguar, and a Mercedes. Some bank accounts and maybe some cash—I wouldn't know too much about that. Then, of course, there's the Tuxedo Road house. That was Jack's house."

"When you say it was Jack's house, do you mean it was in his name?"

"Oh—no. He put it in the name of one of his waitresses. He did that just for privacy, I think."

"Objection! Speculation!"

"Sustained."

"Do you know who paid for that house?" asked Emma.

"Yes, I do. Jack paid cash for it. Over three million."

"And do you have any evidence of that?"

"Well, no. But I was at the closing… there in your office, Ms. Faulkner. And I saw him write the check."

"Was anyone else at the closing?"

"Yes. This old couple, the sellers. And Dawn Marie Sterling. She's the waitress I mentioned."

"And do you know whether Mr. Sloan lived in the house—moved his belongings in, took possession?"

"Oh, yes, he did. He definitely lived there. He moved there from his house over in Peachtree Hills right after the closing."

"Okay, ma'am. Do you have any documentary evidence of your relationship with Mr. Sloan?"

"Oh yes. I looked through all my old paperwork and found utility bills in the name of Diana Sloan. I brought a few of them to court. They're from 2002. That was my address at the time—Forty-Two Shepherd's Court."

"Your honor, I tender Petitioner's Exhibit One, utility bills addressed to Diana Sloan at her residence address."

Lebeaux got up and looked at the papers. He shook his head. "No objection," he said.

"Thank you, Ms. Diamond," said Emma. "Your witness, Mr. Lebeaux."

CHAPTER TWELVE

Lebeaux got up, scratching his head like he was puzzled. "Let me see if I understand your testimony, Ms. Diamond. You say you and Mr. Sloan were married for, what…about twenty years, is it? And how long has it been since you lived together?"

"Oh, I'd say about twelve, maybe thirteen years. Like I said, we had an understanding. We didn't have to live together to know we were married."

"I see. Well, you say you saw him put the Tuxedo house in the name of Dawn Marie Sterling, is that right?"

"Yes. It was for convenience."

"And you were sitting right there when he did that?"

"Yes."

"And you were his wife. But he didn't put the house in *your* name, did he?"

"No."

"As his wife, didn't you feel entitled to share in whatever property he owned?"

"Oh, no. Not necessarily. We had our own lives…"

"But now you've filed this petition, claiming to be entitled to everything in his estate, isn't that right?"

Diana looked at Emma, who sat rigid.

"Yes, I filed the petition. I'm his wife. I'm entitled to do that."

"I see. But you knew, didn't you, that Jack Sloan was living with Dawn Marie Sterling?"

"If you say so. She was there at least part of the time, I know that. Like I said, we had an open marriage."

"She and Mr. Sloan were murdered in that house, weren't they?"

"Yes."

"And since the house was in her name, she could have thrown him out at any time, couldn't she?"

"I suppose so."

"And she could have sold the place if she felt like it and pocketed the three million dollars, isn't that right?"

"She wouldn't have done that. Jack wouldn't have let her."

"But he couldn't have stopped her, could he?"

"I guess not."

"And isn't that exactly what happens when you give someone a gift?"

"Objection! Speculation, calls for a conclusion!"

"I'll rephrase that. Ms. Diamond, you are aware, aren't you, that when you give someone a piece of property as a gift, it's theirs to do with as they choose?"

"Yes. I guess so."

"And didn't it concern you that such a valuable piece of property was in the hands of a stranger to your marriage—a mere waitress?"

She shrugged. "Not really, no."

"And if Mr. Sloan had put that house in your name, wouldn't you have considered it a gift?"

"Not necessarily. It would have belonged to both of us because we're married."

"But you just told me that you had your own lives, and you didn't consider his property to be yours."

"Well, maybe I didn't at the time, but now that he's dead, it's all mine. Anyway, I'm definitely more entitled to it than some guy who never even *knew* Jack." She looked over at me.

"We'll let the court decide that, Ms. Diamond. And by the way, while we're on the subject, did Mr. Sloan ever give *you* any gifts?"

She smiled. "Why, yes he did. He gave me a couple of vehicles—a Mercedes and a Lexus SUV. He was very generous with me."

"And he put the titles to them in your name, I assume?"

"Yes, of course."

"But I notice you didn't list either of those cars as assets of his estate."

"No. They're mine."

"Right, because you have title. That's why you believed they were gifts, right?"

"Yes."

Emma was sitting on the edge of her chair, as if getting ready to jump up and object. But she didn't.

"Now Ms. Diamond, I understand that some utility bills were sent to you back in 2002 in the name of Diana Sloan. Have you used that name anywhere else?"

"Not that I can think of right now. I kept my own name. A lot of women do that, you know."

"So your legal name is Diana Diamond?"

"Yes."

"And what was your first husband's name?"

She frowned. "David Diamond."

"So you took the last name of your first husband, but not of your second husband, Jack Sloan. Is that what you're telling me?"

"Yes. You don't want to be changing your name every five minutes."

"I agree. That's why I'm wondering why you would put those utilities in the name of Diana Sloan."

"Objection! Badgering the witness," cried Emma.

"Overruled."

"I withdraw the question. All right, Ms. Diamond, at the time you filed this petition, were you aware that Mr. Sloan and Ms. Dawn Marie Sterling had been married a couple of weeks before they died?"

Diana looked at Emma, who was busying herself with writing something on a legal pad.

"No. I still don't believe it. You sprung that on us just before this hearing."

"But you did see the marriage certificate today, didn't you?"

"Yes, I saw it, for whatever it's worth. I don't believe it's real. Jack wouldn't do that to me."

"But you realize, don't you, that if the document is authentic, it means that Jack Sloan did not consider himself married to you?"

"I don't know how you figure that."

"Well, most people don't get married twice without getting a divorce in between, and you just testified that you were never divorced, didn't you?"

"Yes. If he got married again it was bigamy."

"Bigamy! That's a very harsh accusation, Ms. Diamond. Isn't it more likely that he thought he was single, and there was no reason not to marry Dawn Marie Sterling, whom he apparently held in sufficiently high regard to give her a three-million-dollar house?"

"Objection! Calls for speculation, and I object to counsel's tone. He's badgering again," said Emma.

"Never mind. I withdraw the question. Nothing further."

The judge looked up from his notes. "Any redirect?"

"Yes, your honor," said Emma, rising again. "Ms. Diamond, do you have any idea why Dawn Marie Sterling would have hidden her marriage certificate behind a photograph at her father's house, thereby concealing this alleged marriage?"

"No, it does seem pretty unbelievable."

"And when was the last time you saw Ms. Sterling?"

"A week or so before they were killed."

"Was she wearing a wedding ring at that time?"

"No."

"Did she tell you she was married?"

"No."

"Did she act any differently toward Jack Sloan at that time, as-suming he was present?"

"No, they acted just the same as always."

"Thank you. No further questions."

Lebeaux leaned over and whispered to me. "Joe, I'm going to take a chance. I have a hunch about something."

"Okay," I nodded as he stood up.

"Just a couple of questions on recross, your honor. Ms. Diamond, you've testified that the closing on the Tuxedo property was held in Ms. Faulkner's office; is that correct?"

"Yes."

"And to your knowledge, did Ms. Faulkner represent Mr. Sloan in other matters?"

"Yes, of course."

"Would those be...what? Criminal matters?"

Emma stood up. "Object to the relevance, your honor. This is way outside the scope..."

"Overruled," said the judge.

"How about other matters? Civil cases? Business deals?"

"Same objection," said Emma.

"Overruled."

"Yes. She pretty much represented him in everything," sighed Diana.

"Everything. So she was involved in almost all legal aspects of Jack Sloan's life, wouldn't you say?"

"Yes, I suppose you could say that. She started representing him right after law school, about five years ago."

"So wouldn't you say that Emma Faulkner would have known if Jack Sloan did something as important as getting married?"

Diana smiled. "I don't know. I suppose so."

"And in fact, as Mr. Sloan's trusted advisor, she probably *did* know about the marriage, and therefore knew there was a Nevada marriage certificate somewhere."

"Objection!" shouted Emma.

"Overruled," said the judge, sitting upright.

"I couldn't say. I don't know. Maybe."

"So she really wasn't surprised this morning, to see that this document exists, was she?"

"She acted surprised this morning."

"Maybe surprised to see the document—surprised that Mr. Brock found it—but not that it existed?"

"I don't know."

"Okay. Here's another question. Mr. Sloan was a man of substantial means, correct?"

"Yes."

"And it appears that there may have been a certain amount of danger in his…business dealings?"

"I guess so."

"Well, do you know whether he made a will?"

"I don't think so. No, he didn't."

"Doesn't it seem strange to you that a man in his position wouldn't have a will?"

"Not particularly, no. He knew that everything would go to me because I'm his wife," sniffed Diana.

"I see. Well, let me ask you this: was Dawn Marie Sterling a client of Ms. Faulkner's, too?"

"I don't think so. I don't think they…got along."

"And what gave you that impression?"

Diana looked at Emma for direction, but Emma was focusing on her legal pad again.

"I'm not really sure. I think they might have been...jealous of each other."

Lebeaux did a double take, but you could see Diana retreating, realizing she had stepped in it.

"Jealous? As in *sexually* jealous?"

Emma jumped up. "Objection! Your honor, this is totally irrelevant!"

Judge Mitchell shook his head and smiled down from the bench. "Sustained."

CHAPTER THIRTEEN

The judge called a recess, and Lebeaux took me downstairs and outside the building so he could smoke. But as I walked out the door, I glanced to my left, and there at the end of the sidewalk were three people, huddled together and having a conversation. At first I didn't recognize any of them—a woman and two men. One of the men had his back to me, a guy in uniform. My mouth must have dropped open a mile when that guy turned around. It was Deputy Daryl Spinks.

Daryl saw me right away, said something to the other two people, and then turned back to me and Lebeaux. They sort of nodded to each other.

"Mornin', Joe," Daryl said.

I know I looked confused, because I was. "Good morning. What are you…? I mean, I didn't expect to see you here."

"Oh, I just dropped by to check on you," he said, trying to make a joke out of it.

"But how did you know…who told you about this hearing?"

"I just happened to be talking to my lawyer here, and he thanked me for referring you, and mentioned there was a hearing today. After everything we've been through together, I thought you could use some moral support."

Lebeaux looked uncomfortable. "Daryl likes to be helpful," he said, puffing on his cigar.

"Hey, Joe, don't look so confused. These hearings are open to the public, you know. I come down here quite a bit, just to listen in. A person can learn a lot that way."

I shrugged. Something didn't feel right, all the same. "Who are those people down there?" I asked, gesturing toward the man and woman at the end of the building.

"Who, them? I just met them—upstairs, in the hallway outside the courtroom. Their names are Pete and Gigi, I think. They said they were witnesses in your case, so I thought I'd pump them for some information—just trying to help out, you know?"

"What did you find out?" I asked.

Daryl looked at Lebeaux and then back at me. "Nothing much. They say they're related to this Diana woman—her kids. They knew the dead guy, Jack. Also your daughter. Other than that, they didn't say much."

Lebeaux snuffed out his cigar in the sand ashtray next to the door, and stuck the unsmoked half into his jacket pocket. "We need to be getting back upstairs, Joe," he said, turning toward me.

I thought Daryl looked a little offended. "Hey, I was just looking out for Joe here," he said.

"We're doing all right without any help," said Lebeaux. "It might be better if you went on back to work now."

"Fine," said Daryl. "See you later, Joe."

On the way upstairs, Lebeaux acted peculiar. "I don't think you should be hanging around with Daryl, Joe. He's a nice enough kid, but his judgment is lacking sometimes."

I nodded. "I just met him last week. He took me up to see the Tuxedo house. Seems to know a lot of people."

"Right. That he does," said Lebeaux. I wanted to ask more questions about Daryl, but Lebeaux seemed to want to end the discussion.

After the recess, Emma called Diana's two children to the stand. The daughter, Gigi, was about thirty and looked like her mother—very skinny, with short, clown-red hair and a lot of tattoos. She testified that Diana and Jack had lived together when she was a little girl—and, of course, that she thought they were married. Lebeaux asked her if she had been present at their wedding, and she said no. She thought they were married, anyway.

"So, Miss Diamond, when was the last time you saw Jack Sloan?"

"I don't know, man. Maybe a month ago. Something like that." She looked nervous—kept blinking and sniffing, like she had an allergy. Lebeaux told me later she was probably high on cocaine.

"Where did you see Mr. Sloan?"

"Hey, I don't know. Maybe at his house. Up there in Buckhead." She sniffed a couple of times.

"And was Dawn Marie Sterling present at that time?"

Gigi looked over at Emma. She didn't respond. "I don't remember. She mighta been."

"Were you aware that the house on Tuxedo Road was in her name?"

"No, man. That was Jack's house. Everybody knew that. Even the cops."

"The cops, you say? What makes you think that?"

Emma jumped up. "Objection! This is irrelevant and prejudicial."

The witness looked up and blinked, not catching Emma's warning.

"Overruled. You may answer, ma'am," said the judge.

"Answer?" asked Gigi. "What was the question again?"

"How do you know the cops thought it was Jack's house?"

"Well, there was a search warrant one time, a few months back…and a lot of cops came around that night. The warrant said it was Jack's house. They busted a few of us—possession, you know. They didn't find nuthin' against Jack, though."

"What were they looking for?"

"Objection!" shouted Emma. "Speculation! Irrelevant!"

"I'll sustain the objection as to speculation," said the judge. "Rephrase the question, Mr. Lebeaux."

"Okay. Do you know what the cops were looking for?"

The witness glanced over at Emma, who was looking down at her legal pad and slowly shaking her head.

"No. I don't know. They just showed up. Jack wasn't there that night. There were just a few of us girls there. We all had to wait outside; then they hauled us downtown." She hung her head in her hands.

"All right, Miss Diamond…Are you feeling all right?"

"Sure. Yeah, I'm feeling fine." She didn't look fine, though.

"Okay, then. Tell me, do you know anything about Mr. Sloan's business dealings—what he did for a living?"

Gina looked over at Emma again, apparently waiting for her to object. But there was no objection.

"Well, not really. I knew about his club. That's about all. I worked there for a while. Jack played the piano. He was a real good pianist. That's how he got started."

"And besides the club, do you know anything about Mr. Sloan's assets—what he owned?"

The witness paused. "No. You'd have to ask Pearl about that."

Lebeaux did a double take. "And who is Pearl, may I ask?"

"She was Jack's…business manager. You know. She ran all his businesses."

"He didn't run them himself?"

"No. Pearl did that."

"What is Pearl's last name?"

"I don't know. All I know is Pearl."

Lebeaux turned to Emma. "Your honor, I assume that the witness list we've requested from Ms. Faulkner will include contact information for this individual, this Pearl."

The judge looked over at Emma and nodded. "Miss Faulkner, as we discussed earlier at the bench, I expect complete cooperation in discovery in this case."

"Yes, your honor," said Emma, not looking up from her legal pad.

"And Miss Diamond, who else knew about Mr. Sloan's business dealings, or his assets, or his marriage to your mother?"

The witness rolled her eyes back in her head. It was pretty obvious by now that she was high on something.

Emma stood up. "Objection, your honor. This is not relevant. This witness has testified she doesn't know anything about the decedent's business. We'll provide counsel with a witness list at the appropriate time."

Lebeaux looked at Emma and smiled before addressing the judge. "Your honor, this is vital information. This is an emergency hearing. Time is of the essence. As you know, Mr. Sloan's assets are in a very vulnerable condition at the moment. We're entitled to know everyone who might be a witness to this so-called common-law marriage. If the court appoints Mr. Brock here as administrator, we're going to need to move quickly to preserve the assets of the estate."

"I'll allow it," said the judge. "Miss Diamond, you may testify to whatever you know about Mr. Sloan's business."

"Thank you, your honor. Now Miss Diamond, who else knows about Mr. Sloan's business dealings?"

The witness shrugged and smiled. She had finally caught Emma's signals. "Don't ask me. I didn't have nuthin' to do with it."

Lebeaux frowned. "All right. No further questions."

Then Emma called Diana's son, Pete. He was a tall guy with a little square mustache under his lower lip, maybe a little older than Gigi. He testified that he had been in the military for eight years, so wasn't sure when his mother and Jack Sloan stopped living together. But he, too, was sure they were married.

Lebeaux got up to cross examine.

"Mr. Diamond, can you be more specific about your military service? Where were you stationed?"

"In Iraq for four years, and then Afghanistan."

"And what branch of the military were you in?"

The witness got a peculiar look on his face, looking toward Emma.

"Objection," she said. "Mr. Diamond's military service is not relevant to these proceedings."

"What's the relevance, Mr. Lebeaux?" asked the judge.

Lebeaux looked surprised at the objection. "Your honor, I'm simply seeking to establish the witness's opportunity to observe the relationship between his mother and the deceased."

"I don't know how his military assignment has anything to do with that. Objection sustained," said the judge.

"Well, Mr. Diamond, is there something secret about your service? Something you don't want this court to know about?"

"Objection!" shouted Emma.

"Sustained. Mr. Lebeaux, I've already ruled on this line of questioning. Move on."

"Yes, your honor. Now, Mr. Diamond, when did you return from your military service—what year?"

"That would be 2009—February of that year."

"And that was an honorable discharge, I presume?"

Emma jumped up to object, but the judge cut her off. "Mr. Lebeaux, I've warned you not to pursue this line of questioning. The witness's military service is not in issue here."

"All right, then. At the time you were discharged, was Mr. Sloan in the nightclub business?"

"Yes, he had just opened it."

"Did you work for him at the club, like your sister did?"

"Yes. I was in charge of security there for a while. A bouncer, more or less."

"I see. When you say 'a while,' does that mean a year? Two years?"

"Less than a year. He hired somebody else after that."

"Did he fire you?"

"No. It was mutual."

"And did your mother, Diana Diamond, know you were working for Mr. Sloan?"

"Oh yes. She set me up with him."

"I see. How did she seem to feel about it when you resigned?"

"Well, I didn't exactly resign. I kept working for Jack, except not at the club."

"Oh? What were you doing for him?"

The witness looked over at Emma. She did not respond.

"After I left the club, I was sort of a…I guess you could say I was a bodyguard."

Lebeaux raised his eyebrows. "A bodyguard? And why did he need a bodyguard?"

Pete hesitated, again looking at Emma. This time she stood up.

"Objection, your honor. Mr. Lebeaux is going far afield with this line of questioning. I object to the relevance. And besides, it's clear that a person of Mr. Sloan's means would have every reason to hire a bodyguard."

"Overruled. I'll let him testify to his relationship with the deceased."

Lebeaux looked annoyed. "Well?"

"Like Ms. Faulkner said, it's obvious he was a man of means."

"Did he have a lot of enemies?"

"No, not particularly."

"But obviously he had at least one."

"Yes. Obviously."

"And were you still guarding him at the time of his death? When he was shot to death?"

"Objection! This is argumentative, and totally irrelevant," said Emma, looking flustered.

"Overruled. The witness can testify to his relationship with the deceased at the time of his death."

Pete looked belligerent.

"The answer is yes. I was still his bodyguard. But I was not on duty that night. He didn't want me around that night. That happened pretty often, actually."

"Do you know who he was with on the night he died?"

"No. Besides Dawn and this woman Soraya, I mean. I don't know who else was there."

"And did you know this Soraya—Soraya Romero, I believe it is?"

Pete shrugged and glanced down at the floor. "Not really. I'd seen her around the club sometimes. She was friends with Dawn."

"And I gather you don't have any theories about who might have killed them?"

"No. I gave my statement to the police. Believe me, I've thought about it a lot."

"Yes. I imagine you have," said Lebeaux. "No further questions, your honor."

CHAPTER FOURTEEN

It turned out that Lebeaux was right about the outcome of the hearing. Emma rested her case and then got up and made a closing argument about how she'd proved that Diana was Jack's wife, and that meant everything belonged to her. Lebeaux stuck to the certified documents, like he said he would. That apparently persuaded Judge Mitchell.

"All right," he said. "If there's nothing further, I'll ask Mr. Lebeaux to draw up the temporary order. I find as a preliminary matter that Miss Dawn Marie Sterling was the ceremonial wife of the deceased, Jack Sloan, and therefore presumptively his heir. In addition, I find that the property located at Three-Thirteen Tuxedo Road was a gift from Mr. Sloan to Ms. Sterling. Accordingly, since Ms. Sterling is also deceased, and Mr. Brock is her only heir, he is the preferred administrator of the estate, and the court so finds. Draw that up, and I'll sign it."

Lebeaux was writing furiously while Judge Mitchell dictated these orders. Then the judge looked out over the bench, frowning.

"Now let me add this. Miss Faulkner, I'm ordering you to turn over immediately all information you may possess concerning the assets of the estate of Jack Sloan. That includes a complete witness list, with contact information. I'm frankly concerned about your ethical position in this case, having represented Mr. Sloan and now the petitioner, who claims to be his common-law wife. It seems entirely possible that you may be called as a witness in the final hearing, which of course would be a very unseemly situation. As I told you before we got started, I expect complete cooperation in discovery—that is, if you choose to continue on this case."

He got up abruptly and walked out of the courtroom. Emma sat there with her mouth open for a few seconds, then stood up. You could tell she was fuming but trying to act friendly.

"Well, I guess you win, Jonathan—at least for now. Call me at my office, and I'll fill you in on a few things you will definitely need to know." She smiled that smug smile of hers, with all the big white teeth.

I drove home from the courthouse feeling elated, but also vaguely worried. It suddenly hit me exactly how big a deal this job of administrator would be. Lebeaux had been telling me not to sweat it—that he'd take care of everything—but I wasn't so sure I was ready to accept that. Not that I didn't believe him, but I realized that nobody besides me seemed to care all that much about who had murdered my daughter. To me, that was really the only thing that mattered.

The insurance company had cleaned up my house, but it was basically empty. Most of the furniture had been destroyed by the intruders, and I hadn't had a chance to replace anything except the mattress. I lay down on it, feeling completely drained, and had just about drifted off to sleep when the phone rang.

It was a woman's voice on the line. "Mr. Brock? Mr. Joe Brock?"

"Yes. Who is this?"

"My name is Pearl Magenta. I understand you want to talk to me."

I remembered the name Pearl from the hearing. "Yes, I guess I do. Or rather, my lawyer wants to…"

"No," she said. "It's you I want to talk to. Let's leave the lawyers out of this."

"But the judge said…"

"I know. I heard. But we don't need to be messing around with those people. They're just in it for themselves—for the money. I know things you need to know. I know what happened to your daughter."

My heart started pounding. "What? You mean you know who killed her?"

"Maybe not exactly who, but I definitely know why. There's a lot you don't know about Dawn…Cynthia. She was into some heavy stuff—a lot heavier than she realized."

"Such as?"

"I can't talk about it on the phone. We need to meet. I'll tell you everything you want to know, but only if we can keep the cops and the lawyers out of it."

"Sure. Sure—anything you say," I said, almost in tears with excitement.

"Okay then. I'm in New York on business tonight. Flying home tomorrow. I'll meet you at the Tuxedo house tomorrow night—say around eight o'clock? Do you have a key?"

I realized I didn't. Not only that, but I couldn't get into the place without the security code. Then I remembered what Detective Drake had said about resetting it.

"No, I haven't gotten the keys yet, but I think I can get them."

"Never mind. I have a key. Just wait for me if you get there first," she said.

"Okay, I'll be there at eight tomorrow night."

She hung up without saying good-bye. I leafed through the business cards I'd been collecting and located the detective's card. He'd written his cell number on the back. I dialed it.

"Mr. Brock! Of course I remember you," he said. I was glad to hear a friendly voice.

"Detective, I need a favor from you. The court just appointed me administrator, and I need to take you up on that offer to hook me up with somebody to clean up the Tuxedo house."

"Yeah. Yeah, sure. I'd recommend a company called Good-As-New, over in Decatur. They work a lot of these crime scenes."

"Right," I said, jotting down that name. He gave me the phone number.

"You can tell them I referred you," he said. "Their owner is an ex-cop—a buddy of mine."

"Thanks. Listen, Detective Drake, I'm also going to need that new security code—so I can let the crew in, you know."

"Oh yeah, forgot about that. I don't have that code in front of me right now, but tell you what. I'll meet you over there tomorrow if you like. I'm tied up until three. How does three-thirty sound?"

"That would be great," I said, feeling pretty clever for finagling that code without involving Lebeaux. That was the way Pearl wanted it, and I was too excited about the meeting to object.

I called and left word on the county manager's answering machine that I would be out of the office for a few days. Then I called Lebeaux. His voice mail was on, so I left him a message, too. I said I had arranged for the house to be cleaned up, and he didn't need to worry about it. He didn't call me back.

The next afternoon I pulled up to the Tuxedo Road house and found Detective Drake already there. The yellow crime-scene tape was gone, and Drake's unmarked car was parked up at the top of the driveway. I pulled up behind him, thankful to avoid the long walk up that hill.

"Thanks again for meeting me, Detective," I said, showing him the signed court order from the day before.

"Sure, no problem," he said. "You've bitten off a pretty big chunk with this estate."

"Yes, I've started to realize that. I hardly know where to start. Fortunately, my lawyer says he'll take care of most of it."

"Yeah, they always say that. In the end, you'll have to handle the nasty parts yourself. Starting today."

He pulled a huge jumble of keys out of his pocket and fiddled for the right one. "We took these keys off of the victims," he said. "I checked them out of the evidence room just now. I've never seen such a pile of brass on one key ring. I can't give you the whole mess of them, but I'll let you borrow the front door key to make a copy. I'd recommend that you get all the locks changed right away."

"Sure. Good idea," I said, trying not to gag from the death smell.

He stood there, trying each of the keys that looked like it might fit a door lock. Eventually he found the right one, and we walked in the front door. Right away the alarm started to beep. The detective headed for the panel and entered the code. Then he handed me a card with the numbers written on it.

"You should go ahead and change the code, too," he said. "Never can tell who all has gotten in here. We changed it once, but there seem to be a lot of leaks in this case."

I knew what he meant. I remembered Emma Faulkner exiting the house the previous week. We walked into the front hall. The first thing I noticed was that someone had taken down that big nude photograph from the master bedroom and stood it up in the downstairs hallway. The glass had already been cracked when I saw it before, but now it looked like somebody had peeled back the photograph and its backing, trying to look behind them.

"See what I mean?" said the detective. "I closed this place up the day you and I met, but somebody has obviously been in here since then."

I looked at the picture, which I'd shied away from the first time I saw it because of that enormous penis. Now I looked at it, especially the blond woman standing next to the man. I stepped up closer, not believing what I saw. The woman had a small blue butterfly on her right shoulder.

"Who is that woman?" I asked, more or less to myself.

"We were told that was your daughter, Dawn Marie Sterling," said the Detective, looking at me curiously.

"No, it's not," I said, shaking my head. "It can't be. The tattoo is the same, but the face...it's all wrong. The eyes...well, with all that makeup, it's hard to tell, but those teeth are not my daughter's. She had a cute little space between the front teeth, not that phony Hollywood smile. And Cynthia didn't have breasts like that. She was very small, like her mother...petite."

The detective must have thought I was about to faint, because he grabbed me by the elbow and sat me down in a velvet chair next to the living room entry.

"So you say this isn't your daughter?" he asked, after giving me a minute to catch my breath.

"At least...not the Cynthia I know. This is a different woman." My heart had started pounding again. Could it all be a huge mistake?

Detective Drake pulled up another chair and sat down. I sat there, studying the photograph, still seeing a total stranger.

"Mr. Brock, we have several other photographs of your daughter. All of them are clearly the same woman. If you want to see them, I can arrange for you to meet me down at headquarters..."

I was still trying to figure it out. "Who identified this picture? Or the others?"

"The gardener was the first one. He dealt with her twice a week, and knew her by name. Then there were people who worked at Jack Sloan's club. They all said it was your daughter. We only had their word for it, of course..."

"They're lying. Or mistaken. Or somebody else has taken over her identity. It happens, you know."

"Mr. Brock, I know you're emotional. You couldn't help but be. Everything looks different through the lens of emotion. But I promise you, we have checked it out, and…"

"I'm not emotional," I said. "I know my daughter when I see her. I'm her father, and I'm telling you. This is not my daughter. The woman in that picture is not Cynthia Ann Brock."

CHAPTER FIFTEEN

I sat there, shaking my head, wondering what that picture could mean, with a little spark of hope building up inside—hope that my girl might still be alive.

The detective looked concerned. "Tell you what, Joe. You sit here while I take a little tour of the place. I want to see what else has been going on in this house."

He took off down the hall, but not before drawing his gun from a side holster under his jacket. That made me nervous. I realized that if people had been getting into the place, someone could be in there with us at that very moment. Detective Drake must have realized that, too. My imagination ran a little wild, thinking of the kinds of people who might want to come inside that house.

After a few minutes, Drake came back. "Look, Joe, I don't like the feel of this," he said. "With all this mess, it's hard to tell what's going on, but somebody has definitely been in here. Whoever it is, they're apparently still looking for something. No telling how many people have the key. I'd advise you to get those locks changed

ASAP—today, if possible. In fact, I'd feel better if we called a locksmith over here right now."

Now I was really nervous. I pulled out my new smartphone and handed it to the detective. "I don't know how to use this thing yet. Can you look up a locksmith for me?"

"Sure," he said. "But I know just the guy to take care of it." He punched in a phone number and talked to somebody. Then we waited outside until the truck arrived.

It took a couple of hours for all the locks to be changed out. While I was at it, I arranged for them to change the locks at my house in Jonesboro, too. I called the Good-As-New cleaning company and explained what was going on. They agreed to come out and get started the next day. Everything seemed to be falling into place.

Lebeaux still hadn't called me back. I dialed his number again, and got voice mail again. This time I left a message that I was having the locks changed. After that, it only took two minutes before he returned my call.

"What's going on, Joe? Didn't I tell you I'd take care of everything?"

"Yeah, but the homicide detective thought I'd better get these locks changed right away. He thinks people are still getting in, and apparently they're using a key."

Lebeaux was quiet for a few seconds. "You listen to me now, Joe," he said, sounding angry for some reason. "You're not to be doing things on your own, do you hear? You don't know what you're doing, and you might get yourself in trouble. Anything could happen. It could be dangerous. Your job is just to sign off on whatever I do. Is that clear?"

I didn't understand what had him so hot under the collar. "Well, I might as well tell you that I've already arranged for a company to clean the place up…"

"You *what?*"

"Yes. It needs to be done, and this is a reputable company. The police detective gave me their number."

He was silent again. I could hear him breathing heavily on the phone.

"Mr. Lebeaux? I don't understand why this is a problem. I'm just taking care of things…"

"All right, all right," he said. "You didn't know any better. I should have told you not to…anyway, are you at the house right now?"

"Yes. They're almost finished changing the locks."

"Okay. When you get the keys, you need to drive by my office and leave me a set of them."

"Sure, I can do that," I said, thinking this guy was certainly a control freak.

"And then stay away from that house. I mean it. You don't need to get mixed up in this."

I hesitated, thinking about my appointment with Pearl just a couple of hours later.

"Okay, fine," I said, figuring what Lebeaux didn't know wouldn't hurt him. I started to tell him about the photograph of the murdered woman who didn't look like Cynthia, but something told me not to—not just yet.

When the locks were finished, I asked the locksmith to help me reset the alarm code. He said I had to call the security company to do that. After a little argument about who I was, they let me change it. I set it to my daughter's birthday: 11-14. The detective had already taken off, and I didn't want to be alone in that place, so I drove down to Peachtree and had dinner. It was after six o'clock, and I figured Lebeaux's office was probably closed, and he could wait until the next day to get his keys.

While I ate dinner, I thought about that photograph. What if it really wasn't Cynthia who was murdered? It occurred to me that if she *wasn't* dead, I didn't have any business being involved in this whole mess. On the other hand, I knew that the Tuxedo Road house had been titled in the name of Dawn Marie Sterling, who was definitely the same person as my daughter, Cynthia—unless, of course, someone had impersonated Cynthia to get that name change. But why? And if so, where *was* Cynthia? My mind kept chasing down different paths like that, getting nowhere. It was all so baffling. But I have to admit that as I sat there over dinner, turning over all the possibilities, I did chuckle to myself, realizing that this was the most excitement I'd had in my whole life, and I didn't want to see it end. I decided that no matter who the murdered woman was, I had to get to the bottom of it.

At about seven thirty, I finished dinner and drove back over to Tuxedo. There was a white Mercedes parked in the driveway. As I pulled in behind it, I saw a woman sitting in the driver's seat. I got out and walked up to the car.

"Pearl?"

She looked up at me. "That's right. And you must be Joe," she said. She was not smiling as she got out of the car. I thought she looked a lot younger than I would have expected—not much more than thirty. She had straight dark hair that fell over her shoulders and halfway down her back, and blue eyes—sort of a periwinkle color, actually, with a darker ring around the iris. Her dress was white, strapless, and very short—so short that I could see straight up, almost all the way to her crotch when she got out of the car.

Like I said, she didn't exactly greet me with a smile. "Something's wrong with the locks," she said in an irritated tone. "My key won't work."

"Right. We changed the locks this afternoon."

Now she was really mad. "What the hell did you do that for? I need to get in there. I have business to handle for Jack."

I shook my head. "No, I don't think so. Not anymore. The court made me the administrator, so I'm handling his business now. I have the keys."

She shook her head slowly. "Unbelievable. Last I heard, Emma was going to be taking care of this. I thought she got in touch with you."

"No. I met Emma a couple of weeks ago, right after the murders, but she's not my lawyer. She was representing somebody named Diana in court—somebody who claimed to be Jack's common-law wife. She lost the case yesterday. I won." I felt a little pang of pride that surprised me.

"Diana? Diamond? Says she's Jack's wife? Oh, that's hilarious." She laughed, still shaking her head. "Emma must have figured her odds were better with Diana than you. I guess she bet on the wrong horse."

I wasn't following. "So now I'm in charge of everything," I said.

"Good luck with that." She laughed without smiling. "You'll never figure anything out. You're going to need my help." She didn't really seem to be talking to me but might have been trying to adjust to me being in the picture.

"I'd be glad to have your help. I do have a lawyer, though. His name is Jonathan Lebeaux. He's going to be doing most of the work. I'm just the heir."

"Lebeaux. I know that guy. What rock did you find him under?"

Her attitude surprised me a little. "He's pretty good, if you ask me," I said. "He beat Emma Faulkner in court yesterday. Beat her good."

"Maybe so. But the lawyers don't matter. What we have to talk about doesn't involve the lawyers—either one of them."

We were standing outside in the humidity, with the odor of death wafting out of the house. Pearl didn't seem to be enjoying it any more than I did.

"We don't want to talk here. Let's go get a drink," she said.

I followed her in my car back into town and down Peachtree to Piedmont. After several blocks she turned into a side street and then into a parking lot. In one corner of the lot was a neon arrow pointing down a flight of stairs to a door with a neon sign over it, in the shape of a blue butterfly. Not the words—just the butterfly. I took a deep breath and followed her in.

The club was dark and smelled like stale smoke. Jazz music was playing over a sound system. I saw a stage on one side of the room, with a piano and equipment set up for other instruments, but no one was playing. We sat down at a little table near the stage. There were no other customers in the place. Too early, I figured.

A young, blond waitress came over to take our orders. She was not topless but close to it. Pearl spoke to the girl by name—Carmen, I think—and ordered a bottle of wine. I asked for a Budweiser. I was pretty nervous.

Pearl lit up a cigarette, sat back and crossed her legs, showing most of her right thigh. All these women seemed to like to show their legs. "Okay, Joe. Let's talk," she said.

"Miss Magenta…"

"Call me Pearl. Magenta is a stage name. Jack gave it to me a long time ago, when I was a dancer here," she said, pouring herself a glass of wine.

"Okay then…Pearl, I should tell you that the only reason I'm here is because you said you knew something about my daughter's murder."

"Of course. And I do know something about that—among other things. But first I want to talk to you about money."

I did a double take. "Money?"

"Yeah. A lot of it. Money that you and I could share if we play our cards right." She was smiling now, like a Cheshire cat.

"All right, I give up," I said. "What money are you talking about?"

She narrowed her eyes and looked at me across the table. "Joe, I'm not sure how much you've been told about Jack's business dealings. I don't know how much Dawn would have told you."

"I haven't talked to my daughter for two years, if that helps."

"Okay, so you don't know much. You'll find out soon enough, I guess. Let's just say he was into a lot of...high finance. He handled a lot of cash, not only for himself but for a lot of other people."

"Oh?" The thought hit me that if Jack had a lot of cash, it should be part of his estate. What did this woman have to do with it?

"Yes. The thing is, without me, nobody will ever get ahold of that money. I'm the only one who can find it."

I still wasn't following. "Aren't you legally obligated to turn it over if you know it belongs to Jack...or his estate?"

She smiled again. "True. But it didn't exactly belong to Jack. And I have to find it first. That's where you come in."

"Me? I just told you, I don't know anything about Jack Sloan's business."

Just then Carmen came back to the table with my beer. As she poured it into the glass, her long blond hair fell forward, and I saw that on her right shoulder she had a tattoo. A little blue butterfly.

CHAPTER SIXTEEN

P earl saw my shock and seemed amused. "I guess you've seen that tattoo before, haven't you?"

I didn't know what to say. All I could think about was that nude woman in the photograph on Tuxedo Road.

"Yes. My daughter Cynthia had a tattoo like that. It's how I identified her body. Her face was mostly shot off."

"I can see why it would upset you, then. But Jack made all of his favorite girls get that tattoo. Even me—see?" She pulled the long dark hair away from her shoulder and revealed the tattoo, exactly like Cynthia's.

"Why would he do that?" I asked, trying to put all this together.

"It's a Blue Buddha butterfly," she said. "You know—Blue Buddha? Haven't you ever heard of that?"

It didn't mean anything to me, and I must have looked blank. She shook her head in disbelief. "It's a symbol—a play on words. I can't believe how dense you are, Joe. But it's kind of refreshing, actually."

"I guess I live a pretty conservative life," I said. I know my feelings should have been hurt by being called dense, but I didn't care. I was trying to remember when I first saw that tattoo on Cynthia's shoulder. She had just turned eighteen. I didn't want to think she might have been one of "Jack's girls" back then. Pearl was drinking her wine, looking thoughtful. She must have read my mind.

"So I guess you don't know about Jack and Dawn, do you?"

"No. I never heard of the guy until...*this* happened."

"Okay, do you want me to fill you in? You might not like what you hear."

I nodded.

She finished off her glass of wine and poured herself another one.

"Okay. Well, it started out like you might imagine," she said. She looked at me kind of sideways and smiled. "On second thought, maybe you *can't* imagine. Anyway, Diana brought Cynthia around one night, a couple of years ago. I don't know what Emma told Diana to say in court, but that skinny old whore has worked for Jack for years—long before I knew either one of them. I don't know how it got started, but ever since I've known them, she's been more or less a pimp...recruiter...for the club, and for Jack's more personal interests, if you get my meaning."

This was fueling my worst fears, but I thought I needed to hear it, so I nodded again.

"Jack took an interest in Cynthia right away. I didn't really understand why, except she had that innocent look about her—those big blue eyes. And she fell for *him* really hard. I don't know many women who didn't, actually. Jack was a charmer—so handsome, like a movie star, and so smooth. He could talk his way into or out of anything. And when he played that piano and sang...well, you get the picture."

"Were they in love?"

Pearl smiled. "Well, of course, love is a relative thing. Cynthia definitely loved him, but Jack was very narcissistic. Everything was about *him*, you know? I think he did love her in his own way, but in the same way an artist loves his creation. It was a selfish kind of love. He made her the way he wanted her."

"I'm sorry, you've lost me there," I said.

"Well, to him, she was sort of a blank canvas or a block of clay. He felt like he could mold her into the woman he'd always imagined. He'd burned through a lot of women, and I think he was bored. He'd formed this idealized picture of the perfect female. And about a hundred thousand dollars in plastic surgery later, Cynthia was exactly what he pictured."

"What? That's nuts!" I said. I couldn't imagine Cynthia needing that much plastic surgery. To me, she had been perfect just the way she was. Pearl saw my confusion.

"I know it sounds pretty bizarre, and I guess it was. But he reconfigured your daughter from head to toe, including a whole new set of teeth, cheekbones, boobs, ass—you name it. I should know; I paid the bills."

That nude photograph over the bed came into my head again. Suddenly I was horrified.

"Are you telling me that woman in the pictures on Tuxedo Road was my Cynthia?"

"You didn't recognize her? Well, I guess that proves my point."

"I just don't get it," I said, mostly to myself. "Why would she let him do that to her? It's crazy. And all the dirty pictures and handcuffs and everything. Cynthia was smarter than that."

Pearl reached over and touched my hand. "Joe, I know all this is a shock. But sometimes we think we know people, and we really don't. Sometimes they do things you wouldn't predict. Like I said, Jack had that effect on people, especially women. He drove women a little crazy—even some very smart women."

"So why did she change her name?" I asked, still trying to put the picture together.

"That was Jack again. Once he'd finished his masterpiece, he wanted to give it a name, so he chose the name Dawn Marie Sterling to symbolize her rebirth. Dawn was for a new day, of course. Marie—well, he was Catholic. And Sterling? Purity. He always thought of her as pure. He was heavily into symbols. Like the Blue Buddha butterflies. He got a big charge out of that."

"Okay, I know I'm dense, but why don't you just tell me about that. What exactly were these butterflies supposed to stand for?"

She was on her third glass of wine by this time, and I could tell she was loosening up quite a bit.

"Listen, Joe, we need to have an understanding here. I know you want information, and I can give you plenty. But you need to promise me that it goes no further than us. Not that it really matters that much, now that Jack is dead. But promise me, anyway."

"Okay, I promise," I said, without the slightest idea of where she was going with this.

"Well, there was a time—quite a few years ago, actually—when Jack was dealing weed. You know…marijuana. By the time I started working for him, he had a pretty lucrative little dealership here at the club. His signature product was a variety of cannabis known as Blue Buddha—a very smooth, high-end product that's native to Afghanistan. Well, it so happens that there's this species of butterfly called Blue Buddha that's also native to Afghanistan. So Jack took this butterfly for his personal symbol—sort of an in-joke, you might say."

"I see," I said, remembering the night when Cynthia came home with that tattoo. If only I had known back then what it meant.

She lit another cigarette. "So now you know the basic story, Joe. I know it's hard to accept, but believe me, it's all true."

I ordered another beer. Other customers had started coming in, and the air was filling up with cigarette smoke, in spite of the official "no smoking" signs everywhere. As I sat there, struggling with the image of my daughter, so disfigured and degraded, the anger started building in me again.

"All right," I finally said. "You told me you knew something about how Cynthia died. I'm ready to hear that part."

Pearl sort of shrugged. "Like I said on the phone, I don't really know who did it. I just have a pretty good idea of why."

"That'll do for starters," I said.

"Okay. The short answer is money. I know…surprise, surprise. But it gets a little complicated. And again, I'm taking a big risk telling you about it. If you go to the cops, or even your lawyer, I could be screwed. You'll understand why in a minute. Just promise me."

"I'll promise—if you promise me you weren't involved in the drug dealing," I said, still not understanding what the heck she was asking me to agree to.

"Joe, I was basically a bookkeeper. Jack kept me ignorant. He kept everybody ignorant, except the people in his inner circle— Diana, Emma, and later Dawn. He was pretty smart about that when he started out. That's why he never got caught. But I was pretty smart, too. I knew what he was doing, but I do promise I didn't participate."

For some reason I believed her, and that seemed to make the conversation okay.

"I'll take your word for it, then," I said. "Tell me what happened."

"Well, like I said, Joe had been dealing in weed for a few years. This was maybe 2008 or 2009. I was keeping his books here at the club by then, and I know he was doing pretty well. But all of a sudden, the numbers started going up—*way* up. That was about the time that Diana Diamond's son, Pete, came back from Afghanistan."

"Yeah, he testified in court that he'd served over there."

"I'm sure he didn't testify about why he came back, though, did he?" she said, smiling a little.

"No. I got the impression Emma didn't want him to get into that. She objected."

"I'll bet she did!" laughed Pearl, who seemed pretty close to tipsy by now. She'd gone through most of a bottle of wine in less than an hour. I suddenly realized that she was a very sad young woman.

"Here's the deal, Joe. Pete Diamond got caught shipping weed and opium back from Afghanistan. He got drummed out of the army, but he was never punished. I don't know exactly how he managed that. Maybe some higher-ups looked the other way and got him a discharge without court martial. I don't know how high up this business went."

"Wow," I said. "That's pretty incredible."

"Yes. Bottom line is that since Pete came back, the pipeline of weed and opium has expanded way beyond what he was doing five or six years ago. Way, *way* beyond. That much is pretty obvious." She tipped up the wine bottle and emptied it into her glass.

I couldn't conceal my interest. "So…I gather that Jack got involved in all that? Is that how he made all his millions?"

"Yes, but not like you think. I'm not sure why, but Pete saw Jack as sort of a father figure. He totally trusted him. And of course, Jack had the perfect cover here at the club. Nice cash business, plenty of foot traffic to conceal deliveries. Later on, he also picked up that hotel down by the airport—another nice cash business, which also happened to give him a shipping address where large packages could be delivered. I did the books down there, too.

"Anyway, once Pete got back from overseas, he started introducing Jack to a bunch of his army buddies—guys who had come back and gotten hired by the Atlanta PD, the sheriff's department, security companies, whatever. You know—the kinds of jobs that guys with military training usually gravitate to. There were probably a dozen or so guys. I never knew just how many, or who they were. Like I said, I only know what I saw. But I'm certain they were all in the business of importing drugs from Afghanistan, one way or another."

"People keep telling me not to trust the cops in this case. Now I guess I understand why."

"Yeah. You do have to be careful," she said, narrowing her eyes and looking me over for a moment or two. "But here's the thing. Jack wasn't actually dealing. As far as I know, he never handled any product at all. In fact, I'm pretty sure he even stopped his weed franchise. Within a few months, he'd transformed himself from a dealer into…more or less a banker."

I shook my head, puzzled. "You mean he was laundering money? Drug money?"

She laughed again. "You're catching on—slowly but surely. It was a lot of cash, Joe. And believe me, I know about cash. I know how many hundred-dollar bills you can fit into a suitcase or a trash can. We're talking maybe tens of millions unaccounted for over the last few years. It just kept rolling in. And sure, Jack was spending a lot, but nowhere near the amount that was being moved. He was also keeping his own books. I don't think anyone saw them, except maybe Emma. That's how I knew his business had progressed to a new level."

I know I should have gotten up at that point, paid the bill, and walked right out of that place. But I couldn't. I felt a strange excitement growing in my gut.

"So…didn't you ask him about it?"

"At first I was scared to. Jack had a temper, and he had started drinking pretty heavily. Also using. You know—cocaine? Maybe something heavier, I don't know. It was the first time since I'd known him that he did that. He was also into some very kinky sex. The women he was bringing around were pretty skanky, even for this place. It worried me, because he was getting careless. Sometimes he wouldn't come into the club for days. I don't know where he went."

"So did you figure it out? What was going on?"

"Well, eventually I did ask him, and he blew up. He told me I didn't need to know, and I was better off not knowing. He said he was handling money for a charity—*a veterans' charity*—but it was 'private' and off the books, and I should keep my nose out of it. Of course, that only piqued my curiosity."

I shook my head in disbelief. "Wow. So Jack was a philanthropist!"

"Shit, no. Are you kidding? Jack was in it for Jack—period. I came to believe he had some sort of charity, but I didn't think it could be anything besides another cover. He was stashing all that money somewhere. I could never figure out exactly how or where it was going, but it was coming in at a ridiculous rate. And the joke is that Jack was terrible with money. He could never even balance his checkbook. He'd always had me to do that before this new deal started up. Anyway, about the time I figured out what was going on, your daughter came into the picture."

"Cynthia? What did she have to do with any of this?"

"Nothing at first. But like I said, Jack was taken with her. She became his favorite right away, and he started working on her. She became an obsession, really. I guess part of her innocent appeal was this crazy fantasy world she lived in. It was a fairy land, and she drew him into it. He was more or less her Prince Charming, and she was happy to be his princess. He seemed to forget about his business, all this money that was accumulating—nothing mattered except Dawn. From that point on, I knew in my gut that it was going to end badly."

CHAPTER SEVENTEEN

"Sounds to me like Jack was in over his head," I said.

"You got that right. It felt sort of like the sorcerer's apprentice in that Disney movie. The money just kept coming and coming, and he wasn't paying any attention. Then, about three months ago, things changed. He started getting a lot of strange phone calls, and the money suddenly stopped. Then, out of the blue, the cops raided his house. They turned the place upside down, almost as bad as it is now..." She stopped, no doubt seeing the surprise on my face.

"You've seen the house? Since the murders?" I asked.

"Yeah," she said. "I went in there last week, okay? I told you I have a key, and I was curious. Probably like you. But I turned around and left when I saw the mess."

I nodded. It looked like an awful lot of people had been in that house.

"Anyway," she continued, "the cops apparently didn't find whatever it was they wanted that night. Instead, they arrested a couple of girls for possession."

"And you think those cops had something to do with the drug money?"

"Oh, yes, I'm sure of that. Like I told you, Jack hadn't been dealing any drugs himself for a year or more. Besides, he had been warned about the search, so he and Dawn had left the house that night, about an hour before the cops arrived. I'm positive that the guys who showed up to search the place were part of this so-called charity operation."

"What do you think they were looking for?"

"Maybe money. Or…information. Or they might have meant to finish him off that night or just scare him into giving it up. Who knows? Anyway, it was obvious that the deal had gone sour on Jack, and it terrified Dawn. She called me the next day, and we met for lunch. She told me a lot of things about Jack's business that day— his new business, that is."

"So she was in on this thing?" I was really surprised at that idea.

"Yes. I don't know how long she'd been working for him, but she knew a lot. I think by then she even knew more than Emma. In fact, Emma had sort of disappeared around the time the money stopped coming. It was just Jack and Dawn at that point. And like I said, they were a dangerous combination."

"So…what did she tell you about it?" We were getting to a point where I wasn't sure I wanted to know the details, but somehow I couldn't resist asking.

Pearl smiled. "Not so fast, Joe. What I haven't told you yet is about Dawn and me. We had gotten to be pretty close. Over the past year, she spent a lot of time crying on my shoulder, mostly about Jack and his sexual tastes, which sometimes pretty gross. She didn't like that. At the same time, she was terrified that he'd dump her—find somebody else. I guess she finally persuaded him to marry her, and that probably eased her mind a little. But she also cried a lot about you."

My heart jumped a little. "What? Why would she cry about me? She knew I loved her—always have, always will."

"Yes, she knew that. But she also felt that she'd gone too far, been absent too long, to ever reconcile with you. And also that you'd never understand her relationship with Jack."

I thought about that. I'm ashamed to admit that it was probably true. Although I couldn't imagine the kind of life my daughter must have been living, I probably couldn't have accepted it back then. But as I sat there with Pearl, I would have given anything to have Cynthia back with me, regardless of her lifestyle or how she'd been changed.

"Dawn was very vulnerable back then. Otherwise, I doubt that she would have trusted even me with the things she told me. She gave me enough information to figure out where Jack was stashing that money. Like I said, I don't know exactly how much there was, but I have a pretty good idea of where he was putting it. And that's where you come in."

"Me?"

"Yes. But I'm not going to tell you anything more until I get your agreement on a couple of things."

"Like what?" She had definitely gotten my attention.

"Okay, for starters, we have to agree that this is just between us. No lawyers, no other parties. If I can't trust you on that score, we can just forget about taking this any further."

"I understand. What else?"

"If we do find that cash, it has to be a fifty-fifty split. And it can't be reported to the IRS or the court or anyone else. It has to be our secret."

I stared down at the table. Yes, I was definitely interested in what Pearl had to say. I'd been a faithful civil servant for thirty years and had never expected to get rich during my lifetime. But now I knew I was in line to inherit that big house on Tuxedo Road, plus the Blue Buddha club and this hotel that I'd never seen, down by the airport. That would already make me pretty well off. Was it really necessary to get involved with something clearly illegal like what Pearl was suggesting?

Pearl was watching me, with a scowl on her face. I think she must have guessed what was going through my mind.

"Listen, Joe. Dawn wanted you to have that money—in case anything happened to her, she wanted it to go to you. She loved you, Joe. She wanted to make up for the heartache she had caused you. She wanted you to be happy, even if you couldn't be together."

I felt like I might start crying at that point, but I held it back. Pearl was clever enough to make up that last part of the story, just to suck me in. I recognized that, but it still affected me.

"Okay," I said. "Suppose I do agree to your terms? What makes you think I know anything about this money? I just told you, I hadn't seen my daughter in over two years."

"Right. But she had seen you. She had been watching you for months, looking for an opening to talk to you, but she always lost her nerve. She had a key to your house, and she told me that she'd gone by there several times, just to sit in her old bedroom and remember how it was before she left—and before her mother died. But here's the point: I think she left some things there—some clues to where that money might be."

I still wasn't ready to commit to this scheme, but some irrational part of me couldn't say no, either.

"What sort of clues are you talking about?"

Pearl sat back in her chair. I couldn't tell whether she was drunk or just feeling smug.

"That's for me to know and you to find out—if you agree to my terms, as you put it. I'll just tell you this much. That cash is safely tucked away in bank vaults. I know which banks and where they are. What I don't know is the account numbers. That would be your half of the deal, courtesy of your daughter. That is, if you agree to get involved."

I was getting the picture now. "So you think Cynthia left those account numbers somewhere in my house?"

"I don't just think it; I know it. She was scared to death. Scared Jack would leave her or that he'd be killed. She wanted an insurance policy, so to speak. And like I said, if anything happened to her, she wanted you to have that money. There would be a lot of numbers involved—too many to remember—and after that police raid, it wasn't safe to have those numbers there at Jack's house. Hey, think about it, Joe. You know that she left her marriage certificate there for you to find, didn't she? She wanted you to know she had gotten married, even if it was a secret to everyone else. Why do you doubt that she also left this other information? She practically told me as much the last time we talked. I know you haven't found it yet, or if you did, you didn't know what it meant. But now that you do know, you're in a position to make yourself not just comfortable but very, very rich."

I sat there, frozen in my chair, hearing everything that Pearl was telling me, even believing it, but unable to make a decision.

"And what if I can't find these account numbers? Or what if they don't exist? What then?"

"Well, you're no worse off than before, are you? And there are some bankers who will be very happy to babysit that money until they're able to declare it abandoned."

"I see what you mean," I said. "But I need a little time to think this over. I don't want to get involved in anything...illegal...without being sure that nobody is getting hurt, and there's no chance to get caught."

"I understand," she said. "Take a day or two to decide. I know I said you were dense, Joe, but I can see you're no fool. So let me know as soon as you can. There are other people out there who would like to get their hands on that cash, and I don't know if they have any idea where it is. But I do know they won't stop at much to get it."

CHAPTER EIGHTEEN

The next morning I went to see Lebeaux. He was not in a good mood.

"I waited for you last night, Joe. I thought you agreed to bring me those keys. You could have at least called me."

"Yeah, well, it was late," I said, handing him a duplicate key and scratching down the security code on a Post-It on his desk.

Lebeaux shook his head. "Joe, I'm worried about you. You don't have any business getting mixed up in this case, doing things without consulting me. I guess you realize that it could get dangerous. Whoever killed your daughter could come after you if you get in their way."

"I doubt that. Why would they bother me? I'm just an old fart without a dog in their fight."

"Except that you've just inherited a lot of money—some valuable assets. If I were you, I'd keep a low profile, at least until the cops catch the killers."

I shrugged. For some reason I'd woken up feeling sort of cocky that morning.

"Mr. Lebeaux, I know you think I'm…dense, and maybe I am, a little. But I want to be in on this case. I don't want to just stand by and wait for things to happen."

He was obviously irritated. "And just what do you think you can contribute?"

"More than you think. I'm finding out a lot about Jack Sloan and my daughter."

"Oh yeah? And how are you doing that?"

I felt like I'd gotten his attention. "I have my sources," I said.

Lebeaux got a peculiar look on his face. He reached into his jacket pocket, pulled out a half-smoked cigar, and lit it up.

"Listen here, Joe," he said, leaning across the desk and glaring at me. "You hired me to represent you—remember? If you look at our contract, you'll see that there's a paragraph in there about 'cooperation.' That means you agree not to do anything that could interfere with my representing you properly. So if you have information pertinent to this case, I need to know it—now."

I hesitated, thinking about Pearl and the things she'd said about not trusting the lawyers. On the other hand, Lebeaux had impressed me in court. I couldn't afford to do anything to make him withdraw from my case.

"Well, I guess I don't really know much. I've just met some people who might have information, that's all."

"Such as?"

"I met this woman named Pearl. She was Jack's business manager. She probably knows quite a bit about his assets and his business."

"Yes, I'm already looking into that. Patricia McGinnis, a.k.a. Pearl Magenta. I'm bringing her in for a deposition. She was served with a subpoena about an hour ago."

Something about the idea of Pearl at a deposition made me nervous. "When is this deposition supposed to happen?" I asked.

"Day after tomorrow, at nine a.m. You're welcome to come if you like."

"How did you find her? Pearl, I mean."

"Emma faxed me a witness list. The judge ordered her to do that, remember?"

"So does that mean Emma will be at the deposition, too?"

"Of course. Both parties and their lawyers are entitled to attend. A deposition is just an opportunity to put witnesses under oath, to get information—evidence. That's something we're pretty short on right now."

"I see," I said. I knew Lebeaux couldn't get Pearl to talk about the money, but Emma apparently knew enough to ask the right questions. And from the way Pearl acted the night before, evidently they weren't close. A deposition might be the only way Emma could make her talk.

"I've got some other depositions lined up all next week," said Lebeaux. "Diana Diamond and her two kids, Pete and Gigi. That covers the pathetic witness list Emma sent, but the way it works, you get information about further witnesses by questioning the ones you know about. I also have my investigator out nosing around. He's good. If there are any other assets out there, he'll find them."

Fat chance, I thought. As far as I knew, Pearl was the only other living person who knew about the "other assets." But now that I knew about Pete Diamond's history, I was worried. I knew he wouldn't tell the truth in a deposition, and I wasn't sure I could keep quiet about that.

"Shouldn't we talk to the cops?" I asked.

Lebeaux shook his head. "Nah, they're not helpful. They seem to have lost interest in this case. Or else they don't feel like sharing their info with us."

"I thought the lead detective was pretty helpful, actually," I said.

He shrugged. "By the way, Joe, I'm filing a new petition in the probate court today. We need to petition for the estate of your daughter. There shouldn't be any opposition to that, since she didn't have any other heirs."

I noticed that he had a brown accordion file on his desk with my name on it.

"Okay, fine. What's in the file?" I asked. I was still feeling pretty bold.

"Just copies of all these court papers, petitions, notices, what have you. And the judge gave us back our evidence, of course, until the final hearing. You know—the certified documents we submitted."

"Could you make me copies of all that?"

"Sure," he said, but he still sounded irritated. He took the file into the next room and came back a few minutes later with a stack of paperwork in a manila folder.

"Joe, I'm giving you this because I believe in keeping my clients informed. But I'm going to say this one more time. You don't need to be involving yourself in the legal end of this. That's my department."

"I understand. I just want to feel included," I said.

I left Lebeaux and drove to my office down in Jonesboro. I hadn't been there for a couple of days; for that matter, I really hadn't been paying much attention to my job since they found the bodies. But I wasn't prepared for what happened that day. The minute I walked in the door, I was handed a message that the county manager, Guy Zickert, wanted to see me. I walked into his office, and he motioned me to sit down.

"Joe, I'm sorry to hear about your daughter," he said. I thought he was just calling me in to give me the standard condolences.

"Thank you, sir. It was quite a shock, but I'm slowly getting back to normal."

He shifted in his chair. Zickert is a big guy who used to play college football. He still looks like an athlete and always wears short-sleeve shirts that show off his biceps.

"That's what I wanted to talk to you about, Joe," he said. "We've noticed that lately you haven't been putting in the performance we've come to expect from you."

"Right," I said. "I know I've been slacking off here lately. But like I said, I'm recovering from the shock..."

"Joe, I'm not talking about just the past couple of weeks," he said, picking up the Styrofoam cup on his desk and blowing on the black coffee inside. "We certainly understand why your recent terrible loss would set your performance back. But you know the budget has been cut back this year because of the economy. The county is basically bankrupt. The union is fighting to keep our pensions. So we're in the unfortunate position of having to decide which of our personnel to keep and which ones we have to let go."

I stared at him. This wasn't making sense. I knew I wasn't turning out the volume of work I'd produced when I was younger, but I was the most experienced guy in the office. They'd be crazy to fire me.

"Mr. Zickert, I don't understand," I said. "This doesn't make any sense..."

"It's just a fact of life, I'm afraid. We have to cut personnel by ten percent this year, and I know it's very bad timing for you, but unfortunately the commission has decided to let you go."

I knew better than that. The commission didn't make personnel decisions without input from Zickert. He was in charge—the hatchet man. It was just plain cowardly of him to blame it on the commissioners.

"Look, Joe, you've got your pension and a lot of sick leave accumulated. The commission voted you two months of severance pay. And we hear that you're about to inherit quite a nice windfall, too. Most of the guys in your department are supporting families, living paycheck to paycheck. It's tough out there. We had to make some decisions..."

After that, I wasn't hearing anything he said.

CHAPTER NINETEEN

I packed up my office in two little banker's boxes. Strange that twenty-five years could be reduced to such a small package. But to tell the truth, after the initial shock of it, I wasn't upset about being fired. For some reason, it seemed more like a relief than a setback. And like I said, I had started out that day feeling bold.

By the time I got home, it was nearly noon. I pulled out my new smartphone to call my brother Charlie and fill him in about everything, but noticed that I had somehow managed to turn the thing off without trying to. When I turned it back on, I saw that I had three voice-mail messages, one from Lebeaux and two from Pearl. I listened to Pearl first.

"Joe, I need to talk to you. It's urgent. Call me as soon as you get this."

The second message was an hour later. Pearl sounded different—very upset. "Joe, you need to call me right away. Your lawyer just served me with a subpoena. I can't go to this deposition. Things have changed. You need to forget everything we talked about last night. I mean it, Joe. For your own safety, forget everything I told you. They know that we talked. Call me and I'll explain. It's a matter of life and death…" And then the message cut off.

Then I listened to Lebeaux. "Joe, we need to talk. Come back by my office this afternoon if you get a chance. We've got a whole new set of problems."

I hit the callback button for Pearl and got her voice mail. I tried again and got the same thing, so I just left a short message. But that panic in her voice stayed with me.

Then I called Lebeaux. He picked up right away. He sounded pretty upset, too.

"Listen, Joe, you need to get over here. The case has just gotten more complicated. I'll explain when you get here."

When I arrived at his office, Lebeaux was sitting behind the computer, typing away at something. I realized that I'd never seen a secretary or any support personnel in his office.

"Sit down, Joe. I've got a shocker for you."

I sat. "I don't know how many more shocks I can take today, to tell you the truth," I said.

"Sorry about that. But here's the deal. It turns out that Jack had a sister—an older sibling named Jillian Farrell. Lives out in Los Angeles. The two hadn't spoken for years, and I'm not sure how Emma found her, but this morning Emma dismissed her case for Diana and filed another petition, alleging that Jillian is Jack's sole heir."

My head had started spinning. "Okay…I guess I follow that. But I thought you told me that since Cynthia and Jack were married, she would be his only heir."

"Well, that's right, as far as it goes. The problem is that it depends which one of them died first—Jack or your daughter. If Jack died first, then Cynthia would have inherited everything, and you would inherit it all from her. On the other hand, if Cynthia died first, then Jack would have inherited everything she owned, including the Tuxedo Road house, and that would mean you're cut out altogether. Jack's living heirs—in this case, Jillian—would inherit everything."

"Jesus," I said. "This is way too complicated. Give me the bottom line."

"Okay, then. We're going to have to get someone to testify that Jack died first. You can bet that Emma will have somebody testifying that Cynthia died first. It's basically an expert pissing contest."

"So who wins? What if the judge can't decide between them?"

"Ah! Very good question. Fortunately or unfortunately, depending on how you look at it, the law has an answer for that. If the court can't determine which one died first, then there's a presumption that each one survived the other. It could get even more complicated in our case, but basically, whatever is titled in each person's name goes to the heirs of that person."

"But how can Emma represent this Jillian person with a straight face after she's just been in court representing Diana?"

Lebeaux laughed. "I know. We lawyers are scum, aren't we?"

I didn't answer him. I was thinking about Pearl, wishing I'd been able to reach her. Also, I was suddenly having visions of everything slipping away—all the property, all the money. And now I didn't even have a job.

"So who can we get to testify that Jack died first?" I asked.

"Good question. Didn't you mention that the Detective—Drake, is it?—had a theory about how the murders happened?"

"Yes, that's right. He said he thought the killer would have shot Jack first and then aimed at the two women on the couch. He said it could have happened in less than three seconds."

"Hmm. That might be helpful, but it still wouldn't prove which one *died* first. For that we'll need a pathologist to testify to how long a person would live with a given kind of wound. It gets pretty technical, but the autopsy report should be helpful. I imagine the fact that the bodies sat there for three days makes it that much harder. Nobody saw any of them alive after they were shot."

I thought about Cynthia's body there in the morgue. That memory made this whole legal game seem unbelievably morbid and absurd.

"Okay. So what do you need from me?"

"Nothing now. I'm drafting up a response, but frankly, if this Jillian person is legit, we've got a whole new case on our hands. I'm sending my investigator out to California today to check on her. We should know by tomorrow whether she's for real."

"And if she isn't?"

Lebeaux smiled. "If she's a ringer, then our pal Emma is going to have a lot of 'splainin' to do."

I left Lebeaux's office and started back home; then, on an impulse, I turned off the freeway toward the Atlanta police headquarters. Fortunately, I caught Detective Drake in his office, writing up a report.

"Sit down, Joe. How can I help you?"

"Wow, I don't even know where to begin," I said. My conversation with Pearl was going through my head—also her voice-mail message—and I knew Drake might be able to verify a few things for me. Then I remembered how paranoid Pearl had seemed about the police, and I decided not to bring any of the conversation up with Drake, even though I had no reason not to trust him.

I told him about the new wrinkle in the probate case and that we were going to have to prove which one of the victims died first. He seemed interested and reenacted the scene for me again. He seemed to enjoy doing that. Then he hit me with some news.

"By the way, Joe, we just got back an ID on that third victim. The Romero gal? Turns out her real name was Sandra Spinks. She's from Texas. We're trying to locate her next of kin. Any idea why she might have been hanging out with your daughter and Jack Sloan?"

"No—no idea. *Spinks*, you say?" That name was familiar. Then it hit me. Daryl Spinks. It seemed like an unusual name to be just a coincidence. "Detective, I know somebody with that last name who lives here in town somewhere. He works for the Fulton County Sheriff's Department, at the jail."

"Oh? And you think they might be related?"

"Well, I don't know about that, but don't you think it might be worth checking out?" I didn't tell him about the night Daryl and I broke into the Tuxedo Road house.

"Maybe. I'll make a note of it," he said, but he didn't seem all that interested.

I drove home, thinking all the way about how fast everything was happening and how the law didn't seem able to keep up with it. Lebeaux sitting there drafting his legal response. Detective Drake sitting there writing his report. Nobody seemed to be very interested in finding out what really happened on Tuxedo Road. To them, it was all routine—black-and-white lines, like the data I used to love so much in my job. But to me, it was much more than that. To me it had become just what Pearl said on the phone—a matter of life and death.

CHAPTER TWENTY

After trying to reach Pearl a couple more times and getting her voice mail, I sat down at my kitchen table to eat the dinner I'd picked up at Taco Bell. It was still early, still plenty of daylight. Trying not to focus on the empty, barren shell of my house, I thought about what Detective Drake had said about the third murder victim. Could she be related to Daryl? If so, what had she been doing at the Tuxedo Road house? And even more puzzling, exactly how deeply was Daryl involved in all this?

I remembered the first time I met the guy—the night of Cynthia's funeral. That was the time he persuaded me to drive up to Buckhead, when I later saw him leaving the bar with Lebeaux. Could that mean that Lebeaux was involved somehow with this Sandra Spinks? It began to feel like all the strange coincidences I'd been experiencing lately were far from coincidence. I kept turning it over in my head, and before I realized it, I'd finished most of a six-pack. Feeling even bolder than earlier in the day, I decided to call Daryl.

"Hey there, Joe!" he said, like we were long-lost buddies. "I've been hoping you'd call."

"Really? Why is that?"

"Well, I was hoping you'd catch me up on your case. How is it going?"

"That's hard to say. Things are moving pretty fast. I'm trying to keep up," I said. I was thinking he might volunteer some information about this mystery woman, Sandra, but then realized that I was going to have to bring up the subject myself.

"So Daryl," I said, "I found out this afternoon that the other girl who was murdered up in Buckhead wasn't named Soraya Romero, after all. Her name was Sandra Spinks. I thought that was quite a coincidence, since your name is Spinks, too."

There was a long pause on the other end of the phone. "Joe, we need to talk. Not on the phone. Can you meet me somewhere?"

I started feeling that same excitement I'd felt when I discovered that my daughter owned the property on Tuxedo Road, or when Pearl called me out of the blue. "Sure. How about the Fuzzy Navel? You know, the bar where we met the first time?"

"Okay. Give me an hour. I'll meet you there," he said and hung up.

I sobered up a bit before we met, thinking I didn't want to do anything foolish where Daryl was concerned. But when we sat down at the Fuzzy Navel, I ordered another beer. Daryl ordered whiskey.

"So you found out about Sandra," he said. "You surprise me, Joe. You're on the ball."

"Well, I haven't exactly found anything out. Except that you have the same last name. Are you related?"

He nodded with an ironic little smile. He opened his wallet to a photo of a pretty brunette. "Yes. Sandra was my twin sister."

Actually, I had expected as much. The murdered woman was about Daryl's age, and with that last name, what were the chances they weren't related? But I wasn't prepared for what he told me next.

"I guess there's no reason for me not to tell you about her. Joe, Sandra was an undercover cop—well, not really a cop, but an investigator for US Army CID. We grew up in Houston and enlisted together, but we ended up here in Atlanta at the same time for different reasons. I got the job with Fulton County when I got out of the service. Sandra stayed in Afghanistan until about a year ago; then they brought her back and assigned her to this job in Atlanta. It was just luck that we ended up in the same city."

"Let me understand this. Do you mean your sister was investigating Jack Sloan and...Cynthia?"

"Well, yeah. But nobody knew that. At least, we didn't think they knew. But after the murders, I gathered the killers either knew or suspected her. I've waited all this time to claim her body because the army asked me to. Now that they've ID'd her, I guess it's not a secret anymore. The brass must figure there's no longer any point in keeping it under wraps."

"When did you find out about her undercover assignment?"

"Oh, I knew about it right after she moved back here. She hung out at the Blue Buddha until they hired her on as a waitress. She even let them tattoo that little butterfly on her shoulder. I knew she was still with CID, so I asked her about it. Little by little, over several months, she filled me in on what was going on. She trusted me. We were always close."

I was annoyed. "So, do you mean to tell me that you knew all about this when we met that first night? You let me think you were just some random guy who felt sorry for me?"

"Afraid so. I didn't have any choice, Joe. I couldn't blow Sandra's CID cover at that point, but I was just as curious about the Tuxedo Road house as you were, and for the same reason. That's why I talked you into going up there."

"And what about Lebeaux? Did he know about it, too?"

Daryl hesitated. "Why do you ask that?"

"Because I saw the two of you together that night. I drove back around the block and saw you and Lebeaux coming back in here together."

He nodded, thinking it over. Like he was trying to decide what I knew and what I was just guessing. "Well, yes, Lebeaux knew about Sandra. He was my lawyer. I had told him about her CID assignment."

I wasn't sure just how far to take this, but pieces of the puzzle were starting to come together. "Was that before or after she was murdered?"

"After. I didn't have anybody else to talk to about it."

"Yeah? And what's in it for him?"

"In it? I don't know what you mean." But the look on his face told me he was holding back something important.

"Lebeaux isn't the empathetic type," I said, remembering how he'd brushed Daryl off at the courthouse. "I can't imagine he'd get involved in this unless he thought there was a buck to be made somewhere."

"Well, Joe, he stands to make quite a tidy sum representing you. Don't forget I referred you to him."

"Right, but that wasn't until later. That first night, when we met, I wasn't in the market for a lawyer."

Daryl looked sheepish. He hadn't given me credit for thinking all this through.

"Okay, then. Here's the truth. We followed you from the funeral—Cynthia's funeral. We saw the notice in the newspaper. We saw you leave your car in the parking lot and figured you'd be back for it. Lebeaux wanted to talk to you about the Tuxedo Road house. He knew it was worth a lot of money and figured you'd eventually need somebody to claim it for you. He had researched the title and wasn't sure whether you realized at that point whose name it was in. That's all there was to it. He was ambulance chasing, and

I was…helping him. He was going to give me a finder's fee. And like I said, I was curious about Tuxedo Road, too. Sorry if it caused you any worry."

It sounded plausible, in a sleazy sort of way. I breathed a little easier.

"So…what did your sister tell you about Jack and my daughter?"

"Oh, not much. Just that he was throwing a lot of money around—you know, Jack was a drug dealer. But Sandra's assignment went further than that. The army's interest was much deeper. It seems Blue Buddha was not just the name of Jack's club. It was a code name for a bunch of ex-military guys. They were bringing in drugs from Afghanistan, and Jack was handling money for them. That's pretty much all Sandra told me."

That last beer had hit me pretty hard, and I wasn't sure my brain was up to processing all this information. Although the picture was getting clearer, there were still a lot of questions in my mind. I know I should have shut up right then, but I was irritated that Daryl seemed so far ahead of me in figuring out this mystery.

"What do you know about a woman named Pearl?" I asked.

The question seemed to shake him up a little.

"Hmm, seems to me I've heard the name, but that's about all. Wasn't she the bookkeeper or something?"

"Yes. She was Jack's business manager. She knew a lot about his business."

"Such as?"

Right then I wished I had kept my mouth shut. Daryl was looking at me funny.

"Well, she says he wasn't dealing any drugs recently," I said. "Maybe it was all a big misunderstanding."

"When did you talk to her?" asked Daryl.

"Yesterday. I met her for drinks. Anything wrong with that?"

"No. Of course not. But you need to be careful, Joe. From what Sandra told me, there are some dangerous characters lurking around the Blue Buddha. I don't think you're prepared for what you might get into."

"I can take care of myself. I'm smarter than I look."

I said that to impress Daryl, but it turned out I wasn't really very smart.

CHAPTER TWENTY-ONE

The next day was scheduled for the cleanup on Tuxedo Road. It had been almost a week since I'd been up there, and I had agreed to meet the cleanup crew to open the place up for them. When I pulled into the driveway at a little before nine in the morning, I was surprised to see that little red Maserati parked in front of the garage. Emma was standing on the front porch with a woman of about forty, with long blond hair and a slim build. She was wearing a yellow sundress. I did a double take when I saw this gal, as from the back she looked almost like Cynthia. But of course it wasn't my daughter. It was Jillian Farrell.

"Good morning, Joe. It's good to see you," said Emma, as chipper as could be. I thought her friendly tone was pretty hypocritical under the circumstances and didn't respond.

"Joe, this is Jack Sloan's sister, Jillian," continued Miss Hypocrite. "She's from California. I guess you already know that she's filed a petition for her brother's estate."

I nodded. "Lebeaux told me," I said. Jillian smiled. She was very pretty, with wide-set blue eyes and a creamy complexion. Even from the front, she reminded me of Cynthia.

"Lebeaux is on his way. I phoned him this morning to let him know we wanted to see the place. Jillian is entitled to see her brother's property."

I couldn't very well argue with Emma, and didn't see any harm in it, so I unlocked the front door and deactivated the alarm. Emma charged right in, but Jillian hung back. I could tell she was overwhelmed by the smell, which, if anything, had gotten worse.

"I think I'll just wait outside," she said. "I don't need to see the inside."

As she spoke, the cleaning crew's truck pulled up the hill and stopped next to the sidewalk. A man and a woman got out, wearing white jumpsuits, with some sort of gas mask hanging from their necks. We introduced ourselves. Their names were Kevin and Tonya, apparently a married couple.

"If you want to go inside, you can use one of our masks," said Tonya, gesturing toward the truck. "We always carry extra."

I looked at Jillian, who really seemed like she was about to pass out from the smell. "What do you say? You've come all this way… you should really go inside at least once," I said. She smiled at me, sort of shyly. I knew it was ridiculous, considering that we were adversaries and everything, but I couldn't help liking her.

Tonya fitted both of us with masks, and we started to go in. But about that time, Lebeaux's Mercedes pulled up and stopped on the street. There wasn't room left for him in the driveway. He started jogging up the hill with his necktie flying, and I could tell he was royally pissed. When he got to the top of the driveway, he didn't stop, even to say hello. He marched right through the open front door.

"Emma? Where the hell are you? Get down here—now!" he shouted into the house.

She appeared at the top of the stairs, smiling that toothy, phony smile.

"Good morning, Jonathan. You got my message, I see."

"Damn right. Thanks for the all the notice. I should be down at the courthouse now, filing a motion for sanctions. You don't have any right…"

"Oh, come on, Jonathan. You know very well that it wouldn't have taken ten seconds for old Judge Osgood to sign an order allowing my client to view the place. It's only a technicality. Why put everyone to that trouble?"

"I might have agreed to it if you hadn't just shoved your way in, as usual," said Lebeaux. He was still hopping mad.

"Now, now. There's no point in arguing in front of our clients. What will they think of us?" said Emma, tipping her head almost flirtatiously.

"Come on down here. Let's do this in a halfway orderly way," said Lebeaux, apparently conceding Emma's point.

She came down the stairs, and we all gathered in the entry hall. The place looked the same as the last time I'd seen it—a total disaster. I was conscious that Jillian must be experiencing quite a shock, just like I did the first time I walked through that house. I stuck close to her as we toured all the rooms, and the two lawyers walked together up ahead, Emma pointing out the rooms like a tour guide. They were both taking a lot of notes, not paying any attention to us. Jillian and I couldn't talk with those masks on, but she seemed to appreciate my concern for her. At least I thought I saw gratitude in her eyes behind that mask.

When we got to the top of the basement stairs, I took hold of Jillian's elbow, shaking my head. She seemed to understand what I meant. We both walked back toward the central hallway and out the front door.

"You don't want to go down into that basement," I said, lifting my mask. "That's the scene of the murders."

"I figured as much," she said. She had removed her mask, too. "Pretty awful, I imagine."

"It's worse than you imagine, I guarantee that," I said.

"Thanks for warning me. I don't know how I would have reacted. I'm sort of a baby about things like that."

"You don't have to be particularly sensitive for that place to gross you out. The whole house gives me the creeps. Frankly, I have trouble believing that the cleaning crew can ever make this place livable."

She nodded. Then we stood there for a moment sort of awkwardly, not knowing what to say to each other.

Finally I thought of something to say. "I'm really sorry about your brother. Were you close?"

She shook her head, a little sadly, I thought. "No. I hadn't seen Jack for over five years. The last time we spoke, it ended in a huge argument."

What a sad coincidence. I felt like I might cry. "You know, my daughter and I argued, too, just before she left home. I'll never forgive myself for letting her go. This might not have happened…"

Jillian touched my arm. There were tears in her eyes, too. "Joe, I'm so sorry. I guess we don't appreciate how precious our family is until we lose them. Especially like this."

I wanted to hug her, but I knew that wouldn't be appropriate. Besides, about that time, Emma and Lebeaux came through the door. They were still arguing, but they stopped when they saw Jillian and me standing together.

"Let's go out to the garage and check on the cars," said Emma, flashing a remote garage opener she must have picked up inside the house.

I hadn't even considered that there might be vehicles involved, but when we opened the three garage doors, we found a Jaguar sedan, a BMW sports car, and a Mercedes SUV parked inside, like nothing had happened.

"These are all titled in Jack's name," said Emma, sort of smugly.

"Fine," Lebeaux snapped back at her. "Part of the estate."

Just then, Emma's cell phone rang. She walked away from us and came back a few minutes later, looking a little frantic.

"Listen, Jillian, I'm going to have to call you a cab. I know you're staying down by the airport, and I have to get back up to my office ASAP. It's up in Vinings, the opposite direction…"

I jumped in. "Don't do that. I'm going past the airport. I live down in Jonesboro. I can give Jillian a lift."

Lebeaux and Emma looked at each other nervously.

"Are you sure?" asked Jillian. "It's not out of your way?"

"I'll be glad to drop you off. No point in wasting forty bucks on a cab," I said. I was surprised at how firm I sounded.

Lebeaux and Emma both started to object. It was obvious that neither of them liked the idea of their clients getting together. But Jillian cut them off. "That's so kind of you, Joe. Thanks so much!"

I left a key for Kevin and Tonya, the cleanup crew, and showed them how to set the alarm. Then Jillian and I took off, leaving our lawyers standing in the driveway, still arguing about something.

When we were on the freeway, I turned to Jillian. "Have you had breakfast?"

She smiled. "No. I'm on West Coast time. It was a little early when I got up."

"Well then, we both need to keep our strength up, and I know where we can get a great stack of pancakes," I said, turning off the freeway toward the Denny's I'd discovered days earlier.

We ordered a pot of coffee and a couple of Grand Slam breakfasts. I think we were both conscious of the irony of the two of us sitting there, having breakfast like old friends, while our lawyers did battle up in Buckhead. Once she relaxed a bit, Jillian was even prettier than I had realized. She smiled a lot, and she had dimples. I tried not to pay too much attention to that.

"Are you married, Joe?" she asked. Neither of us was wearing a ring.

"No. Widower. My wife died of cancer several years ago. How about you?"

"Same. My husband was killed in Afghanistan two years ago. He was a captain in the army."

The mention of Afghanistan got my attention. It seemed I'd been hearing about that place an awful lot lately. But the news that Jillian wasn't married made me ignore it.

"I'm sorry," I said. "So are you from California originally?"

"Yes. Jack and I grew up there, out in the San Fernando Valley, but I live on the beach now. Ever been there?"

"No, but then I haven't traveled much of anywhere else, either. I'm sort of a homebody, I guess."

She smiled, showing her dimples. "I've been pretty much of a homebody lately, too. This is the first trip I've taken since Greg died—Greg was my husband."

Things seemed to be going well, and I didn't want to spoil the mood, but I couldn't resist bringing up the subject we both had on our minds.

"How did Emma find you?" I asked.

"I'm not exactly sure, but she's a resourceful lady. She knew Jack was from California, so she had somebody research the public records out there. Somehow she tracked me down."

"Did you know Emma tried to put up another woman as Jack's wife? Filed a petition in court, saying she was his common-law wife. Lebeaux shot it down."

"Yes, she told me about that. She said they just didn't have enough evidence to prove their case, and that was a problem in a lot of common-law marriage cases. Apparently under Georgia law, if there's no living spouse, the siblings are next in line to inherit. That's why she contacted me."

"So you'd never met Diana before? Like when they were supposedly married for all those years?"

"No. I met her for the first time in Emma's office. She signed some sort of waiver so Emma could represent me. I was surprised, to tell you the truth. Jack was not the marrying kind. He was very... promiscuous. I was shocked to hear he'd married your daughter," she said.

"So, from what Lebeaux has told me, the court case is going to depend on which one of them died first. Is that how you understand it?"

Jillian raised her eyebrows. "Yes. Emma seems to think she can win everything, no matter how it goes. She says the least we can get is everything but the house. She made me sign a contract for a forty percent fee."

"Yeah, Lebeaux is pretty confident, too. And he got the same deal from me. Seems like the lawyers are carving out a big chunk of the estate, either way."

"Sure does. What a racket, huh?"

We both laughed. Then we talked awhile longer, long after we'd finished our breakfasts and a second pot of coffee. She told me she was older than she looked—forty-six. She was an artist, living in a beach town called Laguna. She had a disabled son named Benjamin. Neither of us talked much about our spouses. I figured the subject was as painful for her as for me.

Just before noon, I dropped Jillian off at her hotel. Then, without really planning it, I drove to the mall. It was time I got some new furniture for my house. And while I was at it, I thought I'd get myself some new clothes.

CHAPTER TWENTY-TWO

Pearl had never called me back, even though I'd left half a dozen messages since I got her voice mail. I would have suspected she was just brushing me off, but the tone of her voice in that message was worrisome. I listened to it several times over those two days. She sounded more than nervous—she sounded scared.

Pearl's deposition was scheduled for that next morning at ten. I dressed myself in a new pair of jeans that were cut a little closer than my old Levi's, with a white shirt and a brown leather jacket that I'd picked up on the way out of Macy's the previous afternoon. Nothing too fancy, but I'd had a good night's sleep for a change, and I thought I looked pretty good as I headed out the door for Lebeaux's office.

Jillian had told me she would be there, but Diana was out of the picture as her case had been dropped. The judge had combined the two probate cases—Jack's and Cynthia's—at Lebeaux's request. I gathered that's standard procedure in a case like ours, involving a deceased married couple. When I walked into Lebeaux's conference room, Emma and Jillian were already there.

"We're waiting for the witness," said Emma. The court reporter was setting up her equipment.

I nodded to Jillian, and she smiled back. Emma looked back and forth between us and didn't seem pleased.

Lebeaux was on the phone in the other room, but at about ten fifteen, he walked into the conference room. "Where's Miss McGinnis?" he asked Emma, as if she ought to know.

She shrugged. "I haven't talked to her."

"She was served with a subpoena two days ago. She had plenty of notice. I hope she knows she'll end up in jail for contempt if she doesn't show."

Emma smiled. "Jonathan, don't be so dramatic. I'm sure she'll show up. She's probably stuck in traffic."

But Pearl never did show up. We waited for almost an hour, with Lebeaux pacing around the office and calling his investigator and the judge's chambers. Nobody seemed to know where Pearl was. Emma got up and walked outside with her cell phone. Jillian and I chatted for a while; then we basically sat there and watched the clock ticking. Thinking about that voice-mail message, I was getting worried. But something told me not to say anything about it.

Finally Lebeaux came in and told the court reporter she could leave. He was pissed again. "We're going to have to reschedule this," he said. "That woman is going to be sorry she stood us up. She's just run up a couple grand in attorney fees and reporter fees, and by the time I get her into court on contempt, it's going to be three times that much. I hope she has a big bank account."

I had to smile at that last remark, of course. Emma was already halfway out the door. Jillian got up to leave.

"Say, do you have anything planned for the rest of the day?" I asked Jillian. I don't know where I got the nerve.

"Not really. I was hoping you'd ask," she said and smiled.

"It's a beautiful day. Feels like fall. Do you feel like walking?"

"Sure," she said. "Let me just go tell Emma I won't need a ride home."

She caught up with Emma outside. The news that Jillian and I were hanging out together again must have been a shock. Emma spun around and glared at me—a mean look, almost threatening. But I wasn't in any mood to be intimidated.

We walked around downtown Atlanta for a while and then ended up at a nice little Mexican restaurant off Peachtree Street. I started to order my usual beer, but Jillian said she didn't drink, so I passed on the alcohol and ordered iced tea.

"You realize we're making our lawyers nervous," I said.

"Yes. I'm sure they don't know what to make of this connection. To tell the truth, neither do I," she said and laughed. "We ought to be enemies, but I can't get very enthusiastic about this probate case. My brother and I were never very close as adults, so I don't feel like I much deserve an inheritance from him."

"I feel the same way about Cynthia. Maybe more so. I didn't even know your brother, Jack."

"Then there's the question of where all this money came from. I can't get that out of my head," she said.

"Yeah. I felt that way at first, but now I've gotten used to the idea. Somebody has to claim it, so why not us?"

She nodded and then paused, focusing on the piece of lettuce on her fork. "Joe, I don't know how to bring this up, but something has been bothering me. I can't put my finger on it, but…do you get the feeling there's something wrong with this whole picture?"

"Wow, I sure do. I've felt that way from the very first. Why do you ask?"

"Well, remember I told you that my son, Benjamin, is disabled? What I didn't mention is that he's a wounded veteran. Ben was in college when my husband was killed. He took it really hard—crazy with anger at the Islamic terrorists for killing his dad. Finally, he dropped out of school and signed up in the army. Two weeks after he was deployed, they shipped him home with a terrible brain injury—shrapnel from a roadside bomb. We were devastated."

"Wow, I'm sorry to hear that. I hear there are a lot of young soldiers coming back with that sort of injury."

"Yes, but what you don't hear about is the shameful way they're treated. We ran into nothing but roadblocks from the government, trying to get help for Ben. His doctors said he could be rehabilitated, but it would take a lot of therapy—*expensive* therapy. The VA wouldn't pay for that. They were satisfied to have him sitting in a wheelchair, pumped full of drugs. He couldn't work, and I had to stay with him twenty-four-seven. The medical bills drained the last of my husband Greg's death benefit from the VA. I was at the end of my rope."

I wasn't sure how any of this followed from our conversation, but I could see she was very emotional. I reached across the table and took her hand. She smiled a little and sighed.

"Then one day I got a call from someone named Pete who claimed he knew Jack. He said he was with a private charity called the Blue Buddha Brotherhood."

"No kidding? Blue Buddha? That's the name of Jack's nightclub," I said.

"I know. That's what I meant about how weird everything seems. I found out about the name of the club when I got back here and saw it all over the paperwork for his estate. But Joe, I never made any connection between this charity and Jack's shady business. If I had, I would have refused their help. But as it turned out, Blue Buddha was a godsend for my family. They wired twenty thousand dollars into my bank account a week after I talked to this guy Pete—no questions asked. Then they kept wiring funds—five to ten thousand a month. It kept our lights on and Ben's bills paid, and it even allowed me to get out of the house a little and restart my life."

Suddenly my conversation with Pearl two days earlier popped into my head—what she'd said about Jack claiming he was funding a veteran's charity. Maybe he was telling Pearl the truth.

"Did you find out anything about this group—who they were?" I asked.

"That's just it. I never could get a straight answer. I'd get calls from people who said they were with Blue Buddha, asking about Ben and how we were doing. They never really identified themselves. None of my military wife friends had ever heard of it. I know I should have checked it out, but honestly I was so grateful that I didn't dare push it."

"Well, who could blame you? These people must have seemed like guardian angels," I said.

"Exactly. They were lifesavers. But then, all of a sudden, a couple of months ago, the money stopped. No explanation, no notice. Ben and I were right back in the same fix—flat broke, desperate, and unable to get any help from the VA. Frankly, that's the only reason I agreed to come back here and file this claim for Jack's estate. I'm desperate."

I looked across the table at Jillian, wondering whether I should divulge my conversation with Pearl. Pieces of the puzzle were definitely falling into place as we spoke. Jack must have been telling the truth about the veterans. But why had the funding stopped? And why had it all ended in murder? There were still way too many unanswered questions. So, even though I had started to trust Jillian, I decided not to let her in on what I knew.

CHAPTER TWENTY-THREE

I had agreed to meet the furniture delivery truck at four that afternoon, so I dropped Jillian off at her hotel again and drove home. Once the furniture was off the truck and in my house, I sat down to think things over. It was good to feel like my house was more than just an empty shell again, but the new living-room sofa and chairs were much more modern than anything I'd ever had before, and I wasn't at all sure I'd made the right choices.

I had just popped a beer and put my feet up on the new ottoman when the doorbell rang. Peeking out the window, I saw Daryl and his cop friend Hugo standing on the doorstep. I didn't see any reason not to let them in.

"Hey, Joe. You remember my buddy Hugo?"

"Sure."

Hugo nodded, and I offered them both a beer. We all sat down on the new living room furniture. They both seemed a little nervous.

"So what's up, Daryl?" I asked.

"Hugo here has some questions for you. Unofficial, of course. It's about the murder case."

"Oh? I thought Detective Drake was handling that," I said.

"Well, he is," said Hugo. "I'm not involved directly. But I'm following up on a few leads, trying to figure out motive and that sort of thing."

"I don't see how I can help you there," I said. "I don't know anything about Jack except what the other police officers have told me."

"Except Daryl here tells me that you've been doing some investigating on your own. Is that right?"

I hesitated. What was he getting at? "Not really. I'm just keeping my ear to the ground. Unofficial, of course."

"Right. For example, I understand that you've talked to this woman named Pearl," he said.

"Pearl?" I asked, trying to act disinterested, even though I was alarmed. "Oh, you mean Jack's bookkeeper. Yes, I did talk to her briefly a few days ago. Just over drinks."

"And what did she have to say?" asked Hugo. Daryl was leaning back on the sofa, staying out of it.

"About what?"

"About Jack's business."

"Not much. Just that he owned the Blue Buddha club, and a hotel, and had made a lot of money. I already knew that."

"What did she say about the money, Joe?" Something in Hugo's tone seemed suddenly menacing.

"I don't know what you mean," I said.

"Yes, you do. You discussed Jack's business with Pearl. Pearl knew a lot about that subject. She knew a lot about how much money he had and where it all went, didn't she?"

My mind was freezing up with confusion. "Maybe. But I wouldn't know anything about that," I said.

"So who set up the meeting? You or Pearl?"

"She called me. It was totally her idea. Like I said, I didn't know anything about Jack's business."

"Joe, Pearl would never have talked to you voluntarily unless you had something she wanted. She was...is...very secretive about money. She was paid to be that way."

"So...how do you know Pearl?" I asked, trying to make sense of this interrogation. I felt like I was getting the third degree.

"I don't," he said, sounding a little defensive himself. "I just know she worked for Jack, and from all indications, his business was less than legitimate."

"Maybe so. But I'm just an ordinary guy—not mixed up in anything illegal. I hadn't seen my daughter in over two years. Daryl knows that. Isn't that right, Daryl?"

Daryl nodded. "Relax, Joe," he said. "You're not under suspicion."

"Then why all the questions? I don't get it."

Hugo shifted in his chair, evidently frustrated. "Look, Joe, we know that Pearl had information about Jack's assets—information that nobody else would have had. The investigation has narrowed quite a bit. We know that Jack was laundering money for some people—some veterans who were running some sort of drug-smuggling operation from Afghanistan. It would have been a lot of money—maybe tens of millions."

"Oh? Why would Jack be laundering money? I thought he was a drug dealer himself," I said.

"Good question. That's the sort of question that we'd like Pearl to answer. But she won't talk to us, Joe. She's avoiding us. We think she's concealing material evidence about the murders."

"Why don't you bring her in for questioning, then, instead of wasting time grilling me?"

Hugo shook his head. "There's no reason to be hostile, Joe. We're just doing our jobs here—looking for evidence wherever we can find it."

I wasn't convinced. I've always respected the police, but something didn't seem right. I decided to play along.

"Okay, then, what if she did tell me about the veterans and drug smuggling? You seem to already know a lot more than I do about that."

"No we don't," said Hugo. "We don't know the critical part—where the money is now."

My heart started beating faster. "What does that have to do with the murder investigation? Why would the police care where the money is?"

"You're avoiding my question, Joe. I'm not happy about that," he said, frowning.

"You haven't answered my question, either. What do you care where the money is?"

Hugo looked a little surprised at my aggressive tone. I was surprised, too. Then his surprise turned into a dark scowl.

"Listen up, Joe. You seem to think you can just waltz in and scoop up this cash like you were entitled to it, just because Jack and Dawn are dead. But that money didn't belong to Jack. It belonged to other people. Those people will go to great lengths to recover it. They're ruthless, and they have resources. They're out there somewhere, looking for their money. If I were you, I'd be worried about that."

"There's no need to shout," I said. "I told you, I don't know anything about the money. And I doubt if Pearl knows anything, either. If she does, she hasn't told me."

"I don't believe you, Joe. I think you're holding out on me. You and Pearl. You're going to regret the day you ever got mixed up with that bitch, I promise you that."

Daryl had moved to the edge of his chair and looked very uncomfortable.

"Hugo, leave him alone. He doesn't know anything. I can vouch for Joe here. He's a straight shooter."

Hugo and Daryl exchanged looks.

"Okay then. I guess I have to take your word for it. But think it over, Joe. Give me a call if you change your mind."

We got up and walked to the door. Hugo stormed out ahead of us.

"I'm sorry, Joe," said Daryl. "I didn't have any idea he'd come on so strong. I guess he's just trying to earn his chops in the Atlanta PD."

"That's all right," I said. "Just don't bring him around here anymore. I don't like the guy."

As soon as they left, I fished out Detective Drake's card. He answered right away.

"Detective, I just had a visit from a member of your department—a guy named Hugo. Do you know him?"

"I'm not sure. Why?"

"He was here asking me a bunch of questions about the murder case," I said. "He wanted to know about this woman named Pearl, who was an associate of Jack Sloan's."

There was a pause on the other end of the phone.

"That's funny," he said. "We just had a report about that woman from the NYPD."

My heart jumped. "The New York police? What sort of report?"

"Well," he said, "They fished her out of Long Island Sound this morning. Somebody tossed her out of an airplane after they chopped off a couple of her fingers and blew her brains out."

CHAPTER TWENTY-FOUR

"What? Pearl is *dead*? Are you sure?" I couldn't believe what I was hearing.

"Afraid so. Patricia McGinnis, a.k.a Pearl Magenta—she washed up this morning, along with a guy named Peter Diamond. His body was mutilated, too; I guess I don't need to go into details about how. Anyway, it's for sure it wasn't the fish that got those body parts. Those two people were obviously tortured."

"Tortured? My God!"

"Somebody was apparently after information from them. Maybe the same people who ransacked the Tuxedo House. It's starting to look like all of Jack Sloan's close associates are on somebody's serious shit list."

Close associates? I thought of Jillian, Jack Sloan's sister. But surely she was safe.

"When did this happen?" I asked.

"A couple of days ago. Pearl was due to come in for questioning that afternoon but didn't show up. Now we know why."

That would have been the day she left me the voice mail. No wonder she was scared.

"But doesn't that seem like a strange coincidence? That she would be killed on the same day she was supposed to be questioned?"

"Good point," he said. I'm starting to wonder about all the leaks in this investigation. Maybe more than leaks. Anyway, the next witness on our list is Jack's hot lawyer, Emma Faulkner. Do you know her?"

"Yes. Unfortunately, I've had some dealings with her."

"Well, we hear from some of the lawyers in the DA's office that she and Jack were quite close. You might say closer than your typical attorney and client. It was apparently the subject of a lot of gossip at bar gatherings." He laughed, sort of a sleazy laugh.

"Really? You mean they were sleeping together?"

"I don't know that they did much sleeping—but everything else, apparently. It had been going on since she was in law school. And the way I understand it, they were still an item when the guy was murdered."

"But he married my daughter! And Emma claimed in court that another woman was Jack's wife!"

Drake laughed again. "What can I say? Some men are pigs. Some women, too."

"Poor Cynthia. I'm sure she didn't appreciate that," I said, more or less to myself.

"Few women would," said the detective. "Anyway, Faulkner had to know all about Jack's business dealings, both legal and illegal, so she's a pretty obvious witness in the murder case, assuming it was a mob hit, as we suspect."

"When are you going to question her?"

"Unclear. I called her a couple of hours ago to set it up. Told her about those two bodies up in New York and offered to take her into protective custody under the circumstances. She refused. She also refused to be interviewed—claiming the attorney-client privilege bullshit. Our legal advisor says it won't fly in this case, since the privilege dies with the client, but it works as a stalling tactic for her. If the case ever goes to court, the judge will shoot it down. I imagine she'll end up taking the fifth."

"Do you have any other leads?" I asked.

"Not really. I've never been too optimistic about solving this case. Jack was suspected of dealing marijuana from his club, but we didn't have any recent evidence of that. Whatever he was up to, he must have gotten in over his head, since the crime scene had all the earmarks of a professional hit."

"I heard your officers searched his house a couple of months ago. Do you know anything about that?"

"Oh? No, I hadn't heard that. I'm in the homicide division, so it wouldn't routinely have crossed my desk. But it didn't come up on our records search, either. There was a warrant, you say?"

"I believe so—a couple of months back. At least, that's what was said in court. And I think Lieutenant Frank Dupree mentioned it when I was down there at headquarters that first day. He said there were a couple of arrests for drugs that night, but they didn't find anything they could use against Jack. I'm surprised you didn't know about it."

He sounded sort of irritated. "I'll look into it. Probably not related to the homicide case. But I'm interested in this police officer you mentioned—the guy named Hugo?"

"Yeah, I don't know his last name. He came by my house and gave me the third degree about Jack Sloan's money—some sort of stash that he'd hidden away."

"Let me run down that name. Can't be too many guys named Hugo in the APD. It sounds like he might be more involved than he says. I can promise you he's not part of our investigation."

"Wow, this sure is a lot to take in at once," I said.

"Sorry about that, Mr. Brock. How have you been holding up?"

"Okay, I guess. It just seems like every time I start to figure things out, something else throws me off balance."

"I understand," he said. "That's how it is with police work, too. Well, hang in there, sir."

I thanked him and hung up. It had been one hell of a day. First Pearl's no-show at her deposition, then there was the inquisition from Daryl and Hugo, and now this. I sat down with a sheet of paper and tried to put everything into some sort of order. The police might be clueless, but I knew—or strongly suspected—why she had been killed. It had to be about those millions in cash that Jack had stashed in banks somewhere. Now it looked like whatever information she had about that money was gone, along with her.

I pulled out my phone and replayed the voice mail Pearl had left me, probably just hours before she was tortured and killed. Why would she tell me to forget about our conversation? She didn't say it wasn't true, just that I should forget it "for my own good." From the sound of it, she probably wished she could forget about it, too. She was certainly right about one thing: for her, at least, it turned out to be a matter of life and death.

There's something about me that you might not have figured out by now. I'm stubborn. Sometimes too stubborn for my own good. I got to thinking about that money. Not that I really needed it; that had never really been the case. Even if I lost everything in the probate case, I still had a comfortable pension from my twenty-five years of county service, and besides, I had always lived a modest lifestyle and probably always would. But that stubborn streak kept me focused on the money. For some reason it drove me nuts to think about it somewhere out there, unclaimed until it got forfeited to the bank.

Pearl knew which banks the cash was in. Her killers must have realized that, and maybe they thought she also knew the account numbers. I wondered whether she had broken down under torture and told them where the money was. If she did, they would still need those account numbers. Pearl insisted that I had them—but where? It was a total mystery.

Then slowly something else started to dawn on me. Pearl's message had said "they" knew we had talked. What if Pearl had spilled *all* the beans before they shot her in the head? What if she told them not only where the money was stashed but also the rest of it? *What if she told them that I had those account numbers?*

CHAPTER TWENTY-FIVE

I got up, closed the blinds, and locked the doors and windows. Somebody had already gotten into the house once, and now it seemed more likely than ever that they'd come back. I got my briefcase out of the trunk of my car, rummaged through it for my Smith and Wesson .38 and tucked the pistol into my waistband. I was glad that in Georgia it's legal to keep a gun at home or in your car. I had never used it before, but it made me feel safer, even though I had no idea who or what I was afraid of.

The idea of calling the police kept going through my head. But if there was one thing that was becoming clear, it was that the police couldn't be trusted. I had been doing a lot of thinking about that. Regardless of what Officer Prick said, whoever broke into the house the first time had to have used Cynthia's key. There was only one place they could have gotten that key—from Cynthia herself. Whoever killed her might have stolen it, and that was a frightening possibility. On the other hand, I was pretty sure that after the murders, her purse would have been booked into evidence at the Atlanta PD. Anyone at the police department would have had an opportunity to sneak that key out, without anybody being the wiser. That seemed like a more plausible scenario. Detective Drake hadn't said so in so many words, but he clearly didn't trust all the cops on the case. Regardless of how it happened, though, the more I thought about it, I was pretty sure that whoever broke in had used Cynthia's key, hoping to search the place without my suspecting anything. Then, when they couldn't find what they wanted, they started tearing things up. The result was what I found when I got home that night.

The key didn't worry me anymore because I'd had all the locks changed. But now that Pearl had probably connected me with Jack's money, I knew it was only a matter of time before her killers caught up with me. I paced around the house for a while, getting more and more agitated, until I realized that I was a sitting duck at home by myself and decided to get out of there.

I packed a duffel bag and got into my car, heading north. After passing by the airport exit, I doubled back and pulled into Jillian's hotel parking lot. I was about to call her room to say good-bye when I saw something that stopped me. Somehow, when I dropped her off there both times, I had failed to notice the little sign on the side of the building that said "Fly Away Inn." It must be Jack Sloan's hotel; it even had the little neon blue butterfly next to the name. Realizing that made me uncomfortable. On the other hand, the place might soon belong to me, and it might be a good idea to check it out. Maybe that was why Jillian had booked her room here, as well.

I sat there in the parking lot, turning over my options and looking over my shoulder for anyone suspicious. By then, Jillian was just about the only person I trusted. I had a strong urge to tell her everything—all about the money, the Blue Buddha, the bank accounts, and Pearl. I needed an ally desperately, but was it fair to bring her into this mess? And there was no way I could do that without offering to split the stash with her.

Finally deciding to test the waters a little more, I picked up my phone and called Jillian's room. She met me in the lobby.

"Joe! What a nice surprise! I was just sitting upstairs, dreading the idea of eating dinner alone."

"I'm on my way north," I said. "Thought I'd visit my brother Charlie in Chattanooga for a few days." It was the truth. I didn't have anywhere else to go.

"Oh? Won't our lawyers be needing us?" she asked, looking puzzled.

"Too bad if they do," I said. "I need to get out of town. I just stopped in to tell you I'll be gone for a while."

"So what's the rush? Don't you have time for dinner?"

Her smile with those dimples was so sweet, I couldn't resist. I looked around the lobby. Nothing unusual or sinister about it— just a small inn with comfortable furniture, a front desk, and a small coffee shop. There was nobody else around. It felt safe.

"Okay," I said. "That sounds good."

We ordered burgers and fries, and I ordered a beer. Jillian looked at me and smiled again, but not disapprovingly. I keep forgetting that there are people who don't drink but don't mind if other people do. In the South, you run into a lot of the disapproving kind. It was a relief that Jillian wasn't one of them, and I started to relax.

I looked across the table at Jillian, who was daintily eating fries with her fork and chattering away about trivia. It felt so good to be with her this way, and despite my usual self-doubts, I was beginning to feel that she liked me, too. Still, she was so blissfully ignorant of everything I'd been through since the day of the murders. It broke my heart to realize it, but she deserved to know the facts—at least some of them.

"Jillian, I need to tell you something," I said, clearing my throat. "I hate to spoil our dinner, but you're going to find out about it anyway, and you might as well hear it from me. The woman who didn't show up for her deposition yesterday—the woman named Pearl? Well, she's dead."

Jillian's eyes opened wide. "What? Dead!"

"Yes. She was murdered. They found her body this morning."

"But…why? Do they know who killed her?"

"No. But possibly the same people who killed Jack and Cynthia," I said.

Jillian sat there staring at me, trying to understand. "But I thought this Pearl was a bookkeeper. Who would want to kill a bookkeeper?"

"It's complicated," I said. "It has to do with Jack's business. The drugs. The money."

Jillian was shaking her head, and there were tears in her eyes. "I knew I shouldn't have come back here to Georgia. I don't want anything to do with that money. It's dirty money—blood money."

"I understand how you feel," I said. "I'm pretty nervous about it, too. Somebody ransacked my house right after I got involved in this case. To tell you the truth, that's one reason why I'm leaving town."

"Joe! You need to go to the police!"

"I already have. They said it was just a routine burglary, and not to worry." I was feeling guilty about holding back the whole truth, but I wasn't ready to tell her about the bank accounts, and I wanted to ease Jillian's mind as much as I could.

"That's ridiculous. Joe, this is terrifying! People are getting murdered for my brother's money, and the two of us are right in the middle of it!"

The more I looked into those eyes, the guiltier I felt.

"Jillian, I'm sure you're not in any danger. There's no reason anyone would want to hurt you," I said.

"How do you know?"

"Because you're not involved in Jack's business. You're innocent of all that."

"But so are you!" she said. "And you just told me you were worried. What are you keeping from me? Please don't try to sugar coat this. I want the whole truth!"

I took a sip of my second beer. "Okay," I finally said. "Here's the whole truth. There are some…rumors out there that Jack had a lot of money stashed away. Cash. Nobody knows where. Apparently whoever killed Jack and Cynthia is trying to find that money."

"Rumors? What rumors?"

"All I know is what I heard from Pearl. She said there was some money hidden away."

"And Pearl knew where it is?"

"Apparently somebody thought she did," I said, and took a long drought of my beer.

Jillian pushed her plate away. Her tears had disappeared.

"So you think that's why Jack's house was trashed? They were looking for his money?"

"Possibly. Who knows?" I said.

"Then why would they ransack *your* house, too?"

"I don't know," I said. "It's hard to believe they expected to find much money at my place."

We were both quiet for a while. Then Jillian reached across the table and took my hand.

"Joe, I don't want you to leave. I want you to stay. I'm scared. Please don't leave me."

She was so vulnerable, and I felt so guilty for frightening her, especially without letting her in on the whole picture. I got up and walked around the table, and she stood up to meet me, turning her face toward mine. Then suddenly she reached her arms around my neck and pressed her cheek into my chest. I wrapped my arms around her and felt her slender body relax against me. Right there and then, I changed my mind about Chattanooga.

CHAPTER TWENTY-SIX

When I think back about that first night with Jillian, I still get a little choked up. I hadn't been with a woman since long before my wife died, and I was nervous—worried that the equipment might not work, of course, but also a little scared of being that close to another human being again. As it turned out, I really didn't have anything to worry about on either score. Jillian was very warm and patient—and much more sexual than she seemed. After the most passionate few hours I'd ever spent, we fell asleep, completely exhausted.

I woke up before she did, threw on my clothes, and went downstairs for coffee. When I came back, she was awake.

"Joe! I was afraid you'd gone off and left me," she said, smiling sleepily.

"No chance of that," I said, handing her a cup of coffee. "I didn't know whether you used cream or sugar, so I just left it black. If you like, I'll go back and get…"

"No, this is perfect," she said.

I kicked off my shoes and climbed back into bed with her. "So tell me…how do you like the Fly Away Inn?" she said. "It's probably going to belong to one of us, you know."

"Maybe so. But we're going to have to pay the lawyers somehow. This place might end up belonging to Emma or Lebeaux."

"I know," she said. "And there's something else I've been thinking about. The IRS. What if they come in and claim all the assets? What if they confiscate everything?"

"That could happen, I suppose," I said. Actually, I had been considering the same possibility. That's one reason I was interested in Pearl's story about the stash; no paper trail for the Feds to follow.

"Then we'll have gone to all of this trouble for nothing, won't we?" She chuckled ironically.

I looked at her sitting there, with her hair all messy and with no makeup. She was beautiful. I was amazed that such a woman could be interested in me. "After last night, we could lose it all, and I'd never feel like it was for nothing," I said.

"I feel that way, too," she said and kissed me.

We got dressed and went downstairs for breakfast. The previous night had made me all but forget the fear that caused me to pack up and leave my house. Now, in the light of day, it came back. I realized that I hadn't resolved anything. There were so many questions I needed answers to.

"Jillian, I have to go," I said. "I have to go take care of some things. If I stay here with you, we could both be in danger."

She looked at me blankly across the breakfast table. "But I still don't understand. What are you so skittish about?"

"I can't tell you—not yet. Just take my word for it, I can't stay."

Her eyes narrowed, and a look came over her face that I hadn't seen there before—anger and frustration, and a little bit of contempt. "Joe, don't you realize that you're scaring me more than if you just told me the whole truth? Whatever it is, I can't imagine you're going to solve anything by running away."

I had thought about that, and I saw her point. She thought I was a coward, and I had started to see it that way, too. Obviously I couldn't stay at my brother's place forever. Sooner or later, I'd have to come back and face the problem, one way or another. The house on Tuxedo Road had been sitting there empty for days. I didn't trust Lebeaux to look after it. Besides, Pearl had clearly implied that those secret account numbers were hidden somewhere in my house, and I hadn't even tried to find them. I looked across the table at Jillian, and decided it was time to stop running and take charge.

"Okay," I said. "You're right. More right than you realize. But there are some things I need to do before I tell you anything else. Some questions that need answers."

I got up from the table and laid down some cash.

"Where are you going? You owe me an explanation, dammit! Tell me you're not going to just leave me here!" She looked angrier than before.

"Jillian, you're going to have to trust me," I said, trying to ignore the anger in her eyes. "I'll call you."

I turned and walked out of the restaurant, not daring to spend another minute explaining for fear I'd lose my nerve. I picked up my duffel from the room and got into my car, heading north again. This time I got off at the Buckhead exit. I wanted to check on my daughter's house.

As I turned into the driveway, I saw two vehicles parked in front of the garage. One was a white van. The other was Daryl Spinks's silver pickup truck. I pulled in behind them. The front door of the house was standing open.

"Hello? Who's here?" I shouted into the hallway. Right away I noticed there was something missing—the death smell. Well, at least it was much less noticeable than before. The Good-As-New people had done a pretty good job.

"Down here! In the basement!" shouted a voice I didn't recognize.

I edged my way cautiously down the hall toward the open basement door with a hand on my .38. Daryl had no business being here, that was for sure. And I had no idea who was driving the white van or what he or she might be up to.

"Who's there? Who *are* you?" I shouted.

Nobody answered. I stepped up to the edge of the doorway and stood next to the entrance, being careful not to show myself. Then I heard footsteps coming up the stairs.

"Stop right there!" I said, drawing my gun. I believe I would have fired it, too, if I hadn't seen Daryl walking through the doorway just then with a bunch of papers in his hands.

My heart was beating a mile a minute. "Daryl! What the hell are *you* doing here?" I said.

"Hey, Joe," he said. Then he saw my gun. "*Whoa*! Take it easy, man! Lebeaux sent me. I'm working for him. He gave me the key—see? And the security code. " He reached into his pocket and showed me a key.

"You haven't answered my question. What the hell are you doing?" I asked, putting my pistol away.

He hesitated. "Just...investigating," he said.

"Investigating what?"

Daryl turned around and gestured toward a guy in a suit who had followed him up the stairs. "Joe Brock, meet Mr. Harry Browning of Browning Engineering."

I was completely mystified. "Engineering? What's this about?"

Daryl and Browning looked at each other. We were still standing there awkwardly at the top of the basement stairs. I looked around and realized that all the furniture, rugs and draperies in the house had been removed. The place was basically an empty shell, sort of like a grander version of my own house the previous week. Good-As-New again.

"Come on outside," said Daryl. "Mr. Browning, please excuse us for a minute?" He led the way out to the back patio, where the two of us sat down on some wrought iron chairs.

"Now tell me what's going on. You scared the shit out of me," I said.

"Sorry, Joe. I wasn't expecting you to show up unannounced like that."

"Obviously," I said.

Daryl got that same evasive look on his face that I'd noticed before. "Well, it's like this, Joe. We want to make sure that all the assets are accounted for."

"Huh? And what does an engineering company have to do with that?"

He shifted in his chair. "Maybe I should let Mr. Lebeaux explain it. It's complicated."

"No, Daryl, *you* need to explain it to me—now!" I said, surprised at my tone of voice.

"Okay, then," he said. "All I can tell you is what I know. We've heard some...rumors...that Jack Sloan might have had some money or drugs hidden away. We were just checking to see if it was hidden somewhere in the house here."

"The house is empty, Daryl. No furniture, no nothing. How could anything be hidden in there?"

"All I know is something about a vault. A secret vault. That's what I was told."

"And who told you that? How would Lebeaux know anything about that?"

Daryl stared at the flagstones between his feet. "I'm not supposed to say anything. Mr. Lebeaux said we needed to keep it just between ourselves."

I was furious. "Daryl, I'm the administrator of this estate! I could have you thrown out of here. Maybe thrown in jail! Now tell me what you know about this so-called vault."

"Just let me call Mr. Lebeaux and clear it with him," said Daryl. He punched in some numbers on his phone and walked over to the side of the patio. In a couple of minutes, he came back.

"Mr. Lebeaux wants to explain it to you himself. He says he'll be here in ten minutes."

CHAPTER TWENTY-SEVEN

B rowning was still inside the house. I could hear him banging around down in the basement. I got up, went back inside, and wandered around the house by myself while Daryl sat on the patio out back. The place looked completely different now. All the gaudy furnishings were gone, so you could see the layout much better. It was a nice place, except for one thing. Somebody had punched holes in the sheetrock in every room, and several of the wide floor planks had been pulled up.

After I'd checked through the top two floors, I headed down to the basement. Another shock. This guy Browning had two other men with him, and they had torn out a big section of the block wall behind the bar. There were metal posts holding up the first floor. I couldn't see past the debris to determine what they were doing back there.

Lebeaux finally showed up, and I met him at the front door. He had a defensive look on his face.

"Now Joe, I can explain…"

"Yes, I imagine you can," I said. "Just give me one good reason why I shouldn't fire you for damaging this property without my permission."

"Let's sit down and discuss this like reasonable people," he said. "I'm sure you'll have a different point of view once you've heard the whole story."

"Okay. This had better be good," I said.

We joined Daryl on the patio. I realized that we were sitting almost directly above the basement wall that had been demolished. We could hear them banging around beneath us.

Lebeaux was obviously nervous. "Joe, I know that Daryl has explained to you that the third victim in the homicide was his sister, Sandra."

"Yes, he told me that. What does that have to do with anything?"

"Sandra was working on the case for military law enforcement, and part of her job was to get close to your daughter, Dawn."

"Don't call her Dawn. Her name was Cynthia," I said.

"Okay then, *Cynthia*. Anyway, Sandra succeeded in gaining Cynthia's confidence. In fact, Cynthia confided in Sandra quite a bit. They talked about Jack's…activities."

He hesitated and looked over at Daryl, who was pulling leaves off of an azalea bush next to his chair.

"Go on," I said. "I'm still waiting to hear why you're demolishing my daughter's house."

Lebeaux was choosing his words carefully. "Well, a couple of weeks before their death, Cynthia told Sandra that Jack had been stockpiling cash—a lot of it. They were at the Blue Buddha Club one night, and Cynthia was very upset. She was pretty drunk that night, but from what she said, Sandra pieced together that the money was in a secret place at her house."

"And you think she meant *this* house?" I asked, without thinking.

"Why of course. What other house would she be talking about?"

"I don't know…just asking," I said. "But how did you find out about it?"

"Sandra told Daryl. He knew what she was doing for the army, and he was worried about her. She kept him pretty well informed."

"And when did he tell *you*?"

Lebeaux hesitated again, apparently thinking about how to answer. "He told me after you hired me…when he knew that I'd be representing the estate."

Daryl had gotten up and walked to the other side of the patio, apparently not wanting in on this discussion. I didn't know whether to believe Lebeaux or not. It was all a little too coincidental.

"Okay," I said, as sarcastically as I could. "And exactly when were you planning to tell *me* about it?"

"Joe, I would have told you if we found anything. Really! Why would I keep it a secret?"

"Why indeed?" I said. "I guess we both know why."

"That's completely unfair. What have I ever done to make you believe I'd keep anything from you?"

He had a point. As far as I knew, he'd always played straight with me.

"Okay, then," I said. "Who's going to patch this place up? Looks like several thousand dollars' worth of repairs need to be done."

"I've already arranged that," he said. "It's coming out of my own pocket for now. Of course, if we found anything, I'd charge it to the estate. If you hadn't popped in unannounced today, it would have been repaired before you ever knew anything had happened."

That much I did believe. "And what have these people found? Anything at all?"

"No," he said. "They're working downstairs on a suspicious area. Their instruments picked up a void area behind one of the basement walls."

Just as he said that, I heard a noise behind me. I turned around and saw a large flagstone rise up from the patio. Browning popped his head up.

"Mr. Lebeaux, I think we've found what you're looking for," he said.

We all rushed down to the basement. The wall where the men had been working was half gone. The crew had excavated several inches into the red clay behind the cinder blocks and tapped into another concrete wall, parallel to the house foundation. They had removed several blocks from it and climbed through to a chamber about five feet wide by eight feet long. At the other end of this vault, there was a ladder leading up to the patio. That's where Browning was standing with broad daylight right above him, grinning with obvious pride in his work.

The little vault was dark, but Browning had a flashlight, and as we all climbed in, standing shoulder to shoulder, we could see pretty well. The walls were lined with crudely assembled shelves. On some of them were banker's boxes, most of which had been tipped on their sides and were empty. Other than that, there was nothing in the place except a bunch of papers that had been strewn around on the cement floor.

Lebeaux looked disgusted. "Okay, looks like if there was anything here, somebody beat us to it," he said and crawled up the ladder. Daryl followed him up. I looked around the floor and saw some papers with the name Dawn M. Sterling on them. One was a bill from American Express, dated the previous month. Lebeaux apparently wasn't interested, but something told me not to leave it behind, so I tucked it into my jacket pocket and followed the others up the ladder.

Browning and his team packed up and left. I stuck around while Lebeaux locked the place up and set the alarm. I stopped him as he started to get into his car.

"Mr. Lebeaux, I think maybe I need to look for another lawyer," I said.

"Aw, Joe, you don't mean that," he said. "I've been doing a pretty damn good job for you so far, if I do say so. You'd be making a big mistake to let this little misunderstanding today interfere with our relationship."

"I don't know," I said, shaking my head. "I need to be able to trust you. It seems like there's an awful lot going on that I've been left out of. Every time I turn around, I find out some new and disturbing information."

Lebeaux chewed on his cigar. "Yes, I can see why you'd feel that way," he said. "Joe, we need to have a talk—a heart-to-heart, so to speak. Let me buy you a cup of coffee."

CHAPTER TWENTY-EIGHT

W e drove down to Peachtree and pulled into a diner near Piedmont, just around the corner from the Blue Buddha.

"I know you're having doubts about me, Joe," said Lebeaux. Daryl was sitting next to him in the booth across from me. "Well, you're entitled to be a little skeptical under the circumstances. I think it's time we put all our cards on the table."

I wasn't sure what he was getting at, but I was glad to hear he wanted to clear things up. "Okay," I said. "Let's start with how you and Daryl are connected. Did you really represent him in a traffic case?"

"Yes, that's the truth," said Lebeaux. Daryl nodded agreement. "That was a couple of years ago. I got a pretty nice settlement for him."

"So how did the two of you get mixed up together in this case?"

Lebeaux smiled. "Well, actually, Daryl hasn't been my client for years. More recently, my client was his sister, Sandra."

I must have looked shocked. "What are you talking about? You mean you knew Sandra?"

"Yes indeed," he said, fishing half a cigar out of his shirt pocket. "Like I told you, Daryl learned quite a bit from Sandra about Jack Sloan's dealings, but there's much more to that story. She was finding out things that scared her. She came to me for advice."

"I know about the Blue Buddha Brotherhood, if that's what you mean," I said, but then I regretted it. I told myself to shut up.

Lebeaux looked surprised. "Yes, Daryl told me you'd been talking to this woman named Pearl before she died," he said. "She must have figured some things out on her own. So I expect she told you that Jack was doing business with some military personnel. They were dealing drugs, and Jack was handling their money."

"Right, Pearl told me that, but I don't understand how you got involved," I said.

"Well, first of all, you have to understand that this group was not your ordinary drug-smuggling ring—at least, not at first. Originally, they were on some sort of crusade. It was a group of guys who were pissed off at the US government and the VA for not taking care of our wounded soldiers or the widows and orphans of the thousands who had been killed over there. They were also angry and bitter about the whole Afghanistan war—thought it was a senseless slaughter. So they formed this so-called 'brotherhood' to funnel money to people they saw as victims of the war. Sandra had been told it was only ex-military involved. But once she got into it, she found out that they had people at all levels of the active military, the security contractors over there, and in the civilian government."

I thought about Jillian and what she'd said about the way the Brotherhood had helped her son Ben. It seemed to fit. "Okay, I guess I understand. But what exactly was Sandra afraid of? She must have known it was a dangerous assignment from the get-go."

Lebeaux lit his cigar. "Oh yes, of course she did," he said. "But the more she learned about the Brotherhood, the more she realized it had changed. The organizers had been replaced over the years—in some cases, they'd even been killed off—and the group that was running it were a murky bunch she couldn't pin down. When her intel reports started coming back on her, she started to suspect that somebody in the Army CID might be involved—even the possibility that her real assignment was not to shut down the Brotherhood but to spy on Jack for them. She saw how the organization handled people who had exhausted their usefulness. She didn't know who to trust, and she needed some legal advice, mainly about whether she'd have any legal protection if she had to blow the whistle on people in her own division. So Daryl brought her to me because I'm an ex-JAG officer."

This was the first I'd heard about the workings of the Brotherhood, and I sat there trying to patch together what Lebeaux was telling me with the sketchy information I'd gotten from Pearl and Jillian.

"So exactly what was Jack doing for the Brotherhood?" I asked.

"He was stashing the cash somewhere and washing it through a string of legitimate accounts that couldn't be traced. As for the payments to the beneficiaries, somebody else was doing that—I don't know who. Sandra thought Jack must have been operating this laundry business for several years—until a couple of months ago, that is."

"That's when the money stopped," I said.

"Right," said Lebeaux, looking at me strangely. "Joe, I see you know more about this than I gave you credit for."

"Pearl told me quite a bit about it," I said.

"I see," he said. "Well, I'm not absolutely sure why the money stopped, but here's my theory, based on what Sandra told me. You remember that police raid a couple of months ago, the one that was mentioned in court? I think the so-called search warrant was a ruse, carried out by some police officers who belonged to the Brotherhood."

"Why would they want to search Jack's place if he was such a vital part of their enterprise?" I asked.

"Ah! Now we get to the heart of the matter. It seems that Jack was squirreling away money—skimming off quite a lot of the cash he was handling and stashing it away. He was also making some big purchases, like the Tuxedo house, which he put in your daughter's name. He was acting crazy—using heavy drugs. Sandra reported all this to her CID team. Next thing you know, the Atlanta PD staged that police raid on Tuxedo Road. Sandra saw the connection immediately. They were looking for Jack's stash. They turned the place upside down but didn't find anything. According to Sandra, that vault must have been full of cash at that point, but these rogue cops missed it."

The picture was coming together. "So the Brotherhood decided to cut Jack off?"

"Right, but it's not quite that simple. The organization had split into factions. Jack's biggest ally was this character Pete Diamond, who was one of the original Brotherhood. He had a grudge against the army for a lot of reasons. We know what eventually happened to him, of course. But there were others in the Brotherhood who didn't trust Jack, and they were squabbling for control of the organization. Jack didn't know who to trust, and neither did Sandra. But by that time, she was right in the middle of it."

"So that's when she came to see you?"

"No, not yet. She was still trying to handle it on her own, but after that phony raid coming on the heels of her report about Jack's double-dealing, she started to suspect one of her supervisors, a guy named Hamilton Barnett, of being involved in the Brotherhood. The guy goes by the name Tex. He was with the CID office based right here in Atlanta. Sandra was incensed that she was being played that way. She felt betrayed, but that just motivated her all the more to follow through on her assignment and nail this guy Tex. Bad idea, as it turned out."

"She sounds like a pretty brave woman," I said.

"Yes, she was," said Daryl, nodding. "Sandra was fearless."

"Unfortunately, as they say, discretion is often the better part of valor," said Lebeaux. "Especially true in this case. To me it sounded like the whole Brotherhood operation had degenerated into every man for himself, and they threw out every pretense of military honor. It might have started out idealistic, but greed got the better of them."

"And you got all this from Sandra?"

Lebeaux shook his head. "Most of it, yeah. Some of it I'm just speculating about, based on what happened. But there's one more important wrinkle—something that might explain why it all ended the way it did. Sandra had a specific reason for being scared."

Daryl had been listening to all this without comment. But now he spoke up. "Mr. Lebeaux, we don't need to go into that, do we?"

"It's all right, Daryl. Joe here needs to know everything," said Lebeaux. "So here's what I think happened. Sandra came to me for the first time the day after the phony police raid. She told me she recognized one of the APD cops as a corporal from her unit in Afghanistan. She wasn't sure whether he'd recognized her, but it shook her up."

"Wow!" I said. "So her cover was blown. Except that she didn't know which faction this corporal was working for, so how could she defend herself? What did you advise her?"

"What do you think, man? I told her to get her ass out of there as quick as she could," said Lebeaux.

"But I gather she didn't do that," I said.

"No. Like Daryl said, she was fearless, and she wanted to catch this guy Tex, the traitor in the CID, as she called him. She wanted to set a trap for him. I told her she was being a damn fool. She said it would only take a few days, and then she'd get out. Unfortunately, a few days became a few weeks, and we know how it ended."

I looked over at Daryl. He was hanging his head.

"Daryl here took it upon himself to protect her," continued Lebeaux. "He took some time off work and basically tailed her. He did a pretty good job of keeping tabs on her, but unfortunately something went wrong on the night of the murders."

Daryl was shaking his head with a look of shame on his face. "She knew I was following her and seemed to put up with it—humoring her overprotective twin brother. But that night she jumped my case—told me she could take care of herself. She thought Pete would be there, and she trusted him because he had the hots for her. She said they were just going to grab some takeout and watch a movie. I argued with her, but she said I was too uptight, and I should go out and get laid. So…I did."

Lebeaux patted Daryl on the shoulder. "Daryl here blames himself. You can understand why, of course."

"But I'm not sure I understand your theory. If Sandra thought she was recognized, why didn't the CID take her off the assignment?"

"I wondered the same thing. They left her more or less on her own. But if there was a power struggle going on within the Brotherhood, Sandra would have posed a threat to at least some of its members."

"And apparently she trusted the wrong people."

"Maybe. Here's the bottom line, Joe: I think it may have been Sandra, rather than Jack, who was the target of the hit that night. Jack and your daughter might well have been collateral damage."

CHAPTER TWENTY-NINE

I sat there chewing over what Lebeaux was saying. His theory made a certain amount of sense, but I still had questions.

"Okay," I said. "But who is this guy Hugo? The one that Daryl brought around to see me yesterday."

Lebeaux looked blank. "Hugo? I don't know about any Hugo. Who is he talking about, Daryl?"

Daryl shrugged. "Just a cop I ran into," he said. "He helped me keep tabs on Sandra before she was murdered, and now he's very interested in trying to catch her killer. We both are. That's why he wanted to talk to Joe."

Lebeaux and I exchanged glances. "But that day when the two of you came to my house, he only seemed interested in Jack's money," I said.

"Yeah, I know. I noticed that, too. I couldn't figure it," said Daryl.

"What exactly did you tell him?" asked Lebeaux, looking concerned. "Did you give him any information about the Blue Buddha?"

"Maybe. Or he might have figured it out for himself. He's a pretty sharp guy," said Daryl.

"By any chance did you tell him Sandra was with CID?" asked Lebeaux through clenched teeth, clamped down on his cigar.

"I guess I did. I had to tell him why I was worried about her," said Daryl. "He was law enforcement, and I figured I could trust him."

"And just where did you meet this guy?" asked Lebeaux.

"He was at the jail one day, I'm not sure why. He just introduced himself, and we struck up a conversation."

"And then you told him your sister was undercover CID investigating a drug ring? Shit!" Lebeaux was beside himself.

"No, not exactly like that," said Daryl in a defensive tone. "The subject just came up gradually. We started hanging out together, and naturally he wondered where I was going at night."

Lebeaux pulled the cigar out of his mouth and smashed it into the ashtray on the table. "Oh, Jesus!" he said. "Between the two of you, we've got the complete cast of *Car 54 Where Are You?*!"

"What do you mean?" I asked. I was feeling defensive, too.

"What do I mean!" shouted Lebeaux. "Well, let me see…What I mean is that the two of you need to stop trying to investigate this murder case and mind your own business! You're both a couple of wannabe cops, and you don't have the slightest idea of the trouble you could get yourselves into!"

I was pissed. "Mr. Lebeaux, I think you're forgetting the fact that if I hadn't shown up at the Tuxedo house today, I never would have known about this search for Jack's stash. What if you had found it? For all I know, you'd be halfway to South America with the loot by now!"

Lebeaux seemed to calm down. "Okay, Joe, I already apologized for that, and I told you I understand why you'd be suspicious. All you have is my word for it that I would have given you a full report. I was trying to keep you out of it for your own protection, precisely because I knew you were involving yourself too much in this case."

"And why *shouldn't* I?" I said. "My only daughter was murdered, and everybody seems to have an angle on this Blue Buddha deal that apparently led to her death. The only thing these people have in common is that they don't want me to know about it."

"I think you're being a little paranoid, Joe," he said.

"Sometimes paranoia is the only sensible reaction," I said.

Daryl spoke up. "He's right, Mr. Lebeaux," he said. "I can understand why Joe wants to investigate things for himself. I…"

"Shut up, Daryl! You have no idea what you're talking about," said Lebeaux. "Now listen to me, you two. This case is dangerous. People are dying. You can't let yourselves get involved in it any more than you already have. I suggest that you both go home, get some rest, and let the professionals handle the details."

I thought suddenly about Jillian—how angry she had been when I left her earlier that day. She apparently thought I was overreacting, too. I felt guilty.

"Okay," I said. "I promise I won't take this any further. All I want from you is a promise that you'll keep me informed of what's going on. Keep me in the loop. It's not fair to leave me in the dark."

"Fair enough," said Lebeaux. "As for you, Daryl, I've let you take way too big a role in this. You wanted to help, and I agreed because it was convenient and because I felt sorry for you. Now you need to back off and stay out of this. I mean it."

Daryl was staring into his coffee cup. "Okay," he mumbled, but I could tell he wasn't buying Lebeaux's advice. I wasn't, either.

"All right, then," said Lebeaux. "Now before we end this, you both had better tell me whether there's anything else I need to know about. My ass is on the line here, and I don't want to be walking into any landmines."

I took a deep breath. "There's one other thing," I said, "but I don't think it's important—at least not to you."

"I'll be the judge of that," said Lebeaux.

"Okay, well, for the past few days I've been involved in a relationship," I said. "I guess you could call it a romantic relationship."

Lebeaux's eyebrows went up. "Oh? And who is the lucky lady?"

I knew he wasn't going to approve. I crossed my arms and braced myself.

"The lady is Jillian Farrell, Jack Sloan's sister," I said.

Lebeaux's mouth dropped open. He sat there for a moment or two without speaking. Then he squared his elbows on the table and leaned toward me.

"Joe Brock, you're possibly the dumbest individual I've ever encountered in my thirty-two years of practicing law," he said.

"Thanks a lot," I said. "I really appreciate knowing my lawyer has such a high opinion of me." I was about ready to get up and walk out of there.

"My opinion is irrelevant," said Lebeaux. "I just want you to think about a couple of things before you say any more. First, I want you to consider the fact that this Jillian is your legal adversary. One of you is going to win, and the other is going to lose. No middle ground—simple as that."

"You don't think I've considered that? Of course I realize that we're technically adversaries…"

Lebeaux ignored me. "And then there's the fact that her lawyer is Emma Faulkner. Do you have any idea of what a lowlife legal whore that woman is? I could tell you stories that would curl your hair. You've had your own experiences with her, I gather, so you must know what I'm talking about. The fact that she's on the case alone ought to send up red flags for any sensible person."

I shook my head, realizing that he had a point but certain that none of that mattered.

"That may be true," I said. "But it just so happens that Jillian is the only person in this whole crazy case that has been honest with me. The only person I trust!"

Lebeaux smiled and slumped back in the booth. "You're a damn fool, Joe Brock. A *dumb* fool," he said. "I know you're grieving for your daughter, and I know the facts of this case are terribly upsetting. I also know you're a widower, and you've lost your job. You're down to rock bottom, I guess, and you're desperate for something or someone to believe in."

"This is getting really offensive, Mr. Lebeaux. Whatever you're getting at, I wish you'd just spit it out. I can look out for myself, and I can take care of my own love life, thank you very much. So aside from your worries about my muddying up your case, what can possibly be the problem with my having a relationship with Jack Sloan's sister?"

"Just one problem, Joe," he said. "But it's a big one. My investigator reported back to me this morning from California. Based on what we can tell from the public records, Jack Sloan didn't *have* a sister."

CHAPTER THIRTY

My brain went numb. I stood up and glared at Lebeaux. "What the hell are you talking about?"

"Calm down, Joe," he said. "I know this must come as a shock, but you've got to listen to reason for a change. Jillian Farrell is a ringer. I don't know where Emma dug her up, but there's no birth record for a Jillian Sloan in California. I guess it's always possible there's some other explanation, but knowing Emma the way I do, I tend to believe the most obvious scenario."

"That's crazy," I said, talking mostly to myself. "I may not have known her for very long, but I couldn't be that wrong about her. She's told me details about herself—her relationship with Jack, her dead husband, her disabled son. It just *couldn't* be phony."

"Now you see what I've been warning you about," said Lebeaux. "You can't trust anyone in this case, least of all your admitted adversaries."

I stood there fighting a swarm of emotions that even now I can't express—hurt, fear, betrayal, humiliation, the whole gamut. All I could think to do was lash out.

"That does it," I said. "Mr. Lebeaux, you're fired. Please send me my file and my final bill."

"Come on, Joe," he said. "You're overreacting. Once you have time to think this through you'll realize that I'm only acting in your best interest."

"No," I said. "You're not acting in anyone's interest but your own. Sandra told you about Jack's money, and you saw a chance to make off with a fortune, and I'd never be the wiser. Now that I think about it, that's probably why you sent Daryl into that club to recruit me in the first place and why you kept insisting that I butt out and leave everything to you. Now you sit here insulting me and Daryl, like we're a couple of keystone cops, and causing me to question the integrity of a perfectly innocent woman. I don't know who else is after Jack's money, or who has it now, but I know I can't trust you anymore. You're off the case."

I had started out the door when I heard Daryl behind me. "Wait up, Joe!" he said. "I can't stand this guy any longer, either. I'm coming with you."

Together we got into my car and headed for the freeway. "Where are we going?" he asked after we'd driven a few blocks in silence.

I wasn't ready to answer that. I pulled over to the curb and turned off the ignition.

"Okay, Daryl, it's time you came clean with me. I'm not going anywhere with you until you tell me everything you know about my daughter's murder."

Daryl slumped in the seat, staring straight ahead out the windshield. "Yeah, I guess we do need to get on the same page," he said. "What do you want to know?"

"Everything. Starting with your relationship with this jerk Lebeaux."

"Relationship? There isn't any," he said. "Joe, I know I've made sort of a mess of it, but I've been doing the same thing as you—trying to find out what happened to my sister and your daughter. Lebeaux is nothing but a money-grubbing scumbag."

"If you felt that way about him, why were you helping him look for Jack's stash, tearing the Tuxedo house apart?"

Daryl shrugged. "I don't know. Just playing along, I guess— keeping him honest."

"Honest? That's a laugh!" I said.

He hesitated, looking sheepish. "Joe, I think you need to know some other things about Lebeaux. He met your daughter a few weeks before she died. We both did."

"What? You met Cynthia? How did *that* happen?" I shouted, suddenly furious.

"Calm down, Joe. I knew you'd take it that way. That's why I didn't tell you sooner."

I felt stunned—still reeling from the bomb Lebeaux had dropped about Jillian and now this.

"Tell me what happened—the whole story this time, or I swear I'll physically throw you out of this car."

"Okay, okay," he said. "I apologize for leaving you in the dark. It was Lebeaux's idea. He thought you were too emotionally in-volved to be…reliable. But of course you have a right to know everything."

"So shoot," I said, still seeing red.

"Well, the part about Sandra is all true. She was scared of her own superiors, and that's why she came to Lebeaux in the first place, a couple of months ago. But there's more. It seems that your daughter had gotten nervous, too. When the money stopped com-ing in, she figured the ride was about over, and she decided to jump ship."

"You mean she 'flipped'?"

"Something like that. Dawn confided in Sandra, and Sandra must have trusted her, because she told her about the CID operation. She introduced Dawn to me. One day, about three weeks before the murders, we all went to see Lebeaux. The idea was that he would help Dawn—Cynthia—turn herself in and offer to testify against the Brotherhood in return for immunity, or at least a light sentence. Lebeaux was going to negotiate all this for them."

"But what about Jack? Wasn't she in love with him?"

"Yes. That was her main concern. She wanted immunity for Jack, too, but Lebeaux said that would be impossible. So she did the next best thing—she married him."

I scratched my head. "Why? So she couldn't be compelled to testify against him?"

"Exactly. But in order to carry that off, she had to convince Jack to marry her. I think she basically threatened to leave him unless he made her an honest woman; said she'd been brought up a good girl and intended to die that way. She more or less brought the relationship to a head. For whatever reason, Jack went along with it. I doubt she told him her real reasons, but she might have."

"I can't imagine that the police would let Jack off the hook just because Cynthia couldn't testify against him. He was in the middle of it all!"

"Not really. Jack was just the money man, and after that police raid on his house, he was definitely on the outs with the Blue Buddha Brotherhood. CID was after the organizers in the military and the middlemen who were running the operation. Even after the FBI got involved, Jack might very well have gotten off light."

My brain felt like a pinball machine. "So somebody must have found out that Sandra and Cynthia were working against the Brotherhood."

"Yeah, Lebeaux thinks Sandra's cover was blown, and that's what led to the murders. I'm not so sure. There were other players."

"Like Pete Diamond?"

"Yes. I heard about Pete's involvement from Sandra. You remember that day at the courthouse when I was talking to him and his sister, Gigi?"

"The day Lebeaux brushed you off."

"Yeah. Lebeaux was trying to keep me out of the loop, sort of like he was doing with both of us today. He thinks he's some kind of mastermind and doesn't want anybody else meddling in his game. He has some serious control issues."

"He treated you—both of us—like a couple of bumbling morons," I said. "Like what he said about your friend Hugo, acting like Hugo might have tipped off the Brotherhood about Sandra. Trying to make you feel guilty."

"Right. That's typical. That's why I didn't let him in on everything."

"Such as?"

"Such as, the fact that I talked to Pete after the murders," said Daryl.

"You mean outside the courthouse?"

"Not just there. I had introduced myself to him a week earlier—told him I was Soraya's brother. That was her alias, remember? Soraya Romero. They all apparently had been calling her Sara. I managed to get some information out of him in a roundabout way."

"Do you think he had anything to do with the murders? Wasn't he supposed to be there at the Tuxedo house that night?"

"That's right, and I did suspect him at first. That's why I went after him. But he seemed to have a real crush on my sister. He was pretty shaken up about her death. And after talking to him, I got the impression that he was scared, too. Based on what happened to him and Pearl, he apparently had good reason to be."

"Did he say who he was scared of?"

"Not in so many words. He never really opened up about the Blue Buddha. Probably didn't think I knew any more than what a sister would tell a brother. But he did spill a few other interesting things."

"Like what?"

"Like Jack's relationship with Emma Faulkner."

CHAPTER THIRTY-ONE

"Now *that's* something I've been wondering about," I said. "Detective Drake told me that Jack and Emma had a sexual thing, but that doesn't seem to jibe with Jack marrying my daughter."

"It's hard to figure motives where sex is involved," said Daryl.

"You can say that again," I said, forcing myself not to think about Jillian.

"All I know is that there was bad blood between Emma and Dawn," he continued. "But Emma had more or less disappeared a few weeks before the murders."

"When the money dried up," I said.

"Yeah. I gather she was involved somehow with the laundering operation. According to Pete, she knew everything about Jack's business. He said she was very nervous before the court hearing—probably afraid something would come out that could incriminate her."

"Lebeaux did seem to be probing the witnesses along those lines," I agreed.

"She's another money-grubber. I figure that after the murders, she was scared shitless, but she couldn't resist dragging that old bag, Diana Diamond, into court to try to claim the estate. Emma couldn't stand the idea of all that money going down the drain. I'll bet she got even more nervous after Pearl and Pete Diamond landed in Long Island Sound."

"But she could still be after the money—the stash. From the way the Tuxedo house and my own place were torn up, it's pretty clear that somebody besides Lebeaux is looking for that money."

"She probably feels entitled to it. She and Jack went way back. Pete told me that Jack put Emma through law school—groomed her for his own personal lawyer, so to speak. I guess you could say she was his first 'creation.' Your daughter was his *second* masterpiece—a different kind, of course."

"The guy must have been a roaring asshole. A real megalomaniac," I said, shaking my head.

"Sounds that way, all right. Apparently Emma grew up dirt poor somewhere in Appalachia, but she was always smart. Somehow she found her way to Atlanta, and Jack hired her as one of his 'girls.' She turned out to have more brains than the others and ended up calling the shots for him legally, but somewhere under that business suit, you'll find a little Blue Buddha butterfly tattoo."

"That's disgusting. The whole thing is just creepy," I said. "Jack seems to have had a sadistic need to control women—abuse them."

"I agree," said Daryl. "But of course Emma got a lot out of that relationship—a law degree, respectability, and a nice living. I don't know how much she cared for Jack, but he apparently carried a torch for her through all those years. Jack spent a lot of time at her apartment, right up until the end."

"And where was Cynthia all this time?"

"That I don't know," said Daryl. "She didn't really open up about any of that when I was there in Lebeaux's office. All I know is that there was no love lost between the two women. Lebeaux might know more about it, but now that you've fired him, I guess we'll never hear about it."

I sighed, suddenly realizing that I had no lawyer, and a major lawsuit in probate court, with Emma Faulkner loaded for bear on the other side.

"Okay, I've heard enough," I said. "Let's go."

"Where?"

"How about the police station? I want to talk to your friend Hugo," I said, starting the engine.

"Okay, but I don't think he really knows anything," said Daryl, looking a little defensive.

"Daryl, you have to at least consider the possibility that Hugo is involved in this thing. You have to admit that it's a little fishy."

"Well, if he is, he sure has played it cool."

"What else would you expect?" I said, rolling my eyes.

"Maybe you're right," he said quietly. "I think it's time we confronted him."

We drove down I-75 in silence after that, and turned off at the downtown exit for APD headquarters. The front desk sergeant showed us back to detective Drake's office. I introduced Daryl and told Drake why we were there. We wanted to check on this officer named Hugo.

"You don't know his last name?"

"Sorry, no," I said. "Daryl doesn't remember hearing the last name."

Drake looked puzzled. "What's his involvement in this case?"

"We're not exactly sure. He went out of his way to make friends with Daryl here, and he seemed a little too interested in the details of the Tuxedo Road murders. Then he got Daryl to bring him over to my place so he could question me about…Jack Sloan's finances." I stopped myself. I trusted Drake, but something told me not to volunteer anything about Jack's alleged stash. I wasn't even sure how much he knew about the Blue Buddha, if anything.

"And what exactly do you suspect him of?" he asked.

All of a sudden I felt foolish. "That's just it. I don't know. I just want to verify that he's a police officer, and on the level."

"I see," said Drake, picking up the telephone on his desk. "Max? Have you got a minute? I've got a couple of witnesses here who need to speak to you."

A moment later, another plainclothes detective named Max Heller appeared at the door. He was short and stocky, with a thick blond mustache. Drake introduced us and said we were related to the victims in the Tuxedo Road case.

"Mr. Brock here wants to know whether we have an officer named Hugo on this case," he said.

"The only Hugo I know is Hugo Grassley over in the organized crime division," said Max.

"That might be him," said Daryl. "What does he look like?"

"Tall, thin, little black mustache?"

"Yeah, that sounds like the guy. Is he involved in this case in any way?" I said.

"Not that I know of," said Drake. "If the mob squad had an investigation going on, I'd probably know about it. Do you have any way to contact this Hugo?"

"No. Come to think of it, he always called me, rather than vice versa," said Daryl. "I haven't heard from him for a few days—not since we went down to Joe's house together."

"What's he got to do with the case?" asked Max, apparently interested.

"That's what we're trying to find out," I said. "We just want to verify that he's legitimate."

"I don't know what you mean by 'legitimate,' Mr. Brock. I've known Hugo Grassley for a couple of years, and as far as I know, he's a dedicated cop—former army sergeant. He worked his way up from patrolman in record time. Are you suggesting he might be dirty in some way?" Max looked a little offended.

"Not at all, no," I said. I could feel the color creeping up in my face. "He's probably just trying to help. But if you could put us in touch with him, we'd be grateful."

"You can call the organized crime division and leave a message," said Max. "Do you want me to get word to him to call you?"

"No…no thanks, that won't be necessary. I'll call his department. Thanks for your time," I said. Then I had a brainstorm. "Say, while we're here, is there any way I can track down a search warrant? I mean, a warrant that was issued for a particular house, or a particular person, on a particular date?"

"Sure, that should be public record. You can check the computers in the lobby out front."

We thanked the detectives, both of whom looked annoyed, and headed for the lobby. I remembered Drake saying that he hadn't been notified of any search warrant for the Tuxedo house within a few weeks of the murders, but it couldn't hurt to double-check it. Besides, just because Drake didn't find it didn't mean it didn't exist. And I was sure I could navigate the public records better than he could.

Daryl sat next to me, drumming his fingers on the counter, while I dived into the computer in the lobby. It only took me a second to get into the criminal records section. There, I saw that there were two different classifications of executed warrants—*executed* and *null*. I didn't find anything under "executed," so I looked under the "null" category, figuring this must be where they put warrants that got dismissed or tabled for some reason. The dead-letter file.

I was right. It didn't take long to find the warrant dated May 15, signed by one of the local magistrates. Here's what it said:

Affiant is informed and believes that said property is, has been, or is intended to be the site of unlawful transactions, to wit: the sale and/or distribution of cannabis and/or other substances prohibited by Georgia Law. On information and belief, said unlawful sub-stances and/or contraband may be found in or around the house and/or real property. Affiant's information is derived from confidential sources who have provided reliable information in the past, and are familiar with the property and its owner, Mr. Jack Sloan.

Attached to the warrant was a document labeled a "return," supposedly listing the results of the search. All it said was "Nothing found after diligent search." It was signed by two officers, D. R. Trimble and H. P. Grassley.

I nudged Daryl, who had fallen asleep against the counter next to me.

"Here's our man, Daryl. Hugo Grassley. I think it's time we had another conversation with our friend Hugo."

CHAPTER THIRTY-TWO

As we walked back to the car, I explained to Daryl what I had found.

"Where are we going now?" he asked.

"According to the computer, the organized crime division is in the East Annex of the APD," I said.

"Holy shit, Joe! We can't let this guy know we're onto him."

"Relax. We need information, but so does he. That's why he was grilling me about the money the other day. They didn't find anything in that search of Tuxedo, and he apparently thinks I'm the one who can help him find the stash. Besides, now the detectives on this case know that we inquired about him. We'll make sure he knows that. He won't harm us."

"I'm glad you're so optimistic. We don't know who this guy is connected with. He might even be the killer, for Christ's sake!"

"Yeah, I know," I said, surprised at my own little smile. "But we obviously know more about this case than the cops do, and now we're way ahead of Lebeaux, too. We both got into this to find out what happened to Cynthia and Sandra. We can't get cold feet now, Daryl. We have to see it through."

He was nodding, but half-heartedly. "If you say so," he said. "Just so you know, I have my weapon on me…in case we need it."

"I have mine, too," I said, smiling again. Then I thought about Jillian and felt the smile melt away as a knot of anger twisted my gut. I reached for my phone.

"Show me how to send a text message on this thing, Daryl."

He showed me. "Who are you going to text?"

"This fraudulent female named Jillian," I said.

"Are you sure you want to do that?"

"Yeah, I'm sure." I punched in the message: *On to your game. Not half as stupid as I look.*

Daryl was shaking his head as I started the engine. After a few seconds my phone rang. It was Jillian. I let it go to voice mail.

"Aren't you going to answer that?" asked Daryl.

I shook my head. "No. It's somebody trying to sell me something," I said.

We checked in at the East Annex and found that Hugo wasn't there—his day off, they said. I was disappointed, but Daryl seemed relieved.

"That old boy is pretty popular around here today," said the officer at the front desk. "This is the third time I've had to tell somebody he ain't here."

"Really? Who else was asking?" I said, getting a funny feeling.

"Some sleazy guy in a suit come in just a few minutes ago, and this morning it was a hot brunette carrying a briefcase. She blew in here like she owned the place."

"They didn't leave their names?"

"No. I didn't ask."

"Lebeaux and Emma," I said to Daryl as we walked out of the building. "Check your phone. If Hugo called you, his number should show up there."

"We need to think this thing through, Joe. I'm not…"

"Check your phone," I said again.

Daryl pulled out his iPhone and went through the listing of recent calls. Pretty soon he found a number that looked like it might be Hugo.

"Call him," I said. "Tell him we need to meet with him—today."

"Joe, that's a rotten idea," he said. "If Lebeaux and Emma are both looking for him, you know something is wrong. I've never mentioned him to Lebeaux before today."

"Something is rotten, all right, and I intend to find out what it is. You don't have to come if you're scared, Daryl."

"I'm not scared," he said, but I could tell he was.

I stopped next to the car. "Okay, just spit it out, Daryl. What are you holding back?"

He hesitated, focusing on the pavement. "Lebeaux lied about how Sandra met him," he said. "She met him before I did. He never represented me in a traffic case. He told me to go along with that story. I'm not sure how they got hooked up, but he already knew all about the Blue Buddha Brotherhood when your daughter and I first went to see him with Sandra. To be honest, I felt like he knew more than Sandra did."

I stopped in my tracks. "So you think Lebeaux is mixed up in this thing somehow? You think he's part of the Brotherhood?"

"Could be. I played along with him today, but I've suspected for a long time that he knows more than he lets on."

"But why would he be looking for Hugo?"

"I don't know, but one thing he said today is definitely true. There are a lot of rival factions in that organization now. We know Lebeaux and Emma are enemies, but we have no way of knowing whether Hugo is allied with Lebeaux, or with Emma, or with somebody else altogether. It's a mistake to get mixed up with them until we know what we're dealing with."

"It's time we found out," I said. "Call him."

Shaking his head, Daryl pressed the call button.

"Put it on speaker," I said.

Hugo's number rang twice before he picked up. "Yeah?"

"Hugo, this is Daryl Spinks."

"No shit. I can see your fuckin' caller ID," said Hugo. "What do you want?"

"We...I need to see you. Today if possible."

"What about?"

"Blue Buddha...the money," said Daryl.

There was a pause on the other end. "What about it?"

"I might know where it is."

"Oh? I don't know what you're talking about, man."

"Yes, you do. You were asking Joe Brock about it. I've been talking to him."

Another pause. "Are you alone?"

"No. Joe is with me."

"Where are you now?"

"Your office on Ponce," said Daryl.

"Okay, come over now. I'm in Decatur. Forty-two-oh-six Avery Street."

The call disconnected, and I started the engine.

Daryl looked at me. "Are you sure you want to do this?"

"Sure as shit," I said. "I think it's entirely possible that Hugo Grassley either killed Cynthia or knows who did."

"And if he did? What are you going to do about it?"

"We'll cross that bridge when we come to it. First I want to find out what this guy knows."

"It might be smarter to call Detective Drake," said Daryl.

"No way. I don't trust anybody in that department any more. As far as I'm concerned, they're all crooks. Looks to me like you and I are the only people interested in justice for Cynthia and Sandra."

Daryl nodded, but he still wasn't happy. Just then my cell phone chirped that I had a message. I tapped the text icon. The message was from Jillian: *What on earth are you talking about? Need to see you ASAP.*

I felt the anger flood back into my midsection. This was no time to be dealing with Jillian's pathetic denials. She was a phony, like everyone else in this wretched drama. It made perfect sense. One of the bad guys must have sent her to seduce me into giving up information about Jack's money. I turned the phone off.

By now it was rush hour, and we hit bumper-to-bumper traffic on Ponce de Leon Avenue heading out of the city. We sat at the light at the intersection of Highland for what seemed like an eternity. I got tired of riding the brake and put the car in park while we waited.

"There must be an accident up ahead," said Daryl.

I didn't have time to respond, since right then my car door flew open, and I was being dragged out and pulled to the pavement by a couple of big uniformed cops. I busted my chin against the concrete as they slapped a pair of handcuffs on my wrists, frisked me, and took my gun and phone.

"What the…"

"Shut up," said one of the cops.

"This is crazy! I haven't done anything…"

"I said shut up!" He was digging his knee into the small of my back. I figured I'd better follow orders. Meanwhile, Daryl got out and came around to my side of the car.

"Hey, man, this is a huge mistake. What's he charged with?" said Daryl.

"None of your business. Get back in the car," said the cop.

Daryl backed up. "What am I supposed to do with it?"

"Get it out of here. Clear it out."

I saw Daryl climb into the driver's seat and put the car in gear. Traffic had moved on ahead of us. I watched my car creeping forward. That was the last thing I saw before somebody pulled a bag over my head.

CHAPTER THIRTY-THREE

The siren came on, and the police cruiser made a quick U-turn and then sped up. After a few minutes we stopped, and the cop sitting next to me dragged me out and pushed me into the back of another vehicle. It smelled like cigarettes. I was in the back-seat by myself and realized that the two guys up front were not the two cops who had kidnapped me.

"Get *this*," said one of them. "Thompson said this dork was packing heat."

"No shit. I wonder if he knows which end the bullet comes out of."

They both laughed. After we were back on the road, the engine noise kept me from hearing everything they were saying, but I could tell they were still making fun of me. I should have thought of something clever to say, or at least cussed them out, but instead I sat there, frozen, not daring even to ask where we were going. I kept thinking about Pearl and Pete Diamond, figuring this was probably the end of me. But if they meant to kill me, why had they thrown that bag over my head?

It seemed like we rode for a long time—maybe an hour. Toward the end, I could tell we were off the highway, traveling over a bumpy dirt road, or maybe gravel. Finally the car stopped, and the two guys dragged me out. They led me along a dirt path of some kind, up some steps, and through a couple of doorways. One of them lowered me down onto a tile floor. It was quiet for several minutes; then I heard a door open, and someone walked into the room.

"I hope we haven't inconvenienced you, Mr. Brock," said a deep male voice with a heavy western drawl.

"Who are you? Where am I?" I demanded.

"You're in military custody," said the voice.

"What? I don't believe you," I said.

"Believe it, Mr. Brock. You're here to provide me with some vital military intelligence."

"What intelligence? What are you talking about?"

"Forget the details," he said, laughing. "Actually, you're right. This is more of an *unofficial* inquiry."

"How did you find me? How did you know where my car was?"

"Didn't I just tell you you're dealing with agents of the US government? You're evidently the last person in the country not to realize that if you're talking on a cell phone, you're being... monitored."

"I wasn't talking on a cell phone."

"No, but your little friends were. They're apparently as clueless as you are."

"You're making a mistake," I said. "I don't know anything."

"On the contrary, Mr. Brock. Your government has been watching you very closely. You've turned out to be quite an inquisitive fellow. I think you know quite a lot—much more than is healthy for you."

My wrists had been handcuffed this whole time, and they hurt.

"I need to go to the bathroom. Please take these cuffs off of me," I said.

"You can take a piss when you've answered my questions, and not before."

"Then take this ridiculous bag off my head and speak to me man-to-man."

"I don't think you want me to do that," he said. "If I did, you would be able to identify me. That wouldn't be healthy for either of us. Think of that bag as your friend."

"If this is about the Blue Buddha, I told you I don't know anything…"

"You may not *think* you know anything, but I'm pretty sure you do. My job is to help jog your memory."

"About what?"

"Well, let's start with the basics," he said. "When was the last time you saw your daughter before she met with her unfortunate demise?"

"I hadn't seen my daughter for two years. We weren't speaking to each other."

He sighed. "Mr. Brock, I have it on good authority that your daughter gave you some very important information shortly before she died."

My palms were sweating. "Pearl must have told you that, but Pearl was wrong," I said.

He chuckled. "There—you see? You do know quite a lot, don't you? Pearl Magenta required some…serious persuasion, but eventually she did provide valuable information. Any rational person in her position would have told me everything, so I reluctantly had to conclude that she didn't know any more. The part she didn't know is what I need from you."

"Are you planning on torturing me like you tortured her?"

"Please, Mr. Brock, give me a little credit. I have every intention of letting you go, as soon as you give me what I want. Unless, of course, I think you're lying to me. Then I might lose my temper and do something…extreme. So let's stop playing games. Where are those account numbers?"

"I told you, I don't know. Pearl told me they were hidden somewhere in my house. Somebody ransacked my house right after I found out about Cynthia's death. They probably got whatever you're looking for."

"No," said the voice, "that's where you're wrong. I've already questioned the people who tore your house up. They say they didn't find anything. That leaves you. Whether you know it or not, you must have those numbers."

I shook my head, exasperated.

"Now listen, Joe," he said after a moment. "I know you're an honest guy. You don't have any use for those numbers. You don't know the background—or where those accounts are located. You're not the sort of fellow who would make use of them, even if you did. You'd probably just let that pile of cash sit there unclaimed. That's why I was hoping we could have a rational exchange here. You give me the information, I have my boys drive you back home, and we pretend that none of this ever happened."

"And you clean out those accounts, assuming you can get there first, right? How many other people are after that money?"

He chuckled again. "Too many. That's the whole problem, isn't it? Too many cooks in the kitchen."

"Right. And you can't very well kill all of them off, can you?"

"I recommend that you squelch the sarcasm, Joe. It's out of character."

I felt the blood boiling up in my chest, but somehow my voice remained calm. "Did you kill my daughter?"

There was a pause. "No. I don't know who killed her."

"Am I supposed to believe that? You have to admit, it makes sense."

"That shows how little you do know, Joe. It would have made absolutely no sense at all. The fact that she was murdered is what put us in this awkward position. Some very stupid person made the mistake of killing her and Jack before they figured out where that stash was hidden. That was not professional. It wasn't me."

"Who then?"

"I have my theories, but that's not really important now. Let's get back to the point. I want you to think about the night your house was searched. Had you removed anything from the house before that happened?"

"Like what?" I asked.

"Like anything. Books, papers, documents of any kind?"

"No. I wasn't expecting to be raided. Why would I remove anything from my house?"

"Where did you go that night?"

I had to think about that for a minute. "Nowhere. I just drove around. My daughter was dead, and I was depressed. I'd been drinking. I drove around Jonesboro for a while and ended up at my office."

"Did you go back to the house at all that night?"

"No. I stayed in my office until morning. That was the first time I figured out that the Tuxedo house belonged to my daughter. It was in her name—I mean, the name of Dawn Marie Sterling. I looked it all up on my computer."

"Was that computer a laptop that you'd brought with you from home?"

"No. Nice try. It was on the county computer—the government records software. That computer is not portable. It's wired into the government systems. It's never been anywhere near my house."

The room was quiet for several seconds.

"Joe, I'll be honest," he finally said. "I don't know what to do with you. Either you're lying—and I don't know why you would do that under the circumstances—or there's something we're both missing."

"I don't know any more than I've told you. Honestly, I don't know what else to say."

"All right then, I believe you. I'm going to give you a little break, Joe, while I do some thinking."

Somebody grabbed both of my shoulders and lifted me off the floor. They dragged me through another doorway, told me to sit on the floor, and then closed the door. The room felt small and smelled of bleach—a laundry room? I heard the click of a dead bolt and sat there for a minute or two before I became conscious of another person in there with me.

"Hello, Joe," said a familiar female voice. "Fancy meeting you here."

CHAPTER THIRTY-FOUR

"Who's that?" I said. "Who are you?"

"I'm sure you'll remember me," she said, as she removed the black bag from my head. It was Diana Diamond. I remembered her whiskey voice from the court hearing. Her skinny wrists were bound with plastic cuffs in front of her body. She was wearing tight designer jeans studded with rhinestones and a purple tank top. Her leathery face looked haggard and tired, and her eye makeup was smeared, but it was definitely her.

It took my eyes a second to adjust to the light in the room. "Where are we?"

"I'm not sure exactly. Somewhere in north Georgia," she said, sitting down on a laundry hamper in the corner of the room.

"What are *you* doing here?" I asked.

"Good question. Probably the same thing you're doing—getting my ass grilled by Tex Barnett. He's not in a good mood. Maybe you noticed."

"Tex? Where have I heard that name before?"

"Maybe from your daughter? She had some dealings with old Tex."

"No. Not from my daughter," I said, remembering it was Lebeaux who had mentioned the name Tex. He was Sandra Spinks's colleague at Army CID—the one she suspected of being involved with the Brotherhood. Evidently her suspicions were right.

"What is he trying to get from you?" she asked.

"Information…about money."

"Well, that goes without saying. What sort of information?" Her small eyes narrowed.

I didn't know how much Diana knew, but I was pretty sure I couldn't trust her. I shrugged.

"Come on, Joe. We both know that Dawn supposedly hid something at your house. Tex has had me here since this morning, and I think he's finally satisfied that I don't know anything about this mysterious information."

"Are you the one who ransacked my house?"

She smiled. "Not me. But I do know who did it."

"Our friend Emma Faulkner?" It seemed like a no-brainer. Everybody else had been eliminated.

"Pretty shrewd, Joe. I'm surprised."

"Did she find what she was looking for?"

"No. And she definitely would have told me. Evidently Tex realized that. That's why he's picking on me."

"Why didn't he come after Emma herself?"

"She has bodyguards, and she's too high-profile. Nobody is going to miss a couple of losers like me and you, especially since you're no longer a tax assessor. We're expendable, Joe." In some perverted way, Diana seemed to be enjoying this conversation. She seemed to assume that I knew more than I did about the Blue Buddha. I decided to see how far she would go with it.

"So…were you really married to Jack Sloan?"

She laughed. "Well, that *is* a bit of stretch, I'll admit. We were fuck buddies for years, and we even lived together for a while out in California before he moved back here and made his mark. The common-law marriage deal was Emma's brainstorm. That girl is a plain genius."

"Was she in love with Jack?"

"L-O-L! Does a cat have a tail? Of course she was in love with him. Every woman who ever met him was in love with him. He was the perfect *bad boy*—every woman's romantic fantasy, hand-some as a Greek god, and hung like a horse. He could keep go-ing all night—smooth and sentimental, but with just enough of a cruel streak to make him irresistible. And he even played the fucking piano and sang, for God's sake. No offense, but he was wasted on your daughter. Nobody could figure out what he saw in her."

"Especially Emma?"

Diana smiled slyly. "How true. She couldn't believe Jack would throw himself away on a girl like Dawn. He gave her everything—a new body, a new face, a new name, even a new fairy castle to live in. That's what she called that house, you know—her fairy castle. And she was his fairy princess. As far as I could tell, she didn't give him anything in return but a lot of kinky sex, which he could have gotten from any number of women."

"Maybe he liked her innocence," I said, feeling unexpected tears welling up in defense of my Cynthia.

"You know, you just might have a point there," said Diana. "He didn't know too many *innocent* women. Certainly not Emma. But if her innocence was what attracted him, he sure did everything he could to defile it. And of course, in the end, even Dawn wasn't enough to keep him off the needle."

"He was an addict?"

"All his life. It started out in California, even before I met him, but he was clean for years after he came back here to Georgia.

Then he met Dawn, and things started getting heavy with the Blue Buddha crowd. It was a much bigger deal than he'd ever been involved in. I guess he couldn't handle the pressure."

"I heard that Jack and Emma were still seeing each other right up until the end."

"Yeah, Emma couldn't leave him alone. I know they were fighting a lot, mostly over his habit…and your daughter, of course. Emma is smart, but she has a temper. She can't control it sometimes. It's always gotten her into trouble. Of course, never as bad as what happened that night…"

Diana's voice trailed off. She must have realized from the look on my face that she had said too much.

"What do you mean? What kind of trouble?"

"Nothing. Forget it."

"Tell me, dammit!"

Diana tilted her head and looked at me, as if deciding whether I could handle whatever she had to say.

"Joe, I guess you realize that neither of us is going to get out of this place alive," she said.

I blinked. "No, that's not true. Tex told me he'd let me go if I told him what I know. Anyway, he can't very well kill off everybody connected with this murder…can he?"

"Think, Joe. You're smart enough to figure it out. They put that bag over your head so you'd be encouraged to talk. So you'd think there was a chance they'd let you go. But there are millions of dollars at stake here. Tex has to account for that money. Look how he got the other half of the information he needs, for God's sake! Poor Pearl Magenta certainly paid the price for befriending your precious daughter."

She was crying. A drop of black eye makeup rolled down her wrinkled cheek.

"My son Pete was punished, too," she said, stifling a sob. "The Brotherhood thought he'd stupidly killed Jack and left them scrambling for their money. But they were wrong. My son worshiped Jack. He didn't kill him."

"You sound like you know who did," I said. My hands were sweating again, and my heart had begun to race.

She raised her cuffed hands to her face and wiped away the tear. "Yes, I know," she said. "But the Brotherhood doesn't know, and I'm not about to tell them. You may think I'm a lowlife, but I do have some loyalty. I'm not a rat."

Just then the door opened, and two men walked in. One of them was a tall, middle-aged guy with wavy blond hair and a square jaw like a movie star. He was wearing jeans and cowboy boots. The other guy was a young black man. He was carrying an ironing board, which he placed across the washer and dryer. The end projected over the laundry sink next to the machines.

"Tex! I didn't say anything! I swear!" said Diana.

"Shut up, Diana. You talk too much," said the tall guy. "Well, Joe, I see that Diana has ruined our little privacy agreement by removing your blindfold. That's going to limit my options, I'm afraid. But as long as you've recovered your vision, I have a little show for you."

While Diana and I sat frozen in terror, the two men filled up the laundry tub. Then they picked up all screaming ninety-eight pounds of Diana Diamond and strapped her onto the ironing board. Tex soaked a bath towel in the tub and laid it across her face. Her screams became muffled groans as they tipped the board back into the tub and started the faucet dripping onto the towel. She writhed and groaned for a few seconds—no more than ten—and then they tipped the board flat again and removed the towel from her face.

She sputtered and gasped for breath.

"Now tell me, Diana," said Tex in an exaggerated menacing tone. He seemed to be enjoying this. "Tell me who killed our tomcat friend Jack Sloan and his two little pussies."

Diana coughed several times. "Stop! I told you I don't know!"

"I'm disappointed, ma'am," said Tex. "Somebody killed my buddy, and you and I both know that *nobody* would have done that unless they knew where he kept his...property...now would they? We also know there are several candidates, and you bragged to your friend Pearl that you knew who did it."

"Go to hell!" was her response.

I couldn't contain myself. "Tell them! If you know, you've got to tell them or they'll kill you! You'll drown!"

"See there? Your pal Joe has a lot more sense than you have," said Tex, smiling.

"Eat shit!" said Diana.

Tex made a little tsk-tsk sound with his tongue and then motioned for the other guy to tip the board back again. This time they held her under a few seconds longer, and she came up with water spilling from her nose and mouth. "Okay...stop...I can't take any more!" she sputtered.

"That's more like it," said Tex. He sat her up on the ironing board and patted her back for a couple of minutes while she recovered her breath; then he laid her back down.

Then he spoke softly. "Now for the last time, Diana, tell me who killed our three friends."

Diana looked at me and shook her head, speaking barely above a whisper. "It was not like you think, Tex. Nobody knows where that money is. The money is just...lost. The murders weren't planned. It was all craziness. The person who killed Jack and Dawn wasn't thinking straight. It was all Jack's fault. He did a cruel thing. He announced that he and Dawn were married. He knew how jealous she was. He should have known how she would react..."

"Hold on. Are you saying what I think you're saying?"

"Yes!" screamed Diana. "It was Emma! Emma killed them all!"

CHAPTER THIRTY-FIVE

The room was suddenly quiet except for the muffled sobs of Diana Diamond. She was still lying faceup on the ironing board, her tangled mess of blue-black hair dripping into the sink.

I struggled to stand up, but Bishop, the young black guy, pushed me back to the floor. "Sit down and shut up," he said.

Tex leaned against the countertop. "Unbelievable," he said, shaking his head. "Let me get this straight. You say Emma plugged Jack and his two gal pals just because she was *jealous*?"

Diana was staring up at the ceiling, evidently considering the likely consequences of having given up this information. "Yes," she said. "It was completely irrational. She lost it. She regretted it immediately, but it was too late."

"How did she get the drop on them? It sounds pretty improbable."

"Jack was out of it—dangerously high. He'd been that way for weeks. If he'd been straight, he'd have known better than to break the news to her that way. He was kneeling on the floor in front of the two girls, and his holster was right there on his hip. Emma was standing behind him. When she realized that he was serious about the marriage, she freaked out—grabbed the gun and shot him in the head and then finished the two girls. Jack never knew what hit him. The other two must have seen it coming, but they couldn't react fast enough. It was all over in a couple of seconds."

Tex looked skeptical. "I didn't know Emma was such a sharpshooter."

"Emma is good at everything. She and Jack used to practice at the range together. She was a better shot then he was."

"And how did you find out about all this?"

"She told me. She ran out of the house without even resetting the security system and called me from her car. She was shaken up and scared."

Tex was still sarcastic. "I don't get it. This woman is supposed to be the queen of cool. How could she off Jack and Dawn like that without knowing where to find the money?"

"I admit, it isn't like her," said Diana. "But like I told you before, she's as clueless about the money as any of us. She doesn't know where those accounts are or whose name they're in."

I couldn't contain myself. "So Emma is the one who searched my house?"

Diana looked over at me. "Yeah, that was Emma's people. Dawn was joking that Jack had to marry her because she knew where the money was hidden. Very funny, right? That made Emma furious, of course, but she never thought Jack would actually do it. Then that night, Dawn and Jack invited Emma and that new girl, Sara, over to celebrate. They had tickets to fly out of the country the next day, to someplace in South America—Argentina, I think. Anyway, Dawn mentioned that they needed to stop off at her dad's house to pick up the certificate or some such thing. At least that's what Emma remembered. She thought that must mean Dawn was hiding bank documents at your place, Joe. Emma and her buddies watched your house until they knew you were gone, and then they went through it. But they didn't find anything. She would have told me."

"We've already been over that ground, Diana," said Tex. "I'm satisfied that Emma doesn't know where the money is. She wouldn't be hanging around Atlanta if she'd located the stash."

He pulled her down from the ironing board. "You've done well, Diana—solved some mysteries for us. Now it's up to old Joe here to fill in the details."

Tex and Bishop each grabbed one of Diana's elbows and maneuvered her out the door. She had the look of a frightened animal. I was left there on the floor, waiting for my turn at the water board. Torturing Diana in front of me had had the desired effect. I looked down and saw that I had pissed myself. I was weak with terror, wondering how long I could withstand that treatment.

As I sat there, I kept picturing what must have happened the night Cynthia was killed, and it made my blood boil. I remembered how Emma Faulkner deceived me the first time I met her—how cool and professional she had seemed when she took me to identify my daughter's body at the morgue, all while concealing the fact that she was the one who put her there. Then she turned around and tried to defraud me out of my inheritance. It was hard to imagine the sort of evil that could motivate a person like that.

As usual, anger gave me energy. I managed to stand up and noticed that on the back of the door was a cheap, full-length mirror. Stumbling over to it, I turned around and studied my cuffed wrists, wondering how those blasted painful things actually worked. It looked as though the lock was a kind of ratchet apparatus, with a saw tooth strip that slid against a metal plate. If I could just find something to use as a shim, I could depress the ratchet and pull the lock apart, sort of like what Daryl did with my credit card at the Tuxedo house that first night. The problem was finding something small and flat enough to do the job.

The little room was lined with cabinets, all of which were closed. No way to open them with my hands cuffed behind me. I searched around on the floor, along the cluttered countertop, even between the washer and dryer, looking for anything that I could use as a shim. I was about to give up and sit back down when I glanced over into the laundry tub. Down at the bottom, suspended in a shallow puddle of water, was a black metal barrette, which must have gotten knocked out of Diana's hair when they doused her head in that sink. I raised myself on my tiptoes and groped behind my back as far down into the laundry tub as I could. I could feel the thing, but couldn't quite get it between my fingers. It took me at least a dozen tries to finally snag the thing between my index and middle fingers and shimmy it up the side of the tub.

I went back to the mirror and examined my find. The barrette had two sections that snapped together, connected by a hinge. The top section was a useless ornament, but the bottom piece was a thin, flat, narrow strip of metal that looked just about right. I strained to make my arthritic fingers work together enough to separate the two pieces, and then I went to work. The trick was to insert that little strip into the opening where the ratchet and the slide bar closed together. My old eyes were seeing double as I aimed and poked that metal strip, praying all the while that I wouldn't drop the damn thing. Outside the door it was eerily quiet. I kept imagining what must be going on out there. Were they still interrogating Diana? How much time did I have left before they came back for me? Finally I felt the shim slide into the opening. I pressed against it as hard as I could, squeezing the cuff between my wrist and the mirror and tugging gently at the lock. Then, miraculously, I pulled my hands apart, and they were free. The miserable device dangled impotently from my left wrist. I used the same technique to quickly slide it off.

I looked around again. The only window in the room was above my head—a small, narrow foundation window, just barely big enough for a guy my size to wiggle through. I couldn't tell whether it was locked or sealed, but I had to try. I pulled the ironing board down, opened it as high as it would go, and then positioned it against the wall. It was too high to get up there without a step, so I turned over a bucket and climbed up. The board was cheap and rickety, and I knew that if it fell, the noise would bring the two guys back in. For the same reason, it would be pointless to break the window. My only hope was to get the thing open.

As I stood on the wobbly ironing board, my head was just about touching the ceiling, and the window was at shoulder level. Once again I lucked out. The window was hinged at the top, and there was a small thumb lock along the bottom frame. It was stuck with paint and grime, but I twisted it as hard as I could and managed to get it open. Then I swung the window up and hoisted myself up through the opening. Only when I was clear did I realize that I had never been able to press my own weight like that before.

I stood up and looked around. It was getting dark, but I could see that the cabin was on the shore of a large lake, which could have been any of a number of lakes in north Georgia. In truth, I had no idea where I was, but I knew I had to get the hell out of there. I started around the cabin as quietly as I could, but as I reached the driveway I heard noises inside—Diana's voice, screaming something I couldn't understand, louder and louder. Then there were male voices on top of it, lots of screaming and yelling. Finally there were two loud pops, and everything was quiet again.

CHAPTER THIRTY-SIX

I realized that it wouldn't be safe to run down the driveway, as my captors would expect me to take the road. The shoreline looked just about as obvious, so I decided to head into the woods. I hightailed it into the nearest clump of trees. A few hundred feet into the thicket, I stopped short. Ahead of me was a black BMW. It was parked, but I could hear the engine block still ticking, so I knew its driver must be somewhere nearby. I had crouched behind a large oak tree, wondering which direction to run, when I heard someone whispering my name. Looking around, I saw Daryl and his friend Hugo huddled behind a pile of firewood in the clearing near the cabin. Both of them had their guns drawn. They gestured for me to join them.

Reluctantly, I crept across the space between us and knelt next to Daryl.

"How did you find me?"

"Hugo figured out who must have kidnapped you. He's been here before," said Daryl in a whisper.

Hugo nodded.

"Let's get out of here," I said.

"I think we should try to take those guys out," said Hugo.

I was horrified. "No, we can't do that ourselves. We need to call the police. I think they just shot Diana Diamond."

Daryl and Hugo looked at each other. "What's *she* doing here?" asked Daryl.

"They thought she knew where the money was. They tortured her," I said.

"We heard the gunfire," said Daryl. "We thought you were finished."

"How many are there?" asked Hugo.

"I'm not sure. I only saw two, but there could be more. They're all armed, and they have my gun."

Hugo wasn't happy, but he gestured with his gun toward the BMW. "Okay, let's roll."

It was good and dark by now. We ducked across the clearing and into the BMW. I climbed into the backseat. Hugo gunned the engine with the lights off and hit the gravel driveway at about forty, sending up a cloud of dust. Just as we got clear of the driveway and hit the paved county road, we heard loud voices and car doors slamming, and then a car engine cranked up behind us. I turned around and watched through the back window as Tex and two other guys in a grayish Ford Taurus turned out of the driveway and started gaining on us. Hugo hit the accelerator, and the BMW careened out. We kept up that pace until we hit slower traffic at the bottom of a hill; then Hugo veered around three cars at once without losing speed. The Taurus did the same. We hardly cut speed at all as we wound down a switchback section of road and around some baby lakes. The other guys were following at maybe a hundred yards and gaining on us when we finally hit a straightaway and another line of traffic. It was pitch dark out there, and you could hardly tell one set of headlights from another, except for the speed. We passed a couple of cars as we went around a sharp curve, and then we peeled out, leaving the Taurus several hundred yards behind, so they couldn't see us.

"Hold on," said Hugo, slamming on the brakes and skidding sideways into the parking lot of an abandoned roadside steakhouse. He waited a second for the Taurus to pass, then he hit the gas again and sped out of the parking lot, going the opposite direction. I couldn't see the Ford behind us.

Daryl had turned on his GPS. "Hang your first left up ahead," he said to Hugo. "Highway three-oh-six runs into four hundred."

"Where are we?" I asked, still watching the rear window.

"Middle of nowhere," said Hugo. "Top of Lake Lanier... Buckhorn Mountain."

Hugo made the turn a mile or two later, and we hit a smooth, elevated highway. The Ford still wasn't behind us.

"We must have lost them," said Hugo, "but they'll figure out what we did quick enough. Let's pull off into the woods and give them time to pass us."

We sat behind a stand of pine trees, watching the headlights pass us by for a few minutes. Sure enough, here came the Ford at about eighty miles an hour and flew right by us. Hugo pulled back onto the road, reversing direction again.

"Where did you learn to drive like that?" I asked, finally allowing myself to breathe.

Hugo didn't answer me. He punched the accelerator again, and we flew off down the highway toward I-85. I sat there in the backseat, thinking how I didn't know anything about either of the guys in the front seat, but figuring they came to my rescue, so they must be okay. When we passed the Gainesville exit, I started to relax a little.

"Where are we going?" I asked.

"I haven't decided yet," said Hugo.

"Shouldn't we go file a police report?"

Hugo laughed. "I don't think that would be wise."

"I need my car," I said.

"Don't worry, Joe," said Daryl. "You'll get your car. We have to make sure we aren't being followed."

"So who are those guys?" I wasn't sure I really wanted the answer to that question.

"Sewer rats," said Hugo. "Filthy traitors is who they are."

"I don't get it," I said. "Aren't they the Blue Buddha Brotherhood?"

"Them? No way," he said and laughed bitterly. "They're thieving sons of bitches, stealing bread out of the mouths of war heroes, widows and orphans."

"But they knew all about Jack's money…"

"Yeah, that's *all* they care about," said Hugo. I realized that he had turned off the freeway and stopped the car behind a Shell station at the bottom of the ramp. He turned off the engine and turned around to face me. Daryl looked as surprised as I was.

"Listen, Joe, we need to have an understanding," said Hugo. "You're involved in this thing, whether you like it or not, so it's only fair that you know what you're dealing with. The Blue Buddha is dead. It's been out of commission for nearly a year."

I didn't follow what he was saying. "You mean you aren't involved in it?"

"Not anymore. The merchandise and the money are still rolling in, but now that Pete Diamond is gone, the Brotherhood is finished. He and I started it when he first got back from Afghanistan back in 2009. It was a thing of beauty back then. Pete had the sources covered, and I took care of protection. We did a lot of good for some very deserving soldiers and their families. I'm not sure you know just how rotten the US government really is—or how incompetent the VA system has become. The Buddha was a lifeline for hundreds of families."

My heart jumped. "Did you know any of them personally? Did you know a woman named Jillian Farrell?"

"Yeah, she was Jack Sloan's sister, wasn't she?"

"I'm not sure," I said, a pang of guilt creeping up my spine. "I've heard different stories…"

"In fact," continued Hugo, "Jillian was the reason Pete was able to talk Jack into holding cash for us in the first place. He was nervous about it at first—liked his quiet local gig, with the club and all the women and everything. Then Pete told Jack how much hell his own sister and nephew were going through, and that really tore him up. I guess they hadn't spoken for years, and he felt guilty. So…how do *you* know her?"

"She's here in town, suing me for Jack's estate," I said, feeling miserable. "But Jillian didn't know anything about the Blue Buddha, except the name. At least that's what she told me."

"Yeah, most of the families didn't even know that much. The money just landed mysteriously in their bank accounts every month. We thought it was better that way, for everybody concerned."

"So who's running the Brotherhood now?"

"A bunch of suits and uniforms. Wall Street, the Pentagon. It's way over our heads. As of last winter, the organization itself has been in the hands of some bankers up in New York, but they couldn't function without the help of government—you know, for protection and technology. They're mean dudes. The amount of weed and opium that's coming from those fields in Afghanistan is unbelievable—way more than we could manage. When we started the operation, we had no idea how it would explode and how much cash it would generate. It was only a matter of time before the honchos up north moved in on us. They're not interested in veterans, of course—just lining their own pockets."

"What about Tex and Bishop?"

"They're henchmen, army insiders recruited by these corporate assholes. I know for a fact that they hired Tex to kill Pete and his friend, Pearl. They enticed them up to New York with an offer to split the action. But we know how that negotiation came out."

"So now it's all about the money that Jack stashed away somewhere, is that it?"

"I think Tex is freelancing now. Jack's stash is peanuts to the big boys, but for Tex, it's a bonanza. Pearl spilled the beans about the extracurricular bank accounts, and he saw his chance for some cash action on the side."

"How much money do you think is involved?"

"Hard to say. I was keeping books on everything Jack reported to us, and it was a few million a month. We were turning it over as fast as it came in. But it's all gone now, of course. I'm thinking if he skimmed even half a million a month, there must be ten or twenty million out there somewhere. That's money that would go a long way to help our Brotherhood clients. That's the only reason I'm still in this game."

I sat there feeling overwhelmed with all this information. Thinking about Jillian—how I'd jumped to the wrong conclusion about her, just on the word of that snake Lebeaux. Thinking about the Brotherhood and the people it had apparently benefited. Thinking about all the bloodshed it had caused. Thinking about my Cynthia and the evil woman who had killed her.

"Tell me one more thing," I said. "Tell me how you knew where to find me just now?"

Hugo smiled. "That cabin is where we organized the Brotherhood. It belongs to one of the charter members—an ex-army JAG lawyer. The whole thing was his idea to begin with."

I shook my head. "Don't tell me," I said. "His name is Jonathan Lebeaux."

CHAPTER THIRTY-SEVEN

H ugo turned around, surprised. "You know him? You know Lebeaux?"

"Unfortunately, yeah," I said. "Up until this afternoon he was my lawyer."

"We both know him," said Daryl. "At least we thought we did. The picture is getting clearer by the minute. What a scumbag."

"You don't know the half of it," said Hugo. "Lebeaux represented Pete when the army hauled him up on drug-smuggling charges. Somehow he managed to get Pete off without doing time in Leavenworth. Then he and Pete hatched the idea of the Brotherhood, knowing it would suck a lot of guys in. I don't even know all their names, but most of those original members were good people who got fed up with the war. They heard all the stories about Iraq veterans sleeping under bridges, committing suicide—and how the VA was backlogged for years. It pissed them off enough to step across the line and join Lebeaux's organization. I think he managed to recruit a couple dozen, all up and down the ranks. The highest I heard about was a colonel."

Daryl was quietly shaking his head. "I knew it," he said. "The guy knew way too much about the drug business, even for a criminal defense lawyer. Looks like my sister was just a patsy, providing Lebeaux with intel about Jack while at the same time keeping him up to speed on the Army CID investigation. He was playing both ends against the middle."

"Yeah, I figured that out as soon as I heard about Sandra's undercover operation. She was right in the middle and didn't know it," said Hugo. "But Lebeaux's game had gotten complicated. For the past two or three years, a lot of the original guys had been dropping out. Some of them came home to their families, got regular jobs, and decided the Brotherhood was too risky. Others got 'eliminated,' if you know what I mean. For a while it turned into a real Afghan cartel-style war, including some setup assassinations in the field. Lebeaux had to scratch around for new personnel, and he found some shady military contractors still in country. They hooked him up with this Wall Street crowd, but naturally it wasn't long before Lebeaux got squeezed out like the rest of us."

"So now he's freelancing, too," I said.

"That's about the size of it, as far as I can tell," said Hugo. "Anyway, it's for sure the cash flow from Afghanland has been diverted away from our original purpose, and now the organization is just a cash cow for some slimy-ass white-collar criminals. That leaves a few hundred veterans and their families up shit creek without a paddle."

I sank back in the seat. "And that's why you've been after the bank account numbers? To hand out the missing money to these veterans?"

Hugo nodded. "I figure I'm the only guy left who still believes in the Brotherhood's charter. If that money is out there, it belongs to those soldiers and their families."

We were all quiet for a few moments. Finally Daryl spoke. "So the way I figure it, there are at least three different players out there, not counting us, all looking for Jack's stash," he said. Then his voice dropped, so I could barely hear it above the engine noise. "And apparently, somebody wanted it bad enough to kill for it. That asshole Lebeaux."

I shook my head. "No, Daryl, it wasn't Lebeaux. He's an asshole, all right, but he didn't kill Sandra."

Daryl looked at me, surprised. "How do you know?"

"Because I just heard Diana Diamond tell Tex who the real killer was. It was Emma—Emma Fucking Faulkner who murdered all three of them."

He looked stunned. "But why...?"

"According to Diana, it was all about Jack and Cynthia getting married. When she heard about that, she lost it—shot them all with Jack's own gun."

Hugo and Daryl looked at each other in amazement. "You mean it wasn't about the money, after all?"

"Apparently not. But now Emma is on the hunt for the stash, just like the rest of them," I said. "That's why she had my house ransacked. She was looking for whatever Cynthia supposedly hid there."

Hugo shook his head. "So it all comes down to that," he said, mostly to himself.

I knew he was wondering whether I knew any more than I was saying, and I wondered just how desperate he was to find that money. The weird thing is that even though Hugo was clearly a criminal, and I had no reason to trust him, somehow I couldn't blame him for going after the money. I thought again about Jillian and her son, how the Blue Buddha had relieved their suffering, if only for a short time. The whole picture seemed morally muddy and frustrating.

"So what do you suggest we do?" I asked Hugo.

"How about let's go back to your place? Let's be sure you haven't missed anything—like maybe some clue that's right under your nose."

"I vote for finding Lebeaux and beating the shit out of him," said Daryl. "And then we figure out what to do about Emma."

"No," I said. "This is getting out of hand. We're not vigilantes. Our main worry now is from Tex and his thugs. I say we go report everything to the police."

Hugo did not look happy with that idea. "I'm sorry to hear you say that, Joe," he said. "I know I'm not exactly innocent in this whole deal, but I'm not ready to turn myself in—not yet. First, I need to make sure what's left of the Brotherhood money goes to the right people."

I studied his face for signs that he was lying. What if he was just another freelancer, like Lebeaux, hoping to find the stash for himself? There was no way to tell. But what *was* clear was that if I told the whole story to the cops, Hugo would be the first one they locked up. In spite of his role in the drug-smuggling operation, for some reason, that idea didn't sit right. The other thing that kept going through my head was the question of why he'd told me about the Brotherhood in the first place. He must be pretty confident that I'd either be so grateful for being rescued that I wouldn't turn him in, or else that I'd agree to help him find the money for the Brotherhood. On that score, I still hadn't made up my mind.

"Okay then," I said. "Just take me back to my car, and I'll go home and sit tight. I promise I won't say anything to anyone."

He stared out the windshield for a few seconds. "Sorry, Joe. I can't let you do that, either. It's not that I don't trust you. I just can't take a chance that you'll have a change of heart and hand me over to the cops. It's like I said—now that you know everything, we're all in this together until the end."

"And the end is...?"

"Finding the money. I need you to lead me to that stash. Once we find it and I get it to the people who need it, it won't matter what happens to me. My law-enforcement career is in the toilet, anyway."

"And what if we can't find it?" I said.

"If it's out there, we'll find it. Jack wasn't smart enough to hide that much money very well. He didn't have a clandestine mind."

I didn't respond. All I could think about were those cartons of Cynthia's Nancy Drew novels stashed in my garage. It had never before occurred to me that my daughter's mind might be "clandestine." That started my own mind chasing down some new pathways. I remembered the games she loved to play as a child—"I spy" and "Clue." And then there was the game we made up together, where one of us would hide something in plain sight, and the other one would try to find it. "Humpty Dumpty Strawberry Pie," we called it. Cynthia always won.

"Okay," I said, not yet sure how far I would take things, and not at all confident of what Hugo would have done if I'd refused to go along with him.

Hugo turned to Daryl. "How about you, Spinks? Are you in?"

Daryl had been sitting quietly in the passenger seat, clearly not satisfied with this arrangement. If he wanted to do something else, he didn't say so. He just nodded.

"Okay, then," said Hugo. "Let's go back to Joe's place. But first there's one more thing you both need to know. Emma Faulkner called me this morning in a panic. She'd been down to the precinct looking for me—told me Diana had been kidnapped, and she was scared they would come after her next. I promised her I'd hide her out at my house in Decatur. She's probably there right now."

"How come you're so friendly with Emma? She's a goddamn murderer!" Daryl said.

"Maybe. Maybe not. We only have Diana's word for it that she was the killer. My money is still on Tex," said Hugo, starting the engine.

"You haven't answered the question," I said. "How come you're so friendly with Emma Faulkner?"

"Not so friendly anymore," he said, "but I still feel like I owe her. Emma is my wife."

CHAPTER THIRTY-EIGHT

I didn't believe my ears. "What? She's your *wife?*"
Daryl looked just as shocked. "But I thought she and Jack were an item," he said.

"Yes, apparently so," said Hugo. "Emma and I were married when we were both students at University of Georgia. I dropped out and joined the army. While I was overseas, she met Jack. By the time I got home, she was finishing law school. She introduced me to Pete Diamond, and the two of them got me involved with the Blue Buddha."

"Wow," I said. "How did you put up with what was going on between her and Jack?"

Hugo laughed. "I ask myself that question every day. We never lived together after I got home, but we never got around to filing for divorce, either. Seems everyone knew what was going on except me. Emma was a laughingstock around the APD, but I was dumb enough not to realize it until…just recently. Until then, all along I'd been thinking I could win her back—always was a sucker for her, I guess. Should have divorced her a long time ago."

As we eased back onto the freeway, I sat quietly, trying to absorb all this information. Hugo was a complete mystery at that point. It seemed like the pieces of the puzzle were coming at me at lightning speed and landing in a chaotic heap at my feet. Here I was, riding in the back seat of Hugo's car and, for reasons I didn't understand myself, going along with his scheme to find Jack's money, not even knowing what he might do to me if we did find it. Daryl was another wild card. Why was he mixed up with Hugo at all? He had claimed to be after his sister's killer, but now it seemed he was only after the money, just like the rest of us. One thing was crystal clear: I was somehow in the middle of everyone else's search for the treasure. If only I knew why.

I looked up and noticed that Hugo had taken the off-ramp to I-285. I leaned forward between the front seats. "Where are you going? I thought we were headed south to Jonesboro."

"We need to make a stop at my house," said Hugo.

I was furious. "If Emma Faulkner is there, I don't want to see her," I said.

"You won't have to. I just need to talk to her for a minute," he said.

Daryl looked dark and disturbed but didn't say anything as we headed down Scott Boulevard and turned left into the city of Decatur. I was also quiet, dreading any possible confrontation with my daughter's murderer.

We pulled up into a driveway in front of a craftsman-style house with a broad, covered front porch. These little houses in Decatur are worth a fortune nowadays—three times as much as the same house in Jonesboro. The lights were on in the front room, which in the craftsman floor plan would be the living room. I looked back and noticed my own car parked at the curb, and I sank back in the seat as Hugo turned off the engine.

"Stay here, you two," said Hugo. Then he nodded toward Daryl and added, "Watch him." He jumped out of the car and bounded onto the front porch. Just as he reached the front door, it opened, and I saw Emma standing in silhouette inside. Hugo brushed past her, and the door closed.

Daryl sat in the front seat, drumming his fingers against the console of the BMW, watching the house. We couldn't see anything through the gauzy curtains over the front windows.

"What are they doing in there?" he said after a few minutes. "I don't trust that guy."

"He told us to wait," I said, becoming somewhat agitated myself, and eyeing my own vehicle, which Daryl had earlier left sitting at the curb after I was abducted.

"Yeah. Wonder why. What's he trying to hide?"

The same thought had been running through my own head, and I wasn't feeling much more confident about Daryl than about Hugo, especially because they both obviously thought I needed watching. I wondered what he would do if I bolted, but didn't dare chance it. Then all of a sudden Daryl threw open the passenger door and jumped out of the car. He crept around the side of the house, under the shrubbery and up against the window. He stood there, watching what was going on inside for a minute or two, and then bounded onto the porch and pushed through the front door.

I couldn't contain myself. I got out of the car and stepped up to the front porch, where I could listen to what was going on inside.

"Shut up, Daryl! You don't know what you're talking about," I heard Emma say, her voice loud but trembling.

"No? If you didn't kill them, who did?"

"Put the gun down, Daryl. You're not thinking straight," said Hugo.

"Oh yes, I am. She deserves exactly what she gave my sister."

At that point I heard a struggle—furniture scraping and thudding against the wood floor. Then it was quiet again, except for the sound of Daryl sobbing.

"Now let's be reasonable," said Hugo.

"With that gun pointed at me? You might as well go ahead and shoot," said Daryl through his sobs.

"I told you to wait in the car."

"Yeah, I know. You wanted to protect this murdering whore. What you said was right—you're nothing but a sucker for this bitch!"

Emma said softly, "Don't push me, Daryl. You don't know as much as you think you do."

Just then a set of headlights careened around the corner and pulled up in front of the house. I jumped off the porch into the bushes just in time as Tex and Bishop charged up the front steps with their guns drawn. Bishop kicked in the door. Then I heard a terrific ruckus inside—a lot of yelling and Emma screaming, "Don't! Don't! Don't!" as I ran down the driveway to my car. Thank God, Daryl had left the keys on the driver's seat. I cranked it up, gunned the engine, and didn't look back until I was a mile down Columbia Drive.

I stopped at a traffic light and made myself take in some deep breaths. As much as I wanted to get the hell out of there, I knew I should call the cops. I pulled into a gas station and asked to borrow the attendant's phone. Instead of dialing 911, I pulled out my wallet and found Detective Drake's card. On the back, he'd written his cell number.

It was late, and his voice sounded like I'd gotten him out of bed. "Mr. Brock! I've been trying to reach you," he said.

"Detective, you need to send someone out here to Decatur. It's an emergency. The people who killed my daughter are here. Somebody is about to get killed. It might be too late already."

"Slow down, sir. Where are you?"

"I told you...Decatur. Forty-two-oh-six Avery Street. They're all there...the killers."

"Okay. I'm not sure what you're talking about, but I'll get a City of Decatur patrol car out there right away."

"One isn't enough. Send the whole department," I said, "and no sirens!"

I got back in my car and sat there for a few minutes. Obviously, the most prudent option would be to get away from the scene. On the other hand, I couldn't stand the thought of missing the action back on Avery Street. I turned the car around and slowly circled the block. Both vehicles were still parked in the driveway. As I made my second pass around the block, I saw blue lights coming from all directions, and three patrol cars pulled up in front of the house, blocking the driveway. The officers got out, guns drawn, and headed toward the house.

CHAPTER THIRTY-NINE

I sat behind the wheel about a block away, trying not to tremble, watching the police approach to the house. Two of them went around back, and another two went to the front door and banged on it. After a couple of seconds, the door opened, and the two cops went inside. The last pair sat in their cruiser, positioned across the driveway.

The cops were in there a long time—close to half an hour. Out on the street, everything was quiet except for the squawk of the scanner inside the cop car. The blue lights were still flashing. Several neighbors had come outside and were watching from their lawns. I was wishing I had my phone so at least I could call Jillian and apologize for doubting her. By now I realized that I had been wrong on that score. Either Lebeaux was scamming me, or there was some other explanation, but I should have trusted my intuition about her. Now it might be too late.

Just as I was getting antsy, ready to leave, another Ford sedan came around the corner and parked on the street. It was dark, but I could see that the guy who got out was Detective Drake. I tapped my horn, trying to get his attention, but he didn't turn around. He walked up the steps and was let into the house by one of the cops. Another ten or fifteen minutes passed, and then the door opened and everyone inside sauntered out. I saw one of the Decatur cops patting Hugo on the back, and Detective Drake shook hands with Tex at the top of the steps. Emma Faulkner stood in the doorway and waved good-bye, smiling that big toothy smile. Somehow that rotten crowd of criminals had managed to pull the wool over the eyes of the law. I felt completely helpless, muttering to myself, "This is *not possible*." Then the slow burn started building in my gut.

I waited for Detective Drake to pull away from the curb, and then I eased up next to him, rolled down the window, and motioned for him to stop. We both parked a couple of blocks from the house, and I got out and went around to his side of the car. He was not in a good mood.

"Good evening, Mr. Brock," he said, scowling.

I stood outside his vehicle under a street light, stammering like a fool. "Why are you leaving? Those people murdered my daughter!"

"Mr. Brock, you need to calm down," he said. "We questioned the people in that house, and there was no case to be made against any of them. We checked them out. They're all members of law enforcement and the military, with excellent reputations."

"I know it looks that way, but they're criminals! Emma Faulkner shot my little girl and Jack Sloan. Sandra Spinks's brother is in there, too. He was probably too scared to talk in front of the others. They murdered a woman up by Lake Lanier. You can't just leave without arresting them!"

"Whoa, now. What's this about a murder on Lake Lanier? We haven't gotten any report about that."

"I know. The woman's name is Diana Diamond. She was kidnapped by the two army officers in there—Tex what's-his-name, and the other guy, Bishop. They kidnapped me, too, but I escaped. Diana was tortured. She said Emma Faulkner was the one who killed my daughter and Jack. Then they shot her, and chased me and the other two guys down here to Decatur. Diana's body is probably still up there in that cabin, where they were holding us..."

"Hold on, Mr. Brock. Just slow down. Have you been drinking?"

"No! I haven't had a drink in days!"

"Okay, in that case, I think the stress of your daughter's death is getting the best of you. What you're saying just doesn't make any sense. We don't have a shred of evidence that Emma Faulkner was involved in the murders over on Tuxedo Road. And without a dead body, we can't arrest anyone for the murder of this woman Diana."

"Detective, I'm not imagining things. I was kidnapped this afternoon. Those people in there are all members of a drug ring called the Blue Buddha Brotherhood. They're all looking for Jack Sloan's stash, just like you and I talked about the other day. That's why my house was searched..."

The detective was shaking his head. "Go home and go to bed, Joe. I believe you've had a run-in with these people, or else you wouldn't be calling me in the middle of the night like you did. But I haven't heard anything that would make a case on any of them."

I backed away from the car, wringing my hands. What was the matter with this guy? Why wouldn't he listen to me?

"Goodnight, Mr. Brock," he said, rolling up his window and pulling away from the curb.

I staggered back to my car and started the engine. Behind me I could see the other police cars, turning off their blue lights and leaving the scene. Everyone had gone back into the house. Obviously, there was nothing more I could do.

I made my way back to I-75, heading south. All I could think of was Jillian. The lack of a phone was making me feel all the more helpless. I stopped at a Walmart and picked up a cheap flip phone, and dialed her number. Voice mail answered, but I realized that a message wouldn't be adequate. I had to talk to her in person.

I flew down the freeway to the airport exit, pulled into the parking lot of the Fly Away Inn, and charged up the stairs to Jillian's room. She didn't answer my knock. Back downstairs, I asked the desk clerk to ring her.

"Ms. Farrell doesn't answer," she said. "Now that I think about it, I do recall seeing her leave about an hour ago."

"Did she say where she was going?"

"No. She was with another woman—an older woman with black hair."

My heart skipped several beats. "Was this woman by any chance very skinny, wearing tight jeans?"

She smiled. "Well yes, I think that would describe her pretty well…"

"Oh my God!" I slumped against the desk, fearing actual heart failure.

"Sir? Are you all right?"

"Yes…no. I don't know. Thank you for the information."

I staggered out to my car and sat behind the wheel, just staring out into the parking lot, trying to sort everything out. Obviously, the whole scene with Diana up at Lake Lanier had been a ruse—probably to scare me into talking. But why would Jillian be going anywhere with that woman? As far as I knew, they didn't even know each other. My suspicions about Jillian resurfaced as I thought about Lebeaux's comments again. What if these women were all in it together? Emma, Diana, and Jillian, all trying to get their hands on Jack Sloan's stash, however they could finagle it.

The frustration was just too much. Feeling that I couldn't trust anyone anymore, I started the engine and headed for home. Honestly, I felt so numb that I don't even remember the ride down I-75. The thing that jolted me awake was turning the corner onto my street and seeing a car parked in my driveway—a light-blue Lexus SUV that I'd never seen before.

There was a light on in my living room. I sidled up to the front door and opened it without a key. Someone was obviously inside. Now mind you, I was scared, but also confused. An hour earlier, I would have called Detective Drake, or maybe even the local cops, but after what I'd just gone through up in Decatur, I didn't trust anyone anymore, especially anybody in uniform.

I crept up to the window and looked in. There on my new living-room sofa sat Jillian and Diana, and in Diana's hand was a pistol, held an inch from Jillian's head.

CHAPTER FORTY

I busted through the front door.

"Welcome home, Joe. Figured you'd show up here eventually," said Diana. She was smiling a nasty smile. I noticed her teeth for the first time—small and pointy.

I should have been more scared, but by now I was just plain angry. "What's this about? What's going on?"

Diana was still pointing the gun at Jillian's head with her right hand, and her left hand was behind Jillian's neck, tugging on her hair. Jillian's hands were bound with silver duct tape, and there was another strip across her mouth. She looked at me with those big, round, blue eyes. I could tell she had been crying, and she was taking in big, labored breaths through her nose.

Diana said, "Sit down, Joe. We need to talk."

"I'm through talking to you. You pulled a fast one on me up at the lake—made me think you'd been tortured and murdered. Tried to scare me into talking. You're in on this with all the rest of them, aren't you?"

She laughed again—a wheezy, smoker's laugh. "Not exactly. Not like you think. Sit down, Joe. You're making me nervous. I do crazy things when I'm nervous. I know you don't want that."

I sat on the edge of the club chair across from the sofa, trying to make some sense of this scene. It seemed ridiculous that a gun could make this skinny old hag seem so powerful. Did she even know how to use it? Could this be another trick? Might Jillian even be in on the act?

I finally said, "Okay, I'll talk, but I'm not going to say a word until you put the gun down."

"You know I can't do that, Joe," she said. "I've gone to a lot of trouble to get you here, and I'm not about to give up my leverage now. Emma tells me that you and Miss Jillian here are quite an item. I know your type—mild-mannered tax man who fantasizes about playing hero. Well, here's your chance to save your damsel in distress. I can promise you that if you don't start talking, and quick, your girlfriend here will get the same kind of facelift your daughter got—the Glock 27 special."

That really pissed me off. Strangely, I wasn't afraid. "If you shoot her, you'll have to shoot me, too, and you won't get anything out of either of us. So spit it out, Diana. What do you want?"

"Come on, don't play dumb. You know what I want. You have some information that all of Jack's old pals are trying to get ahold of—information about money that doesn't belong to you. I imagine you'd like to keep that money for yourself, get out of this suburban Atlanta shit hole and make a life for yourself, but it's not going to happen. You need to share that information with me...now."

"I told you up at the lake that I don't know anything. You can't make me give you information that doesn't exist. You can't get blood out of a turnip."

"Bad metaphor, Joe. You may be stubborn, but you're no turnip. You know something you're not telling me. Your daughter was pretty clear on that point."

"What's that you're saying? What about my daughter?"

"I know that Dawn gave you something before she...died. She gave you some sort of map to the buried treasure, so to speak. Come on, Joe, you can't bullshit me. I know for a fact that she did!"

Once again, I searched my brain for anything that might salvage this situation. Diana had it all wrong about the money. The money was nothing. If I'd had the information she wanted, I would have had no problem giving it to her if it would save Jillian. Trouble was, I was drawing a blank.

"Look, Diana. Like I told Tex and his sidekick, I have no idea what any of you are talking about. They turned everything upside down in this house. If I had anything like that, they would have found it."

"Not if you have it in your head. That's a little harder to turn upside down."

I looked at Jillian, who was clearly in distress. She was gagging, like she might throw up, and the gasps were getting more and more fitful.

"For God's sake, Diana, let the poor woman go! Can't you see she's having a serious problem? I swear, if anything happens to her, I'll..."

"You'll what? Kill me? Looks to me like I'm the one holding the gun at the moment." That creaky laugh again as she wiggled the weapon back and forth against Jillian's head to demonstrate who was boss. I was frantic, but knew I couldn't afford to let anger and confusion overwhelm me.

"Let's be reasonable about this," I said. "Tell me exactly what it is you're looking for."

"What I'm looking for? Well, it would be something right in front of your eyes—something about a strawberry pie."

"What? I have no idea what you're talking about," I said, but somewhere in the back of my mind, a light bulb was firing up.

"I think you do. I think you and your daughter had some sort of secret code, and she used it to pass on some clues to you. Maybe she intentionally left it vague because she was planning on coming back home, and she wanted to salvage a little nest egg for herself— an insurance policy, in case things went wrong with Jack. Or maybe she was just being cute. She was always playing cutesy little games like that. It drove all of us nuts—everybody but Jack. He seemed to like her quirks."

"Diana, I wish you'd quit talking in circles and tell me what you want." I was frustrated, but I was listening carefully to everything the woman was saying.

"All right. I wasn't going to use this, but you don't seem to be taking me seriously. Yeah, I'm looking for Jack's stash like everyone else in this game. But unlike the rest of them, I happen to have a little advantage."

She released Jillian's hair, reached into her pocket and pulled out a square pink envelope. It looked like it had been addressed and stamped, but hadn't gone through the mail. Even though I couldn't read it from where I sat, I could have recognized the loopy, rounded handwriting from a mile away. It was Cynthia's.

"What have you got there? Give me that," I said. My heart was threatening to jump out of my chest.

Diana tossed the envelope onto the coffee table. "Slowly, Joe. No false moves," she said, pushing the gun into Jillian's temple.

I picked up the envelope and opened it. Inside was a single folded sheet of pink note paper. I sank back into the club chair, and unfolded the letter. My eyes had started fogging up, and I could barely read my daughter's childish writing.

Daddy,

I was wrong. You've always been my best friend, and I always meant to come home, but now things have gone too far. Daddy, I was a good girl, after all. I've left you proof of that. It's right in front of your eyes. Just look for me the way you remember me, and play our game. There's a prize there for you. Keep your eyes and ears open, and you might find yourself a very rich man. I love you.

Humpty-Dumpty Strawberry Pie.

Cynthia

I read the letter through twice. It was my daughter's voice, but it made no sense. I looked up at Diana. "Where did you get this?"

"I found it at the Tuxedo house. It was on the kitchen table the night your daughter…died."

"What? You were there that night?"

Diana smiled a little nervously. "You heard me. I found it that night."

My mind was running in overdrive. "It's addressed to me! Why did you steal it? What did you hope to gain from it?"

"I just picked it up—figured it might be useful sometime. Looks like now is that time. You daughter was a strange girl. She never told anyone she'd thought of going home to Daddy. In fact, she and Jack were leaving for South America the next day. Jack had been sending her out of the country pretty regularly—must have had her running his laundry. It was pretty obvious to everyone she had squirreled some of the cash away. Probably left the banking info for it here in the house somewhere, thinking she'd be able to access it later. But after they decided to leave the country, she realized she'd never get home again, and she wanted you to have the money. What else could she mean by making you a 'very rich man'?"

"I don't really have any idea," I said. "The Humpty-Dumpty thing is just a silly kid's game we used to play. You're supposed to look for something in plain sight—something that seems obvious once you've noticed it."

"I see," said Diana, narrowing her eyes. I could see the wheels turning in her head as she looked around the room.

"That was pretty nervy of you—picking that letter up, I mean. What if she'd noticed it was missing?"

Diana smiled her nasty smile and shook her head. "That wasn't likely to happen," she said.

A creepy feeling came over me. "And why not?"

She shrugged and rolled her eyes. We sat there looking at each other for maybe four or five seconds as the truth began to sink in.

"So it wasn't Emma who killed Jack and Cynthia after all, was it?"

She twisted her shriveled lips into a half smile. "Emma is not the only woman who knows how to shoot."

"And what kind of gun did you say you've got there? A Glock 27?"

"That's right. It's a good weapon. Small, discreet. It was Jack's favorite."

"In fact, it *was* Jack's, *wasn't* it?"

"You think you're pretty smart, don't you, Joe? I can see where Dawn got her peculiar temperament."

"My daughter had a wonderful temperament. She was an angel. You have no right to talk about her that way!" The rage was building in my throat.

"You're such a tight-ass, Joe. Your daughter was no angel. She got exactly what she deserved. Sure, Jack liked to fool around, but we both knew he would always be *mine*! He promised me years ago that he'd never marry any of these Blue Buddha bitches of his. He lied to me—let your slutty daughter talk him into running off to Vegas."

"I told you not to talk about her like that! Jack seduced her! She was only eighteen years old!" My heart was pounding now.

"Nobody seduced that girl. If anything, she was the one who did the seducing, with those big, innocent eyes of hers. It made everyone sick to watch the two of them. I tried to warn Jack, but he wouldn't listen…"

"Stop! My daughter was a wonderful girl and would have been a wonderful woman if you and your friend Jack hadn't corrupted her…deformed her…*killed her!*"

CHAPTER FORTY-ONE

As I shouted all that, I felt myself rising from the chair and lunging toward Diana. She pointed the gun at me with both hands. Jillian made a squealing noise in her throat and rolled off the couch onto the floor. I stopped maybe a couple of yards away, fearing Diana would shoot if I came any closer, even though it would kill her chance to get the information she wanted. Jillian had scooted on her knees across the room toward the front door.

What happened next is hard to reconstruct, mostly because it all happened so fast, and I've never been able to put it into sequence. Diana and I were staring at each other, a few feet apart, neither of us able to make a move. Then, outside the window, a set of headlights pulled up to the curb, and we heard a car door slam. Neither of us was willing to break our stare down to see who was coming across the lawn. It wasn't until the front door swung open that we both looked up to see the man who had walked in without knocking. It was Lebeaux. He had a large revolver in his hand, and he walked right past Jillian toward Diana.

"Put the gun down, Diana," he said. His expression was serious. His eyes and his gun were trained on her. She shifted her aim in his direction. Now the stand-off was between the two of them, and I was in the clear. I dived behind the club chair and motioned for Jillian to crawl over to me. She held up her hands and I tore off the duct tape with my teeth, then eased the strip off of her mouth so she could breathe.

Diana said, "I might say the same, Jonathan. You're too late. Joe here doesn't know it, but he's already told me where the money is. I'll cut you in if you drop the gun."

"Yeah, like I'm supposed to believe that. Like your word is worth a red cent. Common-law wife? More like common whore!"

"No need to insult me, counselor. I was only following advice of *my* counsel. You may have won the case, but you lost your client—and the jackpot that came with him!"

"That remains to be seen," said Lebeaux. "Where's Emma?"

"I don't know. I imagine she can figure out how to get here the same way you and I did. Tex forgot to disarm the damn drone signal on my phone. That fucking drone led me straight here. I don't know where any of the others are."

"You're lying. You wouldn't make a move without Tex's permission. Tex still has control of the drone, and he's not going to be happy to see you freelancing here."

She scoffed. "You're way behind in this game, Jonathan. Tex doesn't have control any more. The fucking drone is being monitored from Washington now. They're watching all of us from that damn drone. It's out of our hands. They know we're all after the money, scrambling around like a bunch of cockroaches. They're trying to figure out what to do with us. You should pay more attention."

Lebeaux was irritated. "What the hell are you talking about?"

"Just that the big honchos up north don't give a shit who gets the stash. It's chicken shit to them, compared with the big bucks they're making, and Tex is totally out of the picture. He's lost his usefulness to them. We all have. We're nothing but a threat to them now. They're scared we'll blow their cover. They'll eliminate us as soon as they get the chance."

"They have to catch up with us first," said Lebeaux. "Looks to me like it's every man for himself where that money is concerned."

"Well, you could say that. But don't forget I was there the night Jack died. I might have some insight that the rest of you don't have. I do have a brain, you know."

"You couldn't prove it by me."

They stood there, trading insults like that with their guns aimed at each other, for a minute or more. I suppose I should have been terrified, but I just crouched down with my arm around Jillian, staring at the carpet, shaking my head. Such a senseless scenario. Somehow, the idea that a woman like Emma had committed murder in a jealous rage seemed plausible. But Diana? That didn't seem possible. I didn't know what to believe. And Lebeaux? He could only be there for one purpose, the same as Diana's: to find the stash. All this talk about a drone didn't make any sense at all. But I realized that if we hoped to get out of this alive, I needed to appease these crazy people somehow.

"Okay, okay," I shouted from behind the chair. "There's no need for anybody to get hurt here. I'll tell you everything I know."

I stood up and faced them. Diana and Lebeaux both looked at me with surprised expressions, still pointing their shooters at each other. It was almost as if they'd forgotten I was there.

"Stay out of this, Joe. You're in over your head," said Lebeaux.

"We'll see about that. I'm the only one who can lead you to that money. But you both have to put away your weapons," I said, patting Jillian on the shoulder as she knelt beside me. "Put your guns down on the table, both of you."

"Why should we do that?" asked Diana.

"Because it's the only way you're going to get any of that money. We can split it three ways. Or if you prefer, just go ahead and shoot each other, and I'll keep the stash for myself."

They looked at each other for a couple of seconds; then both slowly edged toward the table in front of the sofa and awkwardly laid down their weapons. It was obvious that neither of them was any more skilled at gunplay than I was.

Lebeaux started toward me, opening his arms like a long-lost brother. "All right, Joe, the guns are down. Now let's have a heart-to-heart…"

"Stop right there, Counselor," I said. Surprisingly, Lebeaux complied.

I was on a roll. "Now back away, both of you," I said. "*Way* back—behind the sofa, up against the wall. I'm not going to tell you anything until I'm sure you're not going to hurt us."

Lebeaux had left the front door standing open, and I was maybe fifteen feet away from it. I got up and walked to the fireplace mantel, where I had set down the manila folder that Lebeaux had given me a few days earlier. I had an idea—a very good idea, in fact—that that legal folder was important. Jillian followed me, and I handed her the folder.

Amazingly, Lebeaux and Diana were still following my orders. I guess their greed and desperation had totally taken over their judgment by then. Anyway, the minute both of them were behind the sofa, several feet away from us, I lunged for the coffee table, grabbed both guns, and tucked the Glock into my waistband. Then I took Jillian's arm, and we bolted out the front door, leaving Diana and Lebeaux standing there like a couple of department-store dummies.

But just then, as we reached the front lawn, another set of head-lights pulled up at the curb. I gestured Jillian to duck into the shrubbery, and we watched as Tex and his pal Bishop piled out of their Jeep and darted up the driveway and onto the front porch. They charged through the open front door and slammed it behind them. At that point, I signaled Jillian to run again, and we high-tailed it to my car, which was still parked by the curb.

Everything was dead quiet inside the house. I could only imagine what kind of scene was taking place there—the competing players facing off there in my living room. I expected to hear gunshots any second. We quietly climbed into my car, and I cranked the engine.

But then something astonishing happened. This is where my memory gets very fuzzy, since it still seems like something out of a movie, and I must have been traumatized by the impact of the scene. Just as we pulled away from the curb, there was a blinding flash that lit up the whole block and a huge blast that sounded like a bomb had gone off. I looked back over my shoulder and saw my house engulfed entirely in fire. The flames were shooting up for what seemed like a hundred feet, and there was a huge cloud of smoke rising up over the house.

"What the hell...?" I said, exchanging terrified looks with Jillian.

"Your house just blew up!" she said.

"But how...? What could have happened?"

"I don't know, but let's get out of here!" she hollered, and I stepped on the gas.

CHAPTER FORTY-TWO

It was nearly midnight, but the neighbors had started running out of their houses to see what was going on. By the time we reached the highway, I heard sirens coming from all directions. Jillian sat trembling in the seat next to me, and I confess that I wasn't feeling too steady myself.

"Joe, I think that was a bomb," she said.

"Yeah, it sure sounded like a bomb. But where could it have come from?"

"Remember what they were saying back there? Something about a drone? You don't suppose…"

I shook my head, not willing to believe what seemed obvious. Someone had tracked all of us from the sky and then taken direct aim at my house. A surgical strike, so to speak.

Jillian was still clutching the legal folder I'd given her. "What should we do now, Joe?"

My mind was racing a mile a minute. None of those four villains could have survived the blast back at my house. But there was still one villain I needed to confront.

"We need to find Emma," I said.

"Maybe we should just get out of here—leave Atlanta, leave the state, leave all this behind us!"

I understood why Jillian said that. Part of me felt that way, too.

"No, we can't quit now. I think I might really know how to find that money. I think it has something to do with the marriage certificate right there, in Lebeaux's file. That picture frame was the only thing I took out of the house the night it was ransacked. We need to get to the money before Emma does. Besides, I still think she killed Cynthia and Jack."

"But Diana made it sound like she was the one who did it," Jillian protested.

"I suspect she was bluffing—trying to convince us she was crazy enough to shoot us if we didn't cooperate. She might have been pissed off at Jack for marrying Cynthia, but I don't think she'd have the nerve to shoot them. Don't forget I witnessed what a coward she was when we were both being held captive up at Lake Lanier."

"Except she did have that note from Cynthia. She must have been there at the murder scene, like she said."

"Maybe. Or maybe she was there earlier...or later. Hard to tell."

Jillian was quiet for a moment. "And the guy with the cowboy boots? Tex? What was his relationship with Diana?"

"I can only surmise that Diana was part of the organization, along with the rest of them, but up there in that cabin it sure didn't look like they were working together anymore. Tex apparently killed her son, Pete, along with our poor friend Pearl. I imagine that was enough to turn Diana against the rest of them. When they discovered I'd escaped from the cabin, they apparently just left her there after they fired those shots to make me think they'd killed her. Then she found her way back to your hotel – Jack's hotel. Emma must have told her you were staying there."

"She was driving that Lexus when she picked me up—told me you needed to see me at your house. That car must have been up there at the cabin. They must have lured her up there."

"Yeah. She said in court that Jack had given her a Lexus SUV. I didn't notice any other cars around when we peeled out of there, but I was sort of preoccupied at the time."

"Do you think the drone is still following us?"

"Who knows? On one hand, whoever these so-called honchos are—somewhere up north, I guess, maybe Washington or New York—they must know that we're innocent parties in this whole mess. It looks like what they're wanting to do is kill off anyone who could identify them—blow their cover, like Diana said."

"But on the other hand..."

"On the other hand, whoever these corporate or government big shots are, they definitely mean business, and unlike the rest of these creeps we've been dealing with, they apparently don't care about a few million bucks that Jack or Cynthia might have stashed away. The possibility that I know where to find the money has been our only protection so far."

Jillian still had a puzzled expression. "Won't the cops realize that the explosion back there had to come from a bomb of some kind? Maybe a missile? Only the military would have access to something like that. It should be obvious that someone in the government is up to no good."

"Yeah, one would think so. But then again, you know what I think of the cops in this town. Seems like they're all in on this Blue Buddha scheme, one way or another. I expect they'll cover up the drone attack—maybe say the furnace exploded or some such ridiculous thing."

By this time we were on the freeway, heading north. I really had no idea where we were going, only that I needed to find Emma and confront her about everything that had happened. So I headed for the last place I'd seen her—Hugo's house in Decatur.

I knew Jillian was still terrified after what she'd just gone through. Her hotel, the Fly Away Inn, was on the way.

"You don't have to go with me," I said. "I can drop you off if you'd rather not be involved in this mess any further."

She gazed out the window for a few seconds; then she looked at me and smiled. "You seem to have things under control so far. If you don't mind, I'll stick with you, Joe."

I can't begin to explain how it made me feel, to know that Jillian trusted me that much in spite of her fear.

"Okay then," I said. "But there *are* a few things we need to talk about. Let's stop."

We pulled into an all-night McDonald's just off the freeway. I got into the trunk of my car and grabbed a clean pair of jeans out of the duffel bag I'd packed, as I'd been wearing those pissed-on pants long enough. I changed in the restroom, and then we ordered coffee. It was well past midnight, and the place was almost empty. When we'd settled into a booth, I reached across the table and took her hand.

"First I need to explain why I sent you that stupid text—the one about not being as dumb as I look."

"Yes, that really threw me," she said.

"Well, at that point, I was confused and angry. Lebeaux told me that he'd discovered out in California that Jack didn't have a sister. I thought you were a ringer—in on the plot with Emma and the rest of them."

"I don't know how you could believe that after the night we spent together," she said.

"Now I don't know either, but at the time it was easy to believe that everyone was part of the Blue Buddha crowd except me."

"I understand. Well, there's a simple explanation. Jack and I were foster children. Our parents were killed in a car wreck when Jack was just a baby. We had no other relatives. We lived in a succession of foster homes until I was ten. Then we were both adopted, but into different families. Our names and birth certificates were changed. I didn't see him again until we were both adults, and I found my little brother through a search agency. He was eighteen at the time. We lived together briefly until Jack met Diana, and things turned sour. I never met her, but I'm sure it was through Diana that Emma found me. Jack had probably told her our whole history."

I sighed with relief and more than a little shame. "I should have known it was something like that. Or it could have been as simple as Lebeaux lying to me again. I don't think he was ever honest with me about anything."

"He was after the money, like all of them. And from the sound of it, he was on the outs with the new bosses of the Brotherhood. He must have been desperate."

"Speaking of the money," I said, "hand me that file. I wasn't kidding when I said I might know how to find it."

Jillian's eyes grew bigger. "Really! I thought you were just running a bluff back there."

"No. My daughter must have left me a message on that marriage certificate—something nobody would notice just by glancing at it."

"What sort of message?"

I was sorting through the file as we talked—a thick pile of legal documents.

"Well, Cynthia and her friends loved to play a hide-and-seek game that I taught them. They would hide an object in plain sight, and then as each one spotted it, they'd yell out, 'Humpty-Dumpty Strawberry Pie!' The last one to figure it out would have to hide the object the next round. It was a silly game we made up—nothing particularly mysterious about it."

"Yes! Then that must be what she meant in her letter to you— about the strawberry pie..."

"Right...Ah! There it is," I said, pulling out the copy of the marriage certificate that Lebeaux had made for me. "If I'm right, the clues will be here!"

CHAPTER FORTY-THREE

"Damn! I don't have my reading glasses," I said, passing the document across the table to Jillian. "Can you read this?"

She bent over the paper and examined it. "I don't see anything unusual here. It says State of Nevada, a bunch of info like names and addresses, dates of birth, et cetera, for Jack and Dawn—I mean Cynthia. Honestly, Joe, I don't see anything...Wait a minute!"

Jillian held the document up closer to her eyes and squinted at something on the edge, rotating the paper sideways and upside down.

"This must be it, Joe! Here, in the scrollwork on the border of this certificate. It looks like there's a tiny number written inside each little curlicue in the border pattern. My eyes are pretty good, but I can't make them out very well. Here...take a look."

She passed the document back to me, and I tried to see what she was talking about, but it was hopeless without my glasses, which were in the glove compartment of my car. All I could see was a line of connected, smudged ovals wrapped around the text on the paper like a chain, creating the effect of a fancy border that government agencies use to make things look official.

"How could she write that small? We need a magnifying glass," I said.

We stood up at the same time and headed for the door. Down the block was a Walmart, where we purchased a lighted magnifier for ten bucks. Back in the car, I held the thing up to the border on the marriage certificate. Sure enough, each little oval contained a number. There were maybe a couple of hundred numbers that seemed to be punctuated by a black dot every so often.

"Jillian! There's no doubt that these are the account numbers Pearl was talking about. Looks like a couple of dozen, if you count the numerals between the dots."

She sighed and leaned back against the seat. "I don't see how those numbers will do us much good without knowing where the accounts are in."

Jillian was right. All we'd discovered was a string of meaningless digits that wouldn't take us anywhere without knowing where to look for the accounts. That was the information Pearl was supposed to give me. But I wasn't ready to give up yet.

"All right, let's think about this," I said. "Both Pearl and Diana told me that Cynthia was doing a lot of traveling during the last several weeks. Apparently she was acting as a courier for Jack, maybe to stash away money for the two of them—a nest egg, in case things went south. If we only knew where she was going..."

There are times when you'd swear your subconscious is working completely on its own. For a couple of days, I'd been fiddling absent-mindedly with the paper I'd stuck into my pocket when we were inside that underground vault up in Buckhead—Cynthia's American Express statement. Now, without even thinking, I reached into my jacket pocket and pulled it out. I unfolded it and glanced down at the charges listed for the months of June and

July. There were three first-class tickets on the statement, all to the island of Aruba.

"Look at this," I said, excitement building again. "Cynthia went to Aruba three times during the month before she was killed. That's where we'll find those accounts!"

Jillian looked skeptical. "I don't know, Joe. There have to be a whole lot of banks on that island. I think it's pretty well known for holding shady funds."

She was right again. Still, there had to be a way to sort it out. We were so close to solving the mystery of the missing stash. We sat there for five or ten minutes, racking our brains about how we could ever hope to find that money. Then I remembered where we were going.

I cranked up the car and headed back to the freeway.

"This is a dead end," I said. "Let's go find Emma. I have enough on her now to make her confess. She's the only member of that organization who managed to escape the drone strike. I'm thinking that's not a coincidence. She might be the person responsible for sending that drone after us. She's working for the new bosses up north, giving them the intelligence on how to wipe out their competition."

Jillian frowned. "Maybe. But I've been thinking. Shouldn't we call the police? What if she does confess? There's not much we could do about it on our own. After all, we can't very well arrest her, can we?"

I realized that I hadn't thought the thing through very well.

"Okay," I said. "Maybe you're right." I pulled out my phone and dialed Detective Drake. I knew he wouldn't be thrilled to hear from me, but he was the only person I knew in the police department who seemed to have played it perfectly straight with me. As I expected, he didn't sound happy to hear from me for the second time that night. I put the phone on speaker so Jillian could listen in.

Drake said, "Mr. Brock, I've had about enough of your amateur detective work for one night. I've already told you that there's no evidence at all to implicate Ms. Faulkner or any of the others out there in Decatur. Your imagination is running away with you."

"I don't think so, sir," I said. "A few minutes ago, my house was blown up with four members of this conspiracy inside of it, including two of the people you met a couple of hours ago. You can check on it with the Jonesboro police department. They should be on the scene by now."

There was a pause on the other end of the line. "Blown up, you say? Who blew it up?"

"I'm not sure, but it definitely was no accident. Someone is trying to wipe out the members of the conspiracy I told you about. They got four with one blow."

He sounded interested all of a sudden. "What makes you think Ms. Faulkner had anything to do with it?"

"She's in on this Blue Buddha deal up to her ears—handled most of their business until Jack Sloan got sloppy and they had to get rid of him. I told you before, I think she killed Jack and my daughter, though I can't prove it at the moment."

"Hold on a minute," he said. I could hear him punching in numbers on another phone. There was another pause; then I heard him say to someone on the other end of the call, "Yeah? How long ago? How many fatalities? Any suspects? Okay, thanks."

"You see?" I said, when he seemed to have hung up the other call. "Detective, you have to believe me. This thing is huge. It extends all the way up to the highest levels of the military, the government, and even Wall Street. These people are making millions importing and selling drugs from Afghanistan. They're ruthless. They…"

"Okay, calm down, Mr. Brock. I'll look into it. For now, you need to back off and let the proper authorities handle this thing.

You're not a cop, and if what you say is true, there's no point in putting yourself in danger."

"But…"

"I mean it, Mr. Brock. Find yourself a hotel, check in, and call me back in the morning. I'll let you know if we have any news by then."

He hung up.

I sat there fuming. It may sound paranoid, and maybe it was, a little; but right then it seemed like everyone in a position of authority was either crooked, incompetent, or both. I had no choice but to take this thing into my own hands.

"Come on, Jillian," I said. "We've got a job to do."

This time she didn't argue.

CHAPTER FORTY-FOUR

It took us about half an hour to get back out to Decatur. As I drove up to the house on Avery Street, I cut my headlights. All the lights were still on in the house, including a bright one on the front porch. We parked two doors down and walked back past the two houses, staying close to the shrubbery. From there, we could see inside the living room. Emma was nowhere to be seen. The only people in there were Hugo and Daryl. But there was something else. With his left hand, Daryl was holding his cell phone. With his right hand, he was pointing a gun at Hugo, who was sitting on the sofa, looking scared.

"He must be calling the cops," I said to Jillian. "I hope he has better luck than I had."

She nodded.

At that point, we both sort of breathed a sigh of relief, and I gestured for Jillian to follow me up the front steps. I knocked softly at the door. After a few seconds, Daryl opened it. He had put the gun away and now had a different expression on his face—like he was scared, or maybe just nervous.

"Come in, Joe," he said. "We were just talking about you. I was trying to reach you on the phone."

That was a lie, of course. My flip phone was in my pocket and hadn't made a peep since I talked to Detective Drake a half hour earlier, and Daryl knew that Tex and company had taken the smart phone. Once again, as so often in the previous weeks, my gut started sending out warning signals where Daryl was concerned. In spite of that, Jillian and I both stepped inside.

Hugo was still sitting on the couch, but he was looking down at the floor, picking at a hangnail on his thumb.

"What's going on, Daryl?" I asked, thinking he probably wasn't aware that I'd seen him with the gun.

"We were just discussing what to do about Tex and the others," he said. He turned to Jillian. "I don't believe I've had the pleasure…"

"This is Jillian, Jack's sister," I said. They nodded to each other, but I could tell Daryl was confused.

"So…what are the two of *you* doing here?"

"We're looking for Emma," I said.

"Oh. Well, you're a little late. Right now she's on a plane headed somewhere outside the country. Not sure where."

I glared at Hugo. He was still studying his thumb, looking nervous.

I was furious at both of them. "How did that happen? Why did you let her go? Have you forgotten that she probably killed your sister?"

"Well, that's not exactly settled, Pops," he said. "Why don't you and Jillian have a seat, and we'll talk about this."

"I don't feel like sitting down, and it looks to me like you're the only one who needs to do any talking. Just tell me right now what's going on."

He smiled. "Wow, Joe, you've really grown a pair here lately."

"And it's about time," I said. "So how about cutting the bullshit?"

"Well, I was just discussing with Hugo here that we need to find Tex and his buddy—turn them in for kidnapping you."

I said, "That's not a problem anymore, Daryl. They're dead— blown to bits. Besides, I know that the cops were already here, and they didn't arrest anybody, so your story doesn't hold water."

He looked at me with an expression of respect I hadn't seen before. "And just how do you know all that?"

"Because I'm the one who called the cops, and I watched the whole thing from the street. Somehow all of you managed to pull the wool over their eyes. I guess the military and police cover gets you through almost anything. Professional courtesy, right?"

He smiled again. "And how about the rest of it...the blown-to-bits part?"

All of a sudden I realized that Daryl somehow knew about the drone. I began to get a creepy feeling—even creepier than before. I put an arm around Jillian and pulled her close to me.

"We were there at my house when the place went up in flames. Lebeaux, Diana, Tex, and Bishop—none of them could have survived. Jillian and I barely escaped with our lives. But then, I figure you must know all about that."

Daryl said, "Sit down, Joe. You too, Jillian." Then he pulled the gun out of the shoulder holster under his jacket and pointed it at us. We sat down on the sofa next to Hugo, the three of us all in a row.

Now, mind you, I hadn't forgotten that I had the Glock .27 in my waistband under my jacket. Daryl couldn't have seen it. But he definitely had the drop on us, and I knew if I went for that gun, Jillian would be in danger. I couldn't let anything happen to her. So there we sat, like three ducks in a row, with Daryl standing over us, waving that automatic pistol of his.

"What are you going to do, Daryl? Kill all three of us?"

"I haven't really made up my mind," he said with another little smile. "Of course, I could easily take out all three of you in less than two seconds. I was quite a marksman in the army, you know—part of an elite sniper unit."

"No, I didn't know that," I said, feeling a new kind of dread growing inside me. "For some reason you never saw fit to tell me about your skill with a gun before. But I'm beginning to realize just how much you never told me about."

Jillian and Hugo were sitting quietly, one on each side of me. I could feel Jillian trembling. This was the second time that night that she'd had a gun pointed at her.

"You probably wouldn't want to know everything I know, Joe. You're better off not knowing."

My mind was doing somersaults. What was he getting at?

"So what do you want, Daryl? Are you after Jack's stash like the rest of them?"

He laughed. "That's what I haven't quite decided. I have a job to do, and the pay is good, but not nearly as good as that stash would be. So maybe this is your last chance to open up about it, Pops. If you don't, I won't really have any choice in the matter."

"What about Emma? Did she really leave the country, or did you kill her?"

"Oh, she's gone, all right. Hugo here is a sucker for that bitch—convinced me to let her go in exchange for some information he has about my…employers. He hasn't quite told me about it yet. We were giving Emma time to catch that plane. I took a chance that he was telling the truth. If he's not, well…he knows what will happen."

"And just who are these 'employers'?"

"Interesting you should ask that. That's the very information that Hugo was about to provide me. He says he knows who is in charge of the Blue Buddha now…the people at the top. If he really does, it will improve my negotiating power considerably. I figure they're in positions of power in the government or in business, and they'd pay a pretty good price to remain anonymous."

I was totally confused at that point. "So you're working for somebody whose identity you don't even know?"

"Yeah, it does sound pretty crazy, doesn't it? This is the big time, Joe. If there's enough money involved, you don't ask many questions."

"Even if it means murder? Is that what you're telling me?"

He shrugged. "Sure, why not? I've killed a lot of people—more than I can count, including a lot of so-called 'innocent' people over in Afghanistan and Iraq. So what's the big deal? After a while, killing for a living feels like any other job."

All of a sudden, it hit me—the reason my gut was in knots. It wasn't just the fact that I was sitting there at the business end of a gun, or that sweet Jillian seemed about to have a breakdown.

I said the words slowly. "And for enough money, you'll murder anyone. Even people you know…people you love? Your own family? Your own sister!"

CHAPTER FORTY-FIVE

Daryl waived the gun back and forth. "Shut up, Joe. Don't push me..."

"You killed my daughter, didn't you? You killed your own sister! How could you do that?"

"Shut up, I said!" He was moving closer, looking angrier—no, *colder*. I pulled Jillian closer but kept talking. "And for what? A little cash that you've probably already blown by now, anyway?"

"It was more than a little cash," he said, as if it mattered to him what I thought. "It was half a million. And I never meant to kill Sandra. She was so damn stubborn and bull-headed...I couldn't control her. I begged her not to go over to Tuxedo that night... *begged* her! But she wouldn't listen...said she was getting close to Dawn, and Dawn had all the evidence the Feds needed to bust the Blue Buddha. I didn't have any choice. I had my orders."

I sat there, stunned, realizing for the first time that Daryl had never been truthful with me from the very beginning. His story had seemed to change every time I saw him. I had always figured it was because Lebeaux was manipulating him, but now things were coming into focus.

"So you were hired to do away with the whole Atlanta connection—Jack, Cynthia, and who else?"

"Anyone who got in the way."

"Including Lebeaux?"

"I didn't have any orders on him yet, but it was pretty clear he would be next. He was paranoid about that, but he never suspected me. Thought I was just a dumb cop wannabe—like you."

"And what about Pete Diamond and Pearl? Did you have anything to do with that?"

He laughed. "No, that was Tex's crowd. It was crudely done—very messy. They were after the stash, plain and simple. They jeopardized the operation—got New York law enforcement involved and left a lot of evidence around. It was only a matter of time before they would have been busted for those murders, and that would have meant exposure. That's why they had to be eliminated. You have to admit, that drone deal was pretty creative."

"And you say you don't know who's behind all this?"

"No. I met with a guy in a suit who said he was from the state department. Said the Blue Buddha posed a threat to national security. I met with him three times, but I don't think I could pick him out of a lineup, and I didn't ask any questions. My first assignment was to get all the information I could from Sandra about the CID investigation and everything she'd found out. From there, it sort of escalated. Like I told you, I've just been following orders like any good soldier. I just happened to be paid a little more. But now I've got some options in front of me that I hadn't counted on—the information that Hugo here was about to give me, and now the bonus of whatever you can tell me about that stash. Lebeaux told me you had some sort of secret code…"

I sat upright. "You must be crazy, Daryl! You're unstable—mentally damaged by the war! They're using you! Don't you realize they'll come after you, just like the rest of them? Once you've done their dirty work, you won't be of any more use to them."

Then Hugo sat up. "He's crazy, all right—a sociopath. That's what the army called him when they drummed him out. He liked to kill people too much."

Daryl just smiled again. "So? They teach you to kill; then they get all uppity when you do it too well. And what do you end up with? If you're lucky and don't get killed or maimed yourself, you get a lousy medal or two and a pathetic pension. Yeah, I already figured they'd come after me eventually. That's why I'm building myself an insurance policy and maybe a nice nest egg." Then he grinned at me. "And by the way, Joe, now that you've cracked the case, you might find yourself in the crosshairs, just like the rest of us."

Hugo said, "I just don't get it, Daryl—how you could betray your comrades in arms like that. All the Blue Buddha was ever meant to do was try to help our brothers and sisters who came home broken and helpless, with a government that had no interest in them after they'd sacrificed everything. You sold us out to a bunch of slimy politicians who aren't interested in anything besides lining their own pockets, all while they rant and rave about the Taliban's illegal drug trade. You helped put the Blue Buddha into the hands of a bunch of greedy, murderous, bureaucratic hypocrites!"

Just then, Hugo's cell phone rang. He answered it and mumbled something; then he ended the call and put the phone back into his pocket. "She's on board," he said to Daryl.

Daryl said, "All right then. Your precious Emma is safely on her way out of the country. Now let's have that information you were bragging about. Name me some names."

"Sure," said Hugo, "I've got it right here in my phone." He reached back into his pocket, but as he did so he sprang from the sofa and lunged at Daryl, grabbing for the gun. The two of them started struggling for control of the weapon. It was hard to tell who was winning, as they were scuffling down on the carpet, but Hugo was on top. It took me only a couple of seconds to realize that this was the only opportunity I was likely to get. I stood up and drew the Glock .27 from my waistband, pulling Jillian up behind me, shielding her with my body. Then, just as we were edging toward the door, there was a gunshot. We stopped. Hugo flopped over onto his back, a huge patch of red gushing from his chest, dead eyes staring up at the ceiling. Daryl scrambled to his feet and kicked Hugo out of the way.

"Where do you think you're going? Drop the weapon and sit down." He was pointing his gun at me, and I was pointing the Glock back at him. I should have shot him when I had the chance, when he was off balance. But now we were faced off, and he had the advantage because he was a murderer and I wasn't. Besides, I had Jillian to think about. She was still cringing behind me. I dropped my gun on the floor.

We stumbled back to the sofa, our hands raised.

I said, "How many bodies does that make, Daryl, or can't you count that high?"

He wasn't amused. "I told you to shut up, Joe. Our friend Hugo obviously didn't have much judgment. Apparently he didn't have much information, either, or he would have used it to save his life. I think I'll relieve him of his cell phone, just in case, but meanwhile you should take a lesson from that chunk of meat you see lying there on the carpet."

Daryl knelt next to Hugo's body and took the cell phone out of his shirt pocket, all the while training his gun on us.

"Now let's have a serious discussion about that stash. Tell me what you know about it, or I'm afraid the two of you are going to end up just like our friend here. It would be a shame to leave a mess like that in this charming old house." Hugo's blood was oozing in a pool underneath him, soaking into the rug.

Telling about this now, it's hard for me to believe that I really was not scared at that moment. I had at last found out what I needed to know—how my daughter died and why. Now it was only a matter of getting myself and Jillian out of this situation, and instinct told me I needed a cool head. What seems even more amazing is that Jillian seemed to react the same way. She straightened up, and I heard her breathing slow down, then her soft voice behind me.

She said, "You don't know me, Daryl, but you can take my word for it. Joe doesn't know anything about that money. It's all a ridiculous rumor that's been passed around so many times that everyone believes it. My brother Jack was an addict and a drunk. He spent every cent he got his hands on. He would never have the self-control to accumulate anything, much less a multi-million-dollar stash."

Daryl seemed to look at Jillian seriously for the first time. "Oh? So now I take it that you and Joe here are an item. You're working this thing together, right?"

"No," she said. "We just met a few days ago. We've become friends, and he rescued me from a tight spot a couple of hours ago, but I've talked to him enough to know that he's clueless about that money—as clueless as I am."

Daryl laughed again. "So Joe…it seems you've come a long way from that meek little mouse I met in the bar. Now you're a real tiger. Rescuing damsels in distress? Pulling a gun on a trained killer? And now that you mention it, where did you get that Glock? I left that piece at the scene over on Tuxedo Road, next to old Jack's corpse."

I shrugged. "It seems Jack's so-called wife, Diana, must have showed up shortly after you left. She picked up the gun along with some…personal items belonging to my daughter. I imagine she more or less ransacked the place, looking for money. Probably stole everything of value she could put her hands on. She died in the drone attack back at my house tonight."

Daryl looked surprised, but I'll never know his response, because just as he was about to answer me, the front door crashed open. Suddenly the room was flooded with police, all with their weapons drawn on Daryl. Lights went on outside the house, and I saw out the front window a row of police cars and unmarked cars pulling up to the curb.

"DEA! Drop the weapon and put your hands up!" shouted the first officer in the room.

Daryl complied as at least a dozen officers with various uniforms scrambled into the room.

"Thank God!" said Jillian. We both jumped up and ran as an officer motioned us toward the door.

"Who are you? How did you know...?" I started to ask. Just then I saw Detective Drake come in through the kitchen door. Next to him was another plainclothes officer who flashed a different badge.

Drake walked toward me with his hand out. "Mr. Brock! Man, I owe you an apology. I totally misread this situation."

I nodded, still totally confused. "But what happened? What are all these officers doing here?"

Drake sort of sighed and motioned me and Jillian into the adjoining den as Daryl was being handcuffed on the floor of the living room. We stumbled after the detective.

"It all happened within the past hour," he said. "We got a call from the Feds—DEA, to be exact—that a female involved with the Blue Buddha Brotherhood and the Tuxedo murders had called them and offered to flip in exchange for immunity. She's sitting downtown right now—I believe you said you know her? Emma Faulkner?"

"But...Daryl said she was leaving the country. She was on a plane..."

"No, she wasn't. That was a ruse to get her out of this house. She was calling from the US Attorney's office. They were negotiating a deal. She called her husband's number to tell him she was safe, and to give us time to get out here and make the arrest. It all happened pretty fast, but apparently not fast enough to save that poor guy on the floor in there."

"But what about Emma? What's going to happen to her?"

"Depends on how good her story is. If it's good enough, and they can't make any serious charges against her, she'll probably end up in witness protection somewhere until they pull down the whole infrastructure of this organization. I gather it goes pretty high—cabinet level, I'm told."

"So she will save her skin, after all," I said. Somehow that didn't sit well with me.

"Without her testimony, the Feds probably can't make a case. The organization has killed off everyone else who could have testified."

"I know," I said. "They blew up my house tonight. Pretty scary. Do you think they're still following us with that drone? Are we safe?"

Drake looked confused. "Drone? I don't know anything about that. I heard there was a bomb planted at your house."

"No, there was a drone. It followed me home, and…"

"Shhh," said Jillian. "Joe, we don't need to go into that right now."

I looked at her and understood. "Right. It must have been a bomb. A very big bomb."

CHAPTER FORTY-SIX

Dear Mrs. Cavanaugh:

Please find attached to this e-mail the narrative you asked me to prepare for you. Sorry it took me so long to get it finished. It's all there—the whole story. I warned you it would be pretty unbelievable. The rest of it you already know. I still have mixed feelings about Emma being given immunity, but she did help the Feds hook those twelve big fish in Washington and New York. I guess the Feds have her stashed away someplace safe, waiting for the trial, which you tell me is scheduled for next month. I'm taking your word for it that those twelve are locked up and that they'll probably stay that way for a very long time—at least the ones that don't get the death penalty. Daryl agreed to testify, too, in exchange for life imprisonment without parole, so I'm not really worried about him, either.

I hope I haven't left out anything important. You asked me to tell the story in as much detail as I could remember, and I've always had a pretty good memory. It was your idea to do this, and it's made Jillian feel a lot better about my safety, knowing that I've put the whole thing in writing in case any of the Blue Buddha bigwigs decide to come after me. I try to tell her that a nobody like me isn't likely to seem like much of a threat to them, but she insisted. Yes, of course, you have my permission to have it published. Otherwise it wouldn't do as much good against the bad guys.

It's taken so long to write this that I haven't had time to stay in touch, but our big news probably won't come as a surprise to you. Jillian and I were married last month, and we've brought her son Ben back from California to live with us. He's a great kid. We've hired him a full-time caregiver, and thanks to the quality therapy we're able to pay for now, he's making great progress.

Jillian and I want to thank you for everything you've done for us. As you can tell from what I've written here, our experience with lawyers hasn't been exactly positive. We're grateful that we've finally found ourselves an honest lawyer and that you've finally gotten the two estates sorted out. I know you did everything you could to keep the IRS from taking the Tuxedo Road house, the Fly Away Inn, the nightclub, and all the cars. But then, we expected all along that that stuff would probably end up in their hands. We appreciate knowing that they can't force us to come back to Atlanta to testify.

Maybe I shouldn't tell you about this, but I know you'll keep it under your hat—attorney-client privilege and all that. Those probate "letters" you sent us turned out to be a big help. They gave us authority to take care of all the business matters that Jack and Cynthia could have done themselves. It took us awhile to figure it out, but gradually we realized that with those court documents, we could get all of Cynthia's and Jack's personal information, such as bank accounts, investment portfolios, and credit-card statements. Of course, we didn't know enough about any of that to get very far, with one exception—that American Express statement that I found on Tuxedo Road. I ordered all her past statements, and from there it was pretty easy to trace Cynthia's movements during the several months before the murders. It turned out that Aruba wasn't her only destination. She had traveled all over the Caribbean, including to some pretty nice areas.

It wasn't easy matching those numbers on the marriage certificate with banks on the various islands, and we did get some resistance from those cagey bankers; but after about a month of pounding the pavement, and armed with those probate letters, we finally hit pay dirt—an account in the name of Cynthia Ann Brock (not Dawn Marie Sterling!). Our credentials got us into the vault, and there in the safe deposit box we found the first installment of the stash, a couple of million.

And that's how we ended up here on our private island paradise, listening to the ocean and sunning ourselves outside our cozy little villa on the beach. We've named it the Blue Buddha. That was Jillian's idea, and she and I are the only ones who know the meaning of the blue butterfly she painted above the front gate. Living is pretty cheap here, compared to the States, and we've decided this isn't a bad way to spend our retirement years. Neither of us cares much about luxury, as long as we have each other, but Jillian has developed a pretty extensive network of military families in distress, and we've been using most of the money to help them. Of course, eventually that first stash will run out, but now that we know how to do it, we figure it will be easy to find the next account. After everything that's happened, we've realized how short life really is and how suddenly it can end. We've decided to enjoy it one day at a time.

Helen Christine Anderson
Alangasi, Ecuador

www.ingramcontent.com/pod-product-compliance
Lightning Source LLC
Chambersburg PA
CBHW071132170626
46809CB00002B/584